EDEN

GARDEN OF EVIL SERIES

EDEN – BOOK 1
EXODUS – BOOK 2
GENESIS – BOOK 3
ELYSIUM – BOOK 4

Shade Owens & Ash S-J
www.shadeowens.com

Edited by Nikki Busch
www.nikkibuschediting.co

RED RAVEN PUBLISHING

ISBN: 978-1-990271-06-9

PROLOGUE

The pistol's grip feels hot against my clammy palm. I glare down its rear sight, having a hard time aligning it with its front sight because my hands are shaking. That's when I realize I'm only two feet away from this bastard—I don't need to aim my fucking gun.

He looks terrified. Big beads of sweat drip down his face, darkening his blue collar and red tie, but I don't care. I've been waiting too long for this. And now that I'm here, it all seems so surreal, like I'm not even the one holding the gun.

Yet it is real... I *am* holding the gun, and I *am* standing in the Oval Office of the White House with a gun pointed at the President of the United States of America. His jet-black hair is combed to one side and although I'm sure it's gelled over with some expensive hair product, it looks greasy like he hasn't washed it in weeks.

Maybe he hasn't.

But then again, I doubt even a war would get in the way of his personal needs.

I regrip my gun, remembering why I'm here, remembering everything he's done.

"P-p-p-please," he begs, raising two sweaty hands in the air, and I revel in it.

The sound of a heavy artillery drone suddenly flies overhead, and I know I'm running out of time.

I cock the pistol and press it into his temple.

Everything is about to change.

CHAPTER 1 – EVE

Eve — Present Day

"What happened next?" Scarlet asks, her honey-brown eyes gazing up at me with such fascination.

I smile and gently brush her golden hair away from her porcelainlike face. Behind her, a dozen little girls, no older than eight years old, form a crescent moon in the grass, listening intently to every word I say. Their mothers, too, are drawn to my story, even though I've told it countless times.

"It was a dark world," I say. "A world you wouldn't want to live in." I make eye contact with some of the mothers—they know; they remember. "Men ruled the world."

I see grimaces appear on some of the little faces. Scarlet, the young girl at my feet, sticks out her pink tongue and giggles. "Boys? In charge?"

I smirk down at her. "Strange, isn't it?"

She nods quickly, and the other girls follow suit.

I stand and pluck a large bright red Fuji apple from the tree behind me, then sit back down, rubbing my thumb against its waxy skin. "See this?"

More rapid nods.

"This used to be available in something called a store," I say.

"A store?" one child asks.

"What's a store?" asks another.

They're too young to know or remember the old

world. Two children begin bickering back and forth, but their mothers intervene and tell them to pay attention.

"A store is a place where a person would go to buy food," I say, "like this apple. I would have had to buy it in the store, with money."

"What's money?" one girl asks.

There are subtle smiles on the mothers' faces. What an unusual question. *What's money?*

"Money is something men enjoyed using," I say. "Something that caused a lot of bad in the world."

I know they're too young to understand the concept of greed—of power hunger and pride—but I hope that by describing money as *bad*, they're able to comprehend that it doesn't belong in our new world.

"So, did you destroy the stores?" Scarlet asks, her eyes round, eager to hear more.

"A lot was destroyed," I say. "A lot of people got hurt."

Their smiles slowly turn upside down. These girls know nothing about pain.

"Sometimes," I say, "sacrifices have to be made for good to happen." A butterfly with purple wings suddenly flickers by my face, and Scarlet reaches to touch it. I grin down at her. "That butterfly used to be a caterpillar, you know."

Several girls gasp.

"That little caterpillar had to sit in a tight cocoon for a whole two weeks before growing those beautiful wings."

Their eyes remain glued to me.

"We fought hard—your mothers and your grandmothers—to give you a life full of happiness and peace." I extend a hand out toward the bountiful trees, the multicolored flower bushes, and the cool grass—as vividly green as a granny smith apple—that surround us.

"You fought the bad men?" Scarlet asks.

I admire her bold and inquisitive personality—although only four or five years old, she'll make a strong leader one day.

"We did," I say.

"And you won?" another girl asks. "No more bad men?"

I tilt my head and intently glance at the children's mother s.

"There are still bad men out there," I say, "but that's why I created Eden—a place without any men at all."

Eve – Flashback

"We can't... we can't explain it," the fat man says, loosening his collar. Sweat drips from his dark hairline, soaking his tight white collar. He tugs at his suit cuffs as if stretching his sleeves might help him better fit into his blue overcoat that looks better suited for a kid. It's obvious that television interviews aren't his forte.

I turn up the volume on the touchscreen remote and lean forward.

"Do you think this poses any sort of danger?" the interviewer, a slender, doll-faced woman asks. She looks so out of place, too, with her three pounds of makeup and her light hair so done up it looks like she used an entire bottle of hairspray on it.

The man shakes his head, but not the *I don't know* kind of shake. It's more of a *We're doomed* kind of shake. "We have several hundred research facilities trying to determine the cause, but where's that getting us? They've been studying this phenomenon"—he does an air quote on either side of his double-chinned face—"since 2042. That's twenty years of research since they noticed the change in statistics. And we still can't figure it out. I mean, for the longest time, nature's kept things pretty balanced. You know, fifty-fifty. How the hell"—his eyes dart at the camera, and he clears his throat, no doubt realizing the limitations on the words he can use—"how is it that the ratio's been thrown off by twenty percent in only three years?

Here we are, twenty years later, and seventy percent of the world population is now women. Scientists are speculating that the figure will continue to rise and jump to eighty percent in the next few years."

At the bottom of the screen, there's a black bar with white font that reads, John Gordon: Former Director of the Federal Statistics Department.

I've been hearing about this since I was a kid—how women are going to *take over the world*. It's always been a bit of a joke in school, but over the last few years, it's been getting serious. There's worldwide panic, and every time I turn on the television, that's all I see. It would be nice to get a break, just once. I swipe the remote and change the channel.

"Hey!" Mila says.

I wave a loose hand, urging my sister to keep quiet.

I land on a news channel, where a big red bar is floating at the top of the screen. I'm about to change the channel again, when Mila says, "Wait!"

The banner reads: "New bill to illegalize the abortion of male embryos."

I swing my head around and look at Mila. She's sitting forward with her elbows on her knees, looking the same as she always does on Saturday mornings—with a messy blond bun at the top of her head that's much lighter than her roots and a pair of blue jogs and a white tank top with the same coffee stain she's had for months. Her Caribbean ocean-colored eyes are popping out from behind her thick black-rimmed glasses, so much so that I wonder if they'll smudge the lenses.

When she's freaking out this much, I almost don't notice her birth defect—a triangular-shaped dimple above her right eyebrow. It's around the size of a penny. Kids in school used to make fun of her for it, but I think it adds character. She always wears her hair down in public to hide it, but when she's home, she ties it up. Hopefully one day, she'll stop caring what people think.

Right now, I know exactly how she feels—she's terrified and enraged. The skin of her forehead creases into rolls, and she's breathing hard through big nostrils. I feel the same way. Is this truly happening? I heard about the bill only a few months ago, and I thought it was some big joke—I thought President Price was simply being President Price. I didn't think he'd actually do it.

"Are you fucking kidding me?" Mila spews. She throws her pencil at the wide, holographic television and it goes right through. Dissatisfied by the lack of impact, she tosses her homework all over the floor. "I feel like we're living in the goddamn twilight zone. How is this happening? How does the government have the right to tell a woman she's not allowed to abort based on the baby's gender? This is insane."

I give her the stink-eye. She's thirteen years old going on thirty. Where did she learn to talk like that?

"What?" she says, her thick lips parted. "Don't you see what they're doing? They're trying to gain control of us! They're scared because we're outnumbering them, and they're trying to regain control!"

I know she's right. I can't even argue. I change channels again.

"Is it true?" the news anchor asks, her eyes fixated on the camera. "Is the government considering illegalizing the abortion of male embryos to bring balance to this whole male-to-female ratio?" I can tell she's upset by the way her pointed nostrils flare out. She continues, "And what about female embryos? Are the rumors also true? Is the government planning on reinforcing female abortions in certain states?"

I can feel the heat radiating from my sister beside me.

The screen flips over to a different setting: there's a silver-haired man in a gray red-speckled suit holding a microphone. Other suited men walk behind him and enter what appears to be a hall or a government building. He doesn't respond for a few seconds, then nods his partly bald head and presses a stubby finger against his earpiece.

"Rest assured that the government is doing everything it can to bring about balance in the safest way possible," he says, his voice a deep rumble. "We're currently investigating several approaches to remedy this situation—"

"Remedy?" Mila shouts. I brace myself for a loud bang, but she doesn't throw anything this time. "What is there to remedy? Men are the reason this world is going to shit! Little pussies can't handle there being more of us? It's not enough that they're already in control? Bet you if it were the other way around, though, they wouldn't be panicking like this. They'd be having a field day!"

"Mila!" I growl, my eyes glued to the television. "I'm trying to listen."

She sighs, leans back against the couch's soft plush cushion, and crosses her arms.

"Mr. Paril," the female anchor says, her pencil-thin eyebrows coming close together, "could you please answer the question? Is the government considering the option of labeling the abortion of male embryos a federal crime?"

There's another pause as the screen switches over, and he stares at the camera like an idiot before nodding again. "As I've said, Elizabeth, the government is currently investigating—"

"That's not what I'm asking you," she cuts in. Her nostrils are flared, and her brown skin is pulled back tight on her face.

The screen is now split in half, offering a visual of both the upset anchor and the arrogant man in the suit.

"I'm not at liberty to discuss the nature of the actual investigation," the man says.

"You're not at liberty?" says the female anchor. "You're not at liberty to discuss stripping women of their rights? Abortion has been a controversial topic for decades, and now there are rumors that the government may be stepping in and regulating abortions by illegalizing specific ones only? You do realize that this also means that all women will be obligated to undergo invasive procedures to determine the gender of the baby at an early stage, right? These are human beings, we're talking about." She's glaring into the lens of the camera, a combination of disgust and hatred all over her face. "Who has the right to say it's okay to take a life over another because of its gender? Do you realize the message this is sending to little girls around the world?"

"I understand your frustration, Elizabeth," the man says, and all I want to do is smack him across the face. He's so careless, emotionless. "Rest assured..."

"Rest assured?" she slaps a hand on her desk and points a finger at the screen, but everything suddenly goes bright blue, and there's a white font caption that reads:

We are currently experiencing technical difficulties and are working to resolve the issue. We thank you for your patience.

"What?" Mila bursts out. "She was about to tell him off!"

"Exactly," I say. "Come on, Mila. There aren't any *technical difficulties.*"

She stares at me, and then at the blue screen, her jaw clenched. She digs her fingers into her veiny temples and lets out a low grunt. "I don't understand. This can't be happening."

I'm too in shock to say anything. Government-regulated abortions? Basically, population control. In layman's terms: the government plans to kill female babies and allow only males to be born to tip the scale.

How are they getting away with this? How can they possibly sign off on this? I'd understand if this were happening, say, several hundred years ago when we didn't know any better, but in 2062?

This can't be real.

My heart is pounding, and my palms are clammy.

The news channel flickers back on, but it's an aerial shot of Washington, DC. The sound of helicopter blades echoes out of the speakers, and a caption slides across the screen:

Thousands of women gather around the White House in protest of Bill Z-24.

Flags and signs are popping up everywhere. The camera switches angles, and the television offers a close-up glimpse on the ground, where gathered women are angrily waving their homemade signs in the air and shouting over each other. It looks like something out of a movie.

Another capture slides across the bottom of the screen:

Two dead and three in critical condition as riots continue in Washington, DC.

"Can you—" Mila says, flicking a hand in the air. "Just turn it off."

I sigh and hit the power button, the holographic screen flickering twice before disappearing entirely, leaving only a thin silver frame over our blue-painted walls.

Mila lets out an exaggerated breath. "Where's Mom?"

I cock an eyebrow. "How should I know?"

"Weren't you supposed to work tonight?" she asks, ignoring my question.

I stare at her. God, is she ever hormonal. I don't recall being so full of attitude four years ago when I was her age.

"No," I say sharply. "I had my final exam today. And I already told you, I don't work at Choco-Café anymore."

She lowers her head and stares at me from above her black-and-gold-rimmed glasses. "So, you don't have a job?"

Why does she care?

"I haven't had a job for six months, Mila."

She snorts and leans back into the sofa. "That explains a lot."

"What's that supposed to mean?"

She smirks up at me, and I want to ask her if she's stopped taking her Trisnol—a new drug she's been prescribed to treat her bipolar disorder. But I know if I say anything, she'll snap on me.

"You buy good food," she says, almost embarrassed.

I wasn't expecting that. For a second, I see my little sister in there, somewhere far beneath that teenage demon.

"Mom buys all the cheap shit," she says.

I give her the look—a silent gaze that warns her to be appreciative of the things she *does* have. We don't have much, and I know my mom does her best to support us. The only expensive thing we own is our television, and I spent years saving up to get it.

"I know, I know," she says and raises two open hands on either side of her face. "I liked it when you did groceries, that's all."

I know she's coming from a good place, and I can't be upset with her for sharing her feelings. Instead, I take it as a compliment and smile at her. "I'm looking into starting work at Marshall's this summer. Stacy said they're hiring cashiers, which is pretty awesome considering nowhere else wants human cashiers."

She gives me a crooked smile and looks down at her homework all over the living room.

"Until that happens, though, be thankful Mom's even bringing any food home. You know she makes minimum wage," I say.

"I don't know what you've been smoking, Eve, but Mom hasn't been to work in two weeks. She thinks I haven't noticed, but I followed her the other day. She's been going to those riots—you know, with all the feminists."

CHAPTER 2 – GABRIEL

Gabriel — Present Day

Adam is running his mouth again, teaching these goddamn dogs that women are the reason the world's fallen apart. Most days, I picture grabbing his prickly bald head and smashing it until there's nothing but shards of bone hanging from loose flesh.

But he's established himself here, among the few remaining men, and to turn against him would be suicide. He's wearing a torn, sleeveless shirt, and his tattooed biceps bulge as he animatedly talks to the crowd in front of him, like he's Jesus Christ himself surrounded by a herd of brainless sheep.

He's sitting on an old foldable picnic table—a plastic piece of garbage he seems to think of as his throne. Even from here, I can see the veins in his forehead popping. It's like he's on drugs when he goes off like that. He looks like the type of guy who would take drugs, too. He's scrawny but has a lot of muscle definition. His crazy blue eyes sit in the middle of two dark circles, and the skin around his eyelashes is all red. He has a cracked tooth at the front, but to be fair, most survivors have dental problems. Right now, he's sitting there wearing what he's been wearing for the last two months—a pair of black cargo pants he pulled off a military man, and a white long john shirt that looks like coffee's been spilled on it at least a hundred times. He always keeps his shirt tucked in, and I assume it's because it makes it easier for him to swing his rifle from around his back.

I've never hated anyone more than I hate Adam.

When I'm not fantasizing about beating the living daylights out of him, I'm usually fantasizing about leaving the Rebels. I don't belong here, but I know there's nothing left for me out there.

We've traveled hundreds of miles across cities, hoping we might find other survivors, but everything's become a giant wasteland. So many people died of starvation, disease, and violence. And I'm an ex-marine. I've seen it all, but this world... It's a lot to take in.

What gets to me is these guys. I know what they're looking for, and the thought of it makes me sick to my stomach. For years, they've been hunting for women. It's been said that a certain group of women found their way to some haven. These pricks think that if they find them, they'll get to have their way with them.

Why couldn't I have ended up with a bunch of good men? Who in their right mind thinks about sex in a post-apocalyptic world?

They've already admitted to raping women during the rebellion. In fact, they're proud of it. What kind of sick piece of shit owns up to that? Brags about it?

If I speak up, they'll kill me. All I can do is hold on to the idea that one day, I'll get my chance to take them out, or I'll find a way to run.

"Yo, Gabe!" Adam shouts, leaning his bony elbows on his knees.

I cringe at the sound of his voice. It's an exaggeratedly masculine growl. It's like he's forcing too hard to sound tough.

I make eye contact, but I don't say anything.

"Why aren't you over here?" he asks, pointing his eyes down at his little followers—a bunch of burly men dressed in blood-and-dirt-stained clothes and beards growing out past their Adam's apples. Some try to groom with their knives, but most let it grow, because they just don't care and because they think it makes them look more intimidating, which it probably does.

I look around and realize I'm the only odd man out. I'm sitting against an abandoned schoolyard's rusted chain-link fence, my back to the sun. It's warm on the skin of my clammy neck, and I'm content here.

"Think I caught something," I lie and rub my stomach.

He makes a stupid face at me and keeps preaching.

We're twelve men in total, including me. We used to be sixteen, but two got sick, and two were shot dead by Rebels from a different crew. That's the funny thing about us men—we like to say that women are the reason for this war, but we'll kill each other over territory.

Sometimes, I wonder if it would be easier if I were like Adam's men. Maybe I wouldn't feel so alone. It's an indescribable torture to feel like you don't belong to your own gender. Because in reality, there's a bunch of them and only one of me, so maybe I'm the freak. Maybe I'm too sensitive.

I run my fingers through my long curly black hair and sigh. Any minute now, Adam will get up, hop off the table in his big leather combat boots, and start walking.

Because that's all we do—walk.

Walk, sleep, eat, scavenge, and kill. I avoid the killing part, but some of the men have started giving me weird looks. It's like they're onto me, and they don't like it. They can't stand anyone who isn't exactly like them. Anyone who isn't ruthless and primitive.

I see no point in killing those who aren't part of our crew. It's barbaric. Self-defense—fine. But to kill a group of men to take their food? Their clothes?

I look down at my own leather nine-hole boots. I've been wearing these for years, and although the stitching is starting to come undone, I'll wear them for as long as I can before I steal a dead man's pair. But some of these men wear a bunch of clothes they don't even need. It's like they're proud of themselves for having killed someone. I see no pride in that.

I shift my attention to Masterson. He's probably the heftiest out of all of us, with his slimy belly hanging over his belt and his flabby arms creating pools of yellow stains under his arms. He's munching down on a stale granola bar from one of the expired batches. We raid abandoned stores and buildings whenever possible and only if they haven't already been cleared out by other survivors. Some of the stuff we pick up is expired, which doesn't matter when you haven't eaten in three days, but Masterson tends to abuse his eating privileges.

We just finished going through the school across the field. The sign in front of the school, a molded slab of metal, reads Jackson High. It's amazing what you'll find in high school lockers. There's a lot of stale weed, but most of the time, it's food so rotten it looks like a pile of brown mush and the stench is enough to make me want to run out of the school. Today, we managed to find a few granola bars, chips, chocolate bars, and candy. The rest is pretty much mush. Even sandwiches (I'm assuming they were sandwiches) look like brown soup swirling around in ziplock backs.

I wonder: if we were to run out of food, would the men turn on Masterson? Would they resort to cannibalism, given he's the fattest of the bunch? I pray we don't reach that point, but it's something I have to think about because we're all just a bunch of civilized animals. If cornered in a life-or-death situation, man will always choose life.

Adam suddenly lunges to his feet and spits out a glob of snot. "Let's go find us some pussy."

God, I wish I still had my 9mm. I'd pop one right at his face. Now that the men are fed, they're ready to hunt. Because that's all they can think about—sex. In a postapocalyptic world, they're still thinking about sex.

What a joke.

Don't get me wrong: I miss it, too. A lot. But I

wouldn't go hunting innocent women for it. When I think about rape, it puts a nasty knot in my stomach. I couldn't do it... can't imagine myself holding someone down and forcing them to feel pain so I can get off. It's disgusting. Women aren't toys to be played with by men. They're human beings.

These guys probably used to pick up prostitutes. I can see it on their faces. They're entitled pieces of shit who think the world is owed to them. They think because they're genetically bigger and stronger, they should be in control.

I'm genetically bigger and stronger than Adam—do you see me trying to take his place? I'm not an animal. I have nothing to prove. If I ever do kill him, it won't be out of a desire to be in control or to lead the group. It'll be out of a need to cleanse the world from his worthless, acne-scarred skin.

Masterson shoves what looks like a Twinkie into his mouth, and I cringe because I know that the cream inside is probably all clumpy, if not rock hard. He hops on his feet and laughs like he's crazy or something.

"Yeah!" he says, his mouth grossly full. "Let's find... s... puss...!"

Was that even a sentence? They're like cavemen. What are they going to do if they find a woman, anyway? Knock her out and take turns?

Remember, though: "women are the reason the Earth's gone to shit."

Gabriel – Flashback

"Madre, let me help you with those," I say.

My mom likes to think she can handle everything on her own, but she has a bad shoulder, and the least I can do is help. I pluck the grocery bags out of her stiff hands and bring them into the foyer.

"I could've done it just fine, my Gabriel," she says, her accent not having improved in the slightest since we moved to the United States.

"I know, Mama, but I like to help," I say.

She brushes her fingers against the scruff of my beard and looks at me with her dark chocolate-colored eyes. "How did I get so lucky?"

I smile at her. My mom means everything to me. She's always put me first—always sacrificed her own dreams to give me a life worth living. Sometimes, I wonder what life would be like if my father hadn't been killed at war when I was five. Would I have done father-son stuff? Would I be out playing baseball with him right now? Would I have steered clear of the marines?

Could be I'm still searching for him. My mother hates that I've joined the Black M, or Black Marines, a new division in the US Military, but ever since he died, I've felt a gravitating pull, an indescribable desire to follow in his footsteps, even if it means putting my life on the line.

I feel awful for my mom, though. She lost her husband, and now, her only son is leaving on a mission in a few days.

"I'm gonna miss you, Mah," I say.

She swallows hard a few times, the skin on her neck stretching with every gulp. I don't mean to hurt her—I just want her to know I love her.

She looks at me, and I can almost hear her heart shatter. "Why do you have to go? Why do you want to fight when your father died doing the very same thing?"

I cross my arms and bow my head. "Mah, you know this is something I have to do."

She taps me gently on the cheek, and her fingernails tickle me. "You won't find your father out there."

"I know that."

She smirks, knowing all too well that this is an old song, then walks into the house. I remove my shoes, pick up the bags, and follow her inside.

"Go sit," I tell her. "I'll put this stuff away."

She squeezes my forearm and goes to her favorite recliner chair, where she sits down and picks up a blue-and-black novel sitting on her coffee table.

My mom's not frail in any sense of the word. She's a petite forty-two-year-old woman with olive skin and wavy black hair she keeps tied in a small bun at the back of her head. She has a heart of gold but the temper of a wildcat when provoked.

I pull the bag of milk out of the grocery bag and place it into the fridge's bottom drawer, where my mother always likes to keep it. I personally don't like reaching down to grab milk, but at her height (a short five feet), she doesn't seem to mind.

I put the remaining groceries away and join her in the living room. She still has the same sofa I used to sleep on as a child. It's an orange-and-brown-colored fabric couch that's rough to the touch. It's hideous if I'm being honest, but it's incredibly comfy.

As I look around, I realize that everything is exactly as it has been for the last seventeen years. Nothing's changed. At least, nothing that I can see. She still has her old, yellowwood bookshelf with glass doors cornered by the window, and the walls are still a candy-apple red. Bronze and golden plates hang above the brick fireplace, something my mom's always loved to collect, especially when she goes to Argentina to visit her family. I've tried to introduce her to all the new technology the world has to offer—from holographic televisions to small interior drones that help with household chores—but she wants nothing to do with it.

I glance at her, and she slides off her reading glasses, places her book down, and smiles up at me.

"Are you nervous?" she asks.

"About what?"

"About your mission," she says. "Where are you going?"

She's always been so inquisitive. "You know I can't tell you that, Mah."

Her lips curve up and her eyes narrow on me. "So secretive. I'm your madre, for heaven's sake! Who am I going to tell?"

I rub my forehead, my smile turning into a grin. I've always had such a hard time keeping anything from my mom. She's taught me the importance of honesty, integrity, and respect since I was very young.

But I can't tell her. It's part of my clearance. It's part of the mission. She can't know where I'm going.

"Is it San Diego again?" she presses.

"No, Mah, that was my training."

"You're too young, Gabriel. You're too young to go to battle."

I lean forward, my eyes fixated on hers. "I'll be fine, I promise."

She shakes her head and pouts. "That's what your father said before he left."

There's a moment of silence, and guilt starts to set in. I've been away for two years on a mission in North Korea, and now that I'm back, I'm leaving again. My poor mom didn't know where I was for two years, and I'd rather keep it that way. Not only for her safety but for mine. I don't want to talk about what happened. I don't want to relive any of it.

"Master Sergeant Diego seems to think I have a lot of potential," I say, hoping to make her proud.

"Potential for what?"

I shrug. "To move up. To make something of myself. Mah, if I move ranks, I can take care of us for the rest of our lives. You know that, right?"

"Money doesn't matter to me," she says. "I want *mi hijo* to be safe."

I lean back into the sofa and rest my arms up on the headrest. "I'll do everything in my power to stay safe, I promise you."

She doesn't say anything. That's one thing I hate—when I upset her. But every time we talk about the Black M, the mood turns sour. I don't blame her. I understand where she's coming from and wish I could make things right.

"Can you talk about him, Mah?"

The skin on her face tightens, and her eyes light up. "About Camille? Your father?"

I nod. I've heard the stories time and time again, but when she speaks of him, it's like he's here with us. I want to hear it again before I leave.

"He was as handsome as you," she starts. "Curly black hair. Beautiful big blue eyes with long eyelashes. You look so much like him. You're as big and strong as he was, too. And that deep voice of yours... You got that from him." She stares at me as if she's seeing me for the first time. "He was funny. So funny..." She raises both hands in the air. "But also such a gentleman. You get that from him. Did you know that? Your father had so much respect for women. He was kind and fair. Sometimes I wished he'd never joined the armed forces."

I'm about to stop her and tell her that we don't have to talk about him because I can tell the story's turning dark, but she continues. "It changed him. Made him hard. But the Camille I knew before he went to war..." Her features light up again. "He was one in a million."

She stares off into space, and I sit quietly, letting her enjoy the memory.

"He was so...so..." She quickly glances up at me. "What's that word? Chivalous?"

"Chivalrous?"

She laughs, a full set of white teeth now visible. "Chilavarous," she tries to repeat. "Men aren't like that anymore. But you"—she points a stiff finger at my face—"you were raised to be chilavarous. To be kind. To be gentle with women. You know better than to ever lay hands on a woman. If I ever catch you—"

"Mah!" I cut her off. "I'd never hit a woman. Come on. You taught me better than that."

"I also taught you to open doors for women, and men, too. You show respect to everyone, and you get respect back."

She's still pointing at me. A prominent crease forms between her brows.

"I open doors for people all the time, Mah. I help people when they drop their belongings. I smile at strangers. Going away for thirteen weeks hasn't changed that."

She slowly lowers her hand and raises her chin. "Good."

"You taught me something else, too," I say, inching forward.

She tilts her head and doesn't let go of my stare. "What else?"

"How to cook. Now, what can I make you for lunch?"

CHAPTER 3 – LUCY

Lucy — Present Day

Nola is tightening the back of my fluffy, overlayered dress and going on about how beautiful I look.

I'm lucky even to be wearing this dress. It has a corset-like design at the front, with a silky material on the waist that's creamy blue. Then, at the back, there are white ruffles and frills that puff out. It makes me look older than I am. It looks like the sort of dress I used to read about in history books.

In Eden, a girl can step foot inside the Preparation Room only once. It's a big, office-sized space that was designed specifically for Graduation Day. There's an old wardrobe at the back corner, and although it's full of cobwebs on top of it, the dresses inside are probably worth thousands of dollars. Well, in the old world, anyway. They were found in an abandoned boutique on our way to Eden. I can't remember the name of it, but to this day, women are still wearing clothing they found there.

The mirror I'm standing in front of looks like something out of a movie. Its wooden frame almost looks gold, and it's huge—way bigger than the mirror I have in my room. Then, beside the mirror is a red velvety-looking couch with big yellow buttons on its cushions. I wish my room were as fancy as this one.

"You look just like your mother," Nola breathes.

I know she's right, but I don't want to say it. I've seen pictures of my mom at my age, and it's like I'm staring at her in the mirror. My eyes are a sage green right now, but they change depending on my mood. My mom's eyes did that, too. I could always tell when she was upset because they'd turn a bright pear green. My hair's way longer than hers though, but the color is the same: a dark cherry red that goes light in the sun.

If I look so much like my mom, I wonder if I'll be as tall as her. I'm already Nola's height, and she's already taller than most women in Eden, but I don't know if I'll grow much more.

Nola says she knew my mom, though sometimes I wonder how well she knew her. I doubt they were even friends. Nola's a bit too outspoken for my mom, who never much liked being around overly opinionated people.

"Are you excited?" she asks, her red-lipped grin nearly reaching her ears in the mirror's reflection. She wraps her fingers around my shoulders, and her round face nearly touches mine. Her sandy-brown hair is as frizzy as it always is in this humidity, and it tickles my ear. I can see her body behind mine because she's shaped like an hourglass, so her curves are sticking out. Today, she's wearing a purple dress with black meshing at the front. Nola seems to have an obsession with dresses.

A lot of women wear dresses here in Eden, but they don't have to. Anyone can wear whatever they want. I think dresses are more comfortable for a lot of people. Personally, I prefer wearing pants and a shirt.

"Excited about what?" I ask, and I pull away a bit because I hate having sweaty skin against mine.

She lets out a forced laugh and slaps me lightly on the shoulder. "Always a jokester like your mother."

My mother wasn't much of a jokester, especially before the war, so I don't know what she's talking about.

"My little Gracey would be graduating like you next month," she says, but she quickly turns away.

I try to remember that Nola lost her daughter during the war. I'm convinced that's the reason she's overly attached to me. She always wants to do my hair, dress me up, or meet me in Eden after I'm done with class. She'll never replace my mom, but it's nice to have an adult looking out for me. Her elbows float up beside her shoulders as she wipes her big, almost oversized eyes, and she swings back around with that goofy grin on her face like nothing happened.

"So," she says excitedly, "what's it gonna be?"

"What's what gonna be?"

"Your choice, silly," she says. "You know how it works. The day you turn sixteen years old, you make your decision."

I know what decision she's talking about and already know what I want to do for a living. I want to work with the Technicians. Realistically, it's the most useful trade now that the world has fallen apart. If I need to get away, I'll know how to fix a car and potentially save lives.

"Same thing as yesterday," I tell her. She knows what my answer is, too, but for some reason, she doesn't like it. She might have encouraged her daughter to take a different path, and now that's falling on me.

She makes a disapproving face in the mirror and pulls my long dark hair back behind my shoulders. "Sweetie," she says, "are you sure you want to get your hands dirty like that? It's a dirty job."

I shrug. "I like that."

She looks up at the ceiling and shakes her head. "I can't tell you what to do."

No, *you can't*, I think, but I don't say it.

She tucks her fingers around my hair again and starts combing her fingers through my knots. I've never cared for its upkeep the way most girls in Eden do. I know it tangles often, but it doesn't bother me. I suppose that's why I don't mind becoming a Technician; getting dirty has never fazed me.

"You'd look so beautiful if you braided your hair, Lucy," she says.

Is she trying to say that I'm ugly otherwise? That's not too nice. She must have noticed my reaction because she giggles uncomfortably and says, "You're always beautiful. But you'd look so special. You know—for your big day. Can I braid it for you? For this special day?"

I almost roll my eyes, but I remember that she's looking at me through the mirror's reflection. If it'll make her happy, then I don't see why not.

I shrug and force a smile, my lips feeling like a piece of stale licorice.

She lets out an excited cry and claps her hands over my head.

"You know," she says, separating my hair into three long pieces, "I've braided your mother's hair a few times, too."

Is she telling the truth? I stare at her in the mirror and find it hard to think of any reason she'd have to lie about something like that.

She offers me a sweet smile. "Her hair was as red as yours but not as thick."

My head nods back and forth as she braids my hair behind my neck and down my back.

"What about your dad?" she asks. "Did he have red hair, too?"

My eyes meet hers, and I can't help but wonder: if she was such good friends with my mom, how come she didn't know anything about my dad? Why would she even ask me that?

She must know what I'm thinking, because she rests one hand on my shoulder and says, "She never talked about him, you know."

I believe her.

My mom didn't like talking about my dad. She said he left us when I was a baby. Now that I'm not a little kid anymore, I don't think she was telling me the truth. But I don't know... There's something she never told me, and now that she's gone, I'll never know the truth.

I glance at my reflection, seeing my mother's face in mine: her almond-shaped eyes and her plush lips, her dimple that's barely noticeable on my chin. If there's one thing I can do to honor her memory, it's continue to hide her secret... Whatever it is.

"He had red hair, too," I say, even though I've never known my dad.

Lucy — Flashback

My mom stands in line, tapping her foot and checking the holographic wall clock over and over again.

I look around the store to see what she's so stressed about. I don't see anything.

"Lucy, sweetie, come here," she says and reaches out her hand.

I hate it when she tries to grab my hand in public. "I'm seven, Mom. I'm not two years old anymore."

"Then stay close to me."

"Is that everything?" the cashier asks.

She's a pretty lady with black hair and a silver nose ring that looks a bit too big for her little nose. She's not smiling, but I don't think she even realizes it. I think she hates her job. My mom looks at the black treadmill-looking mat that automatically moves all your items to the cashier. It's empty, so that means my mom has nothing left to buy. She gives the cashier a weird look.

The lady rolls her eyes, pops her bubble gum that smells like cherry, and asks, "Do you need a bag?"

My mom looks around quickly, then nods and twirls her finger in the air that I think means, *Yeah, yeah, hurry it up.*

"That's a dollar more," the lady says.

"That's fine," my mom says.

She's so impatient. I don't get what her problem is.

"Mom..." I try, but she waves a hand, so I shut my mouth. I know better than to annoy her when she's in a bad mood.

The lady pops her gum again, and I can smell the sweet cherry from here. "Twenty-three thirty-eight. Chip or tag."

My mom doesn't believe in getting the payment chip. Apparently, they put it under the skin of your wrist and you can use that to pay. I think it's freaky, and I'd never get it either. There's a beep when my mom taps her key tag in front of the payment machine, and she snatches her bag before the machine even makes the beeping noise. It's a beep that lets you know the receipt's been sent to your tag. Uploaded... I think that's the word.

"Do you want—" the lady says, but my mom's already hurrying through the store's front doors.

"Mom..." I try.

She grabs my arms and starts walking faster. "Get in the car."

Am I in trouble? Did I do something wrong? Why's she acting so mean?

"Mom, what's wrong?"

She doesn't answer me. I climb into the car on the other side of our old two-door Jeep, and my mom goes into her side. She starts the car before I even have time to close my door.

Her eyes are moving around all over the place, so I know she's not mad at me. If she were, I'd know about it right away. She'd be looking at me instead of everywhere else.

"Can you please tell me what's wrong?" I ask.

"Ophelia! Is that you?"

There's a woman standing beside my mom's window. Her hair is bigger than her head, and there's a goofy smile on her face. My mom looks annoyed. She pushes the window's automatic button and forces a smile at the lady.

"Hi, Susan. So sorry, I'm late for an appointment. We'll catch up later!"

The lady is still smiling, and she's about to say something, but my mom puts up her window and pulls out of the parking lot. The tires make a loud squeal noise.

"Mom, please," I try again.

"Put your seatbelt on," she says.

I keep my mouth shut and buckle myself in.

CHAPTER 4 – EVE

Eve — Present Day

I close my eyes, the afternoon sun warming the tip of my nose, and inhale the scent of lavender and lily. The wind is calm, and dozens of finches sitting atop nearby branches are singing a cheerful melody. They move so quickly from one branch to another that I often mistake them for insects.

The sound of laughter surrounds me, and I peel one eye open to spot three little girls playing with a ball constructed of condensed hay. Their mothers are watching them, and when I make eye contact, they smile sweetly at me.

Our very own paradise, I think, gazing around Division Two of Eden.

The funny thing about Eden—or the ironic thing, I should say—is that it used to be a maximum-security penitentiary. But at first glance, you wouldn't even notice it.

My gaze is averted over Eden's wall, and directly at Alpa—Eden's symbolic mountain. When war began destroying our world, the women of the underground revolution were told to look for Alpa—an immense white-tipped mountain distinguished by a steep dip at its very center. Millions of women died of starvation, dehydration, and violence trying to find it, but those who made it have stepped foot inside the golden gates of Earth.

The surviving women gathered in Eden to seed fresh grass and plant hundreds of flowers, fruit bushes, and trees. Iron gates are now entangled with fuzzy green vines and purple flowers, and the ancient concrete walls are covered in rose thorns and dark moss. Apple and lemon trees sprout in nearly every Division, along with garden beds constructed of maple wood filled with an array of vegetables—carrots, beets, tomatoes, cucumbers, peppers, zucchini.

If you crane your neck and look up at the metallic roofs of the prison, you can see solar panels attached. I owe this in part to the warden of the penitentiary, who had the obvious intention of converting the prison into a self-sustained space, but mostly, to a woman named Gail—an electrician who used to work for commercial companies before the revolution.

During the revolution, I made it a point of befriending women with various types of expertise. I was sure their knowledge would prove handy. And to date, we have one Doctor, one Dentist, three Engineers, two Electricians, and four Technicians spread out in various Divisions.

There are eight Divisions in total—meaning eight exterior yards—separated by long, tunnellike buildings that assumedly housed prisoners of different threat levels before abandonment and are now used as living quarters. The Divisions are open to every woman in Eden, however, the women are all to remain out of Division Eight—an isolated Division used only by myself—and away from the front gates.

I watch as a young woman plucks oversized raspberries from a row of bushes nearby, and I smile in admiration. Eden truly is paradise on Earth, and I wouldn't change it for anything.

Suddenly, something cold and wet presses up against my calf and I feel a hot breath blow out against my skin. I laugh before I even have the time to look down. It's Ruby—Eden's most (and only) well-loved golden retriever.

"Hey, girl," I say.

She looks up at me, her droopy lips pulled back into a full smile and her pink tongue plopped out on the side.

"You stirring up trouble?" I tease.

Her entire butt wiggles from side to side, and she lets out a playful bark, her hot doggy breath warming the side of my face. Only a few months ago, we found her in Alpa with her litter snuggled underneath the long hairs of their dead mother's belly. We tried to rescue them all, but Ruby was the only one to survive. Now, she's usually seen running around Eden's cabins or simply lying down beside the children during lesson time.

She even roams the halls of the penitentiary, sometimes seeking affection and other times, food. I always know when she's nearby because her nails tick when she walks across the cement floors. The girls of Eden have been taught to ask their mothers what they can and cannot feed Ruby. Grapes are forbidden as they can be toxic to canines. Most other fruits are acceptable, but the girls are still asked to receive permission, first.

Some days, I miss Google. I miss the freedom to research anything within seconds. I sigh and pluck a fresh apple from the tree above me, then rest myself against the bark. As I gaze around Division Two's courtyard, a sweet taste on my tongue, I realize that I wouldn't trade this place for anything—not even unlimited access to the internet. Not for money, not for gold, not for an endless supply of food.

Eden is truly paradise on Earth. Women around me smile from ear to ear, and I think to myself, *We did it.*

I did it.

We finally created a world in which we're not controlled by men. A world filled with love, hope, and kindness. There's no jealousy in Eden—no fighting over men; no stress caused by lack of money; no desire to compete with one's neighbor. Everyone is treated equally, and everyone receives an abundance of food, clothes, and shelter.

Ruby barks at me again, so I give her a soft pat on the head, but she takes off in a pounce when she sees two little girls playing with the hay ball. I watch as she hops at their feet, her long-haired tail swinging from side to side.

We're a society founded on love, respect, and hard work. The most wonderful thing about living among women is that by nature, we're creatures of nurture.

Where men seek to destroy and wound, we seek to build and heal.

I crunch down on my apple again and inhale a long, calculated breath.

"Eden," I say aloud.

Eve — Flashback

"Can you believe this?" my mom asks me.

She's leaning forward on the living room sofa with a cup of cold coffee in one hand and the television's touchscreen remote in the other. Her blond hair almost looks brown because it's so greasy, and it's hanging on either side of her face like scraggly spaghetti noodles. I can't remember the last time she showered. She's been so involved in politics, she's barely been home.

The television's holographic screen makes it look like we're standing in the interview room, right beside President Price. I'm so sick and tired of seeing his round, sweaty face on TV and the ugly gray suits he always wears. And he always combs his shiny black hair to one side, too, which makes me wonder if it's to hide a huge bald spot.

I scan the scrolling newscast message at the bottom of the screen, which reads, "Riots continue in Washington, DC after President Price signs a new bill to illegalize the abortion of male embryos."

"Who the fuck does he think he is?" my mom spews. Her turquoise eyes look like Halloween candy—perfectly round and much bigger than the average eyeball. "My body, my decision!"

I agree with her, but I'm too tired to bicker about politics. I've spent the last four days studying for today's midterm exams, relying solely on two-hour naps and a dangerous amount of energy drinks. That's what I get for choosing to pursue studies in Information Technology Law. I turn around and make my way upstairs.

"...punishable by ten years in prison. Are you... Is this some kind of joke? What the..." my mom goes off downstairs.

She sounds like Mila earlier this morning.

I close my bedroom door, plop myself onto my bed, and gaze up through my glass ceiling. It looks like the sky's about to dump a waterfall on me any minute now. The sky is black even though it's only midafternoon. Maybe Mother Nature is upset with Price, too.

I'm so tired my ears feel like they're on fire. I know things are bad—that the world is falling apart—but I'm too tired. All I can think about is the long list of internet usage offenses I've had to memorize over the last few days like searching for instructions on how to create methamphetamine, for example—a crime now punishable by five years in prison.

A loud vibration scares the crap out of me. My eyes jolt open. Did I fall asleep? There's a cold puddle of drool beside my face. The vibration goes off again. My phone. It's Ophelia, my best friend.

I slide to answer, still groggy and wanting nothing more than to curl up inside a sleeping bag for days. "Hello?"

"Eve? Did you hear? Is this truly happening?"

I roll my eyes again. Really? Was I woken up only so she could vent?

"Oh, I'm not in the mood right now," I say. I sound like a toad.

"Eve! How're you not freaking out?" Ophelia

asks.

"I'll freak out after I sleep," I say. I don't mean to be rude, but I can't think straight. I hang up while she's still talking, put my phone on silent, and everything fades away.

"Eve, wake up."

I crack open my eyes. It's Mila. How long was I out? She's staring at me with her sky-blue eyes wide open like she always does when she wants something.

"What?" I moan.

"Mom's going out to riot," she says as if Mom went out to riot every night.

I quickly sit up. "What? Why—"

"Everyone's going," Mila says.

"You're not," I say as if I have any control over my thirteen-year-old sister.

She rolls her eyes at me. "I don't want to go. But I don't want Mom going either."

I jump out of bed, my heels making a loud thud as they hit the hardwood floor. "Mom!"

But the front door slams shut and the walls of the house shake.

"Goddamnit," I mutter. What am I supposed to do? Chase after her? How will I even find her? I know my mom—she's small, but she's feisty and crazy as hell. I once saw her spit in a man's face for scoffing at her when she told him she did her own fixes and renovations around the house. She doesn't put up with bullshit, especially when it comes to men.

"This isn't like those feminist parades," Mila

says. "Mom's not gonna go swinging her bra around this time. Women are really pissed off."

"I know, Mila," I say, but I wish I could do more to console her. I can tell she's scared. I'm scared, too. It seems like we're going to war—war against the male gender. The only thing I can pray for is that Congress won't sign off. They can't. They'll realize this is ridiculous, right?

"It's bad," she continues. "Have you seen the news? The riots are getting worse."

I glance out my bedroom window and realize the sun's already set. Where's my mom going at this time, anyway?

"I haven't watched it since this morning, no," I say. I snatch my phone and open my news app. A bunch of articles detail marches and riots that are going on all over the states. Something about women standing up against President Price's bill to illegalize abortion.

The headlines are so many, I can't decide which article to open first. But then I see something. I turn my phone's screen away from Mila so she won't see the headline: *Thirteen women confirmed dead in recent riot due to homemade explosive device.*

CHAPTER 5 – GABRIEL

Gabriel – Present Day

"You know," Castor says, chewing through an old pepperoni stick that looks rotten at one end, "I never thought I'd say this, but I'm happy the world went to shit."

I stare at him. Am I supposed to respond to that? Castor's part of Adam's Rebels. I don't like him, but he's probably at the bottom of my hatred list. He's a bit dumb at times (you know, like an overly submissive dog), but he's not vulgar like the others.

For that, I hate him a bit less than the rest of the crew.

He takes another bite, then licks his thick sausage fingers that are bigger than the stick of meat. "No rules, no laws."

"And that's a good thing?" I ask.

He chuckles, showing me his mouthful of missing teeth.

"No dental care," I add.

He quickly shuts his mouth and gives me the stink-eye, but it isn't long before he starts laughing again. He punches me on the shoulder and says, "I walked right into that one."

"Looks like you walked into something, all right."

He cracks up again, slapping his knee, then points his greasy finger in my face. "You're funny."

That's the one thing I love about Castor. I can

insult him, and he thinks I'm joking. It helps me let out some of my hatred, at least. I could tell him to go fuck himself, and he'd probably laugh at that, too. But I don't say that to him. He's an idiot, but he's not a jackass. I bulk all of Adam's men up in the same category, even though the rare few, like Castor, don't really deserve it.

Sometimes, when Adam talks about the women he's *put in their places*, Castor walks away, usually to find me. He thinks I'm a clown, apparently. I don't smile when I insult him, so I don't understand what he finds so funny.

I gaze around, and I spot Adam searching the school's perimeter. No doubt he's looking for weapons or something. We've walked about sixty miles from our last location, Jackson High School, to find ourselves at another school... Riverside Elementary School.

Adam seems to have a thing for schools. The hateful side of me can't help but wonder if he has a sweet (pedophilic) spot for the young ones or if he likes brick buildings. There's a certain level of safety, I suppose. That, and the cafeterias sometimes still have nonperishable foods.

He fastens his AK-47 over his shoulder and walks out toward the rest of us, his chest puffed out.

"Perimeter looks good," he says.

Seriously? Was that his version of a sweep? Fucking moron.

He drops his gun into his hands. "Let's move in."

He's such a prick. How are the other men not

realizing how unfair it is for him to hold a semiautomatic AK-47, while we're left with our fists to defend ourselves? He likely has a fucking tiny peanut-size dick. A micropenis. He needs to feel like a *big man* with his *big gun.*

I can tell by the way he holds it that he has no prior experience with guns. He's a loose cannon with a weapon. Fantastic.

I've seen him shoot it twice, and both times, he wasted dozens of bullets before hitting his target. If he were smart, which he obviously isn't, he'd hand the gun over to me, the only marine in the crew.

Then again, I'd probably kill him on the spot. So it could be he's smarter than he looks, with his nasty acne-scarred face and gummy smile. Now that I think of it, he looks like a horse. A hairless horse with those big teeth of his.

I picture myself pressing my boot into his throat, my old 9mm pointed at his shiny forehead, and I smirk to myself. My last words to him would be "Hay, hay there, stop struggling. You ain't geddying up."

And with that, BAM, right in between the eyes.

The men around me get up one by one, and we follow Adam toward the school's main entrance. Shattered glass is sprinkled all over the pavement that's smeared by a dark red stain. On the door's stone-blue paint, there's a bloody handprint.

For heaven's sake, this is an elementary school. Why is Adam going in? There were rumors that some men (especially religious fanatic followers of President Price, pretty much all white men) believed that children born of women during the revolution weren't pure... That they were sinful because their mother's generation fought the biggest rebellion in history. And because of this, they thought the children deserved to die.

I saw it on the news, but only once. An elementary school had been infiltrated by a group of men with dark masks and semiautomatics. They killed every girl in sight and took the young boys. No one ever figured out what they did with the boys, but it isn't hard to put two and two together. They were fanatics who wanted to build an army of men. What better way to do it than to raise kids into it? To teach them from a young age that women are nothing but *tools*. Nothing but species used for reproduction and pleasure.

I'm terrified of what I might find inside this school. Adam doesn't seem to care. He's walked over hundreds of dead bodies across the wastelands without so much as a glance. I don't understand him. These dead bodies were once people. They had families. Loved ones.

Adam only cares about himself. He doesn't give a shit about his men, either. He'd kill us all if it meant guaranteeing his safety. That's why he holds that gun. He needs to be in control.

He kicks the front doors open, and the remaining shards of glass sprinkle to the ground as the doors hit the walls on the inside. There's more blood inside, and I'm sick to my stomach.

His leather boots squeak as he cautiously moves forward, his back hunched and his gun improperly aimed in front of him.

Idiot.

The men follow with tight fists and huge eyes, while mine wander to the walls, where massive picture frames are mounted in a perfectly even row. Little plaques indicate the years above them: 2060, 2061, 2062, 2063, and 2064. But that's it. There's nothing else. 2064 was the last year children went to school.

I look at the kids in each picture. They all have silly grins for the most part. Someone on the other side of the camera was trying to make them laugh.

I wonder how many of them are still alive if any. That's what sickens me so much about the revolution... about the war. Women and children weren't spared. There was no mercy. So many men were brainwashed into believing what women spent countless years trying to erase: that men were better than women.

Is it that fucking hard? Is it so difficult for us, as humans, to live peacefully and equally? No one's better than anyone else unless one of them is a complete piece of shit like Adam. Everyone's better than Adam.

But I suppose that's how wars start. Everyone feels entitled to something. Everyone wants to prove they're right and others are wrong.

Just like religion. I fucking hate religion.

All it does is tear people apart. It's like humans can't think for themselves. They need a *higher power* to tell them what's right and what's wrong. But even then, it's twisted, isn't it? It's all left to interpretation. Interpretation of a man-written book.

I clench my teeth and move away from the picture frames. Adam signals us to move closer, lifts his gun at what appears to be a set of cafeteria doors, and kicks it hard. When he enters a room like that, I pray that we have enemies on the other side. I pray that he gets a bullet straight in the head.

Although I hate our crew, except for Castor, sometimes I wonder; would they behave differently if they had a better leader? They are sheep, after all. Their brains are moldable. What if I led them? Could I teach them that they're a bunch of pigs? Could I also *unteach* them? It's hard to imagine me teaching grown men a lifetime of values my mother taught me.

But, it might be possible. I have to believe it is because I don't want to be alone in this world, and I don't want to be with men like this, either.

Adam takes a step toward the open doors but quickly throws his arm over his mouth and nose. "Jesus Christ."

I don't need to step foot into the cafeteria to smell it. I'd know that smell anywhere. I've smelled countless times on my missions. It's a foul, stomach-churning stench that makes you want to vomit out your entire stomach.

"Nothin' good in here, boys," Adam says, and he continues down the hall.

As the men walk away, I stop at the cafeteria entrance and peer inside. Castor quickly glances back at me, a look of despair in his eyes.

Big plastic tables are sprawled throughout the giant room. Some have fallen over, or maybe they were pushed over to be used as shields because there are black bullet holes in them.

But what's around these tables is what makes me want to drop to my knees.

Hundreds of decaying children, anywhere between the ages of six and twelve, lie still in pools of crusted blood.

Gabriel — Flashback

She doesn't want to let go of me, and neither do I. I don't know when I'll see her again.

"I love you, Mama," I say.

She nods quickly, her face pressed against my chest, then pulls back. Her eyes fill with tears, and her lower lip trembles like boiling water. She places a soft hand on the scruff of my cheek.

"Oh, my sweet Gabriel. I love you more than words can say," she says.

I bend down and kiss her forehead, then throw my bag over my shoulder and climb up on the shuttle bus. I stare out the window, my forehead pressed against the glass. I wish I could tell her that I'm not even leaving the country. That I'll only be a few hours away. But I can't. I can't tell her anything, and it kills me.

She rests a hand over her mouth, then wipes away her tears. The driver closes the doors and drives ahead. My throat swells, but I fight back the emotions. The last thing I need is to show weakness on a shuttle bus full of new marines.

"Gabe?"

I clear my throat and quickly turn to the side. I can't believe it. It's James Walsh, my bunkmate from training. He looks the same as he did when we were training, only his dirty blond hair has grown out a few inches. He has an unsightly scar that cuts through both his pale lips and down his freckled chin. He's wearing his full uniform—a blue, gold-buttoned top with a white undershirt and a tie—the same as mine and every other man's on the shuttle.

"James?" I pull my bags on my lap and he sits beside me, a big deformed grin on his face.

"You're working GENESIS?" he asks.

I nod. "I thought you were posted on the southern coast of Iran?"

He looks around, then leans in, his voice almost a whisper. "No, man. Haven't you heard? They're pulling a bunch of resources from the Middle East to assign them here in the US."

"Why?"

"Same reason they're assigning us to GENESIS," he says. "The riots are getting out of control. Every state has been hit. And the riots are getting violent."

He pulls away and gives me a full up-and-down look. "Don't you watch the news, man?"

I shake my head. "Haven't in the last week. I've been spending time with my mom."

He scoffs like I'm a loser because I'm so close to my mom. "I'm friends with a few of the corporals down at Area 82. Well, they're friends of my father's. Anyways, I hear everything. You'll get a full briefing when we get to Area 82."

I feel like a dog being sent to an adoption center. I have no idea what's going on. I've only heard of Area 82, and it's supposed to be a top-secret compound. Why the heck would they send new recruits of Black M there? The only thing I do know is that I'm obeying a specific order, which was to climb on Shuttle #45 at 9:00 a.m.

That's what I did. But what now? What's this briefing he's talking about? How much has happened that I don't know about?

"Bet you didn't know that the funding for Black Marines has skyrocketed this year. Two-hundred and fourteen billion dollars."

I part my lips to tell him how crazy that is, but he continues. "And, rumor also has it that they're removing women from the military. No one's talking about it, but it's happening."

"What? Why?"

"Why do you think, Gabe? They're outnumbering us. They're infiltrating from the inside."

I almost burst out laughing, but I realize he's serious. He's staring intently at me from behind his yellow-green eyes just like he used to do during training when we were about to tackle a complex, terrorist-themed drill together.

"Come on, James," I say. "Are you seriously buying into all of this? That women are trying to take over? Men are the ones stripping their rights away."

His jaw muscles pop, and he looks away. I hit a nerve.

"Did something happen?"

He shakes his head, but I know he's lying.

I nudge him with my shoulder. "James, come on. What's going on?"

He's staring at the blue leather seat in front of him, his eyes wide and his nostrils flared so much they're red. "Dayna left."

"Your wife?"

He doesn't say anything.

"What do you mean, left?" I ask.

He quickly turns to me, and I can't tell whether he's about to cry or punch me in the face.

"She took off. With Maddison, too. My baby girl. What the fuck? Who does—" He clenches his fist and raises it like he's about to punch something. But he doesn't. He lets out a long sigh. "Said that if I didn't stand up to President Price, I was no better than all the other men out there. Took her fucking bags and left overnight while I was sleeping."

"Jesus, James. I'm so sorry."

He shakes his head again, then rubs his face with his freckled hands. "I've been training for this, you know? It's my career. She wants me to drop everything? And for what? How am I gonna stand up to the government? I'm one man. One fucking man."

I don't know how to console him. I stare at the shuttle's gray floor.

"You know, I spent weeks beating myself up over this. Kept thinking that maybe I should've quit the marines. Maybe Dayna was right, and I was being brainwashed. But then I realized, she's the one who's being brainwashed. She's exactly like all the other women. Trying to take control of men. Trying to dictate how I should live my life."

I don't agree with his view, but James is my friend, so I keep my mouth shut.

"Anyways, there's nothing I can do now. She's gone. I don't know where she went. She's probably joined some rebel group. With Maddison, too. My little girl."

He bites down on his fist.

"I'm sorry," I say. I may not agree with or believe everything he's saying, but he's obviously hurt by the whole thing. And as his friend, I truly am sorry.

"It's fine," he says, and a smile returns to his face. "Goes to show you that women can never be trusted."

CHAPTER 6 – LUCY

Lucy — Present Day

"Do you remember your lines?" Nola asks.

"I, Lucinda Cain, pledge my allegiance to Eden," I say.

"Then Eve will ask you: 'Lucy Cain, today marks the day you decide your role in our society. What trade do you wish to pursue?'"

"I choose Technician," I say.

"Very good," Nola says. "It'll be short, but it's important you get the lines right. Eve is pretty particular about keeping the ceremony traditional."

Particular? Aunt Eve has always been a bit OCD. At least, that's what my mother called it, whatever it means. It's weird to refer to Eve as *Eve* when she's the one who cared for me after my mom died. They used to be best friends. She'd visit us all the time in our apartment to talk about rebellion groups and what we needed to do to stay safe.

I remember her always fixing my mom's picture frames on the walls. She'd open and close our kitchen cupboards, then smile down at me when I'd catch her and say, "Just giving the plates some fresh air. It helps them stay clean."

I believed her then. I was only five. But now, looking back, I know that's weird. My mom tried explaining it to me once. She said something along the lines of *obsessive*, but I never remembered the actual term.

And now, I'm supposed to repeat some lines in front of a room full of women as part of a ceremony. Will Aunt Eve treat me like a stranger? Over the last few years, she doesn't visit me in Division Five as often as she used to. Then, about six months ago, she stopped coming to my Division entirely.

She's been acting a bit funny. I've seen her a few times, but she's usually walking fast and avoiding eye contact. Could it be she's stressed out or something? Or, is her OCD getting worse? I hope she's nice to me at the ceremony. I miss my Aunt Eve.

"Are you ready, sweetheart?" Nola asks.

I slip on my lace sandals, even though they barely fit me anymore, and stand up. "Ready."

She shrugs both shoulders excitedly and grins. "You look marvelous."

"Thanks, Nola."

Her fingers dancing, she extends a hand and I grab it. "Come on now, it's almost time."

She leads me down the corridor of Division Five and into the main hall. It's a big room in the shape of an octagon with shiny white floors. Up top, for a ceiling, there's nothing but glass windows. It fills the room with a lovely natural light.

But we don't cross the main hall. Instead, we turn right and go into Division Four. I've been here a few times. At the end of the corridor, there's a theater room. It looks like one of the rooms we had at my old school, where kids would perform plays. There's a stage and everything. And in front of the stage, there's a bunch of chairs for people to sit on.

When I walk in, I receive a lot of stares and a lot of smiles. Women sit all over the room, and at the front, there's a row of empty chairs. I know these chairs belong to my teachers because they have talked about the ceremony before and about how they always get to sit at the very front. I'm excited to see them. Even though I miss my old friends from school, I'm lucky to have gotten such nice teachers here in Eden.

Nola leads me around the audience and through an old wooden door at the back of the room. I've never been in here before. It looks like an old office or a lounge. There's a small brown suede sofa in the back underneath the barred window, a rack of long jackets beside it, and an empty garbage can that's fallen over. Aside from that, it's pretty bare.

The one thing that surprises me though is that there are no other kids. I suppose it's because, in Eden, I'm officially becoming an adult.

"You can sit, honey," Nola says. She leaves only a crack in the door and presses her face against it, peering out into the crowd.

"What're we doing in here?" I ask.

She smiles back at me. "It's like a school play. You have to wait to be called up."

Part of the ceremony, I realize. I make my way to the sofa, pull up my dress, and plop myself down with a sigh. This is it. There's no going back after today. Will I regret it? What happens if I change my mind in five years? What happens if I don't want to be a Technician anymore?

For the first time, I start to feel anxious.

Why does it have to be so official? Eden is paradise, right? At least, that's what all the women here keep telling me. So why is it that I have to make such an important decision at my age? I'm only sixteen. I'd only be in the middle high school now. But instead, I have to commit to a trade. I have to officially announce what I'm going to do for the rest of my life.

I rest my head back and look up at the rectangle-tile ceiling. Cobwebs line every corner, and the metal brackets holding the tiles have a bunch of rust on them. My heart beats a staccato in my chest. Why am I so scared? Did I make the wrong decision?

But then I see my mother's face form in one of the tiles above me, and I remember what she told me one day before she died:

"Lucy, I need you to promise me something," she'd said, her fingers digging into my shoulders. "Promise me that no matter what happens in this lifetime, you'll always trust this."

She then poked a finger against my chest, right below my heart.

"Always trust your gut, no matter what."

Lucy — Flashback

My mom rushes into our apartment and closes the door behind us with a bang. She locks the chain and the big metal lock thing over the door handle. She only does that when she's scared.

When she drops her purse and keys on the table beside the couch, it sounds like a bunch of metal making music. She pinches the middle of her nose and walks back and forth.

"Mom?"

She ignores me again. Why won't she talk to me? I'm not a toddler. I can handle it.

Then, it's like a lightbulb lights up in her head because she reaches into her purse and pulls out her cell phone. She hovers her hand over it, pokes at something on the screen, and presses it to her ear.

"Eve? It's me." Her voice is all shaky. "There were two of them. I don't know what to do. I think I lost them, but I can't be sure."

She stops talking for a minute, and I can hear Aunty Eve's voice on the other end, but I can't understand anything she's saying.

"Yes, I'm sure. I know. Yeah. Okay. You're right. Okay. I'll be here."

She stands up, drops her phone on the couch, and lets out a long breath.

"Are we in danger?" I ask.

She wasn't expecting that from me. Her eyes become soft and full of love. She wraps her arms around me, kisses my forehead, and says, "No, of course not, sweetheart."

But I know she's lying. I'm not stupid. I can see it on her face. And I know because of the way she drove home and the way she locked the doors. She's scared of something or someone.

"Is Aunty Eve coming over?"

She smiles. "Yeah, she's coming."

I always like it when Aunty Eve visits. She usually brings me something special like a cookie or a cupcake.

"Are you hungry, babe?" my mom asks.

"A bit," I say.

"Let me make you some noodles, okay?"

She gets up and heads to the kitchen. The sound of pots and pans hitting each other bounces around in the apartment, and it sounds like she's whispering to herself.

I want to help. I know I'm just a kid, but if she'd tell me what's wrong, I could help. I don't like seeing my mom this upset.

"My H-Cap's in my purse, Lucy."

Now I know something's wrong. Mom doesn't like it when I play on her H-Cap for more than an hour a day. It's a rule she says is for my own good. Something about my eyes and my brain. It sucks because I love playing Catch Alfred. It's a game she downloaded for me last month. It's a ghost game. You have to stare at the screen until you see something move, and then you poke that spot to catch Alfred. If you miss it, you lose points. If you catch it, you win points.

I'm far along in the game.

My mom hates the game, though. She says it drives her *insane*, whatever that means. But that's only because she's not good at it and she always loses. Every time she plays, she pokes too far, and her finger goes right through the game and messes it all up.

Mom likes to talk about the type of toy she grew up with instead. She says it was a lot easier when they had tablets and gamepads because the screen was solid. The H-Cap (I think it stands for holo-something capsule) looks like a small white handle that fits in your hand, and when you press the power button, it shoots out a screen at one end. You can either play in the air, or you can put the screen against a wall or on your lap. I usually play it in the air like most kids my age do. My mom prefers to have it on something flat.

But she's letting me play with it again even though I already played for more than an hour this morning. That's how I know something's wrong. She wants to keep me distracted. But I don't mind because I want to play.

I stick my hand into her purse and pull out her H-Cap. I'm about to open the game when the apartment's beeper goes off. I hear something loud bang in the kitchen, and my mom swears.

"Mom?"

"I'm okay—just dropped something. Can you answer that?"

I get up and tap the answer button on the security machine. "Hello?"

Aunty Eve's face pops on the screen. She has a

huge smile on her face as soon as she sees me.

"Hey, kiddo!"

"Hey, Aunty Eve! I'm letting you up now."

I press the big green button on the screen, then go to the door and start unlocking the chain, but my mom scares me. She wraps her hand tight around my wrist.

"I got this, Lucy. Go sit and play, okay?"

I'd be lying if I said I'm not a bit hurt that she doesn't think I'm able to answer the door on my own. I sit down on the couch and turn on the H-Cap. I open the app, and the game's music goes off. The sound comes out through the speakers of the handle, and it tickles my hand.

My mom's head is right in front of the door's little peephole as she waits. Aunty Eve doesn't have time to knock because my mom unlocks everything and opens the door real fast. She tells Aunty Eve to come in quickly.

As soon as Aunty Eve is inside, my mom shuts the door hard and locks everything up as fast as she can.

"Jesus, O. You're losing it."

"I'm not losing it!" my mom says, but her eyes turn to me and I quickly look away. I don't want her to know I'm not even playing my game. I want to know what's going on.

She calms down and whispers, "I know what I saw, okay?"

"Hey, kiddo," Aunty Eve says, and she smiles over my mom's shoulder. "Brought you something."

I drop the H-Cap and jump to my feet. She

sticks a hand in her pocket and pulls out a banana oatmeal cookie wrapped in a blue-and-yellow package.

"Thanks!" I say.

"Hey, can you do me a favor?" she asks. "Can you go hang out in your room for a bit? I need to talk to your mom in private."

Even though I don't like being treated like a baby, I like how honest Aunty Eve is. She isn't sneaky. If she wants something, she asks. I like that. So I listen to her, and I take my cookie and the H-Cap into my room.

"I'll bring you some noodles as soon as they're ready," my mom shouts out.

I close my door and press Start on my game, but only so the music plays loud. Then I sit down on the floor and push my ear against the door.

CHAPTER 7 – EVE

Eve – Present Day

I force myself out of bed even though I feel like a pile of bricks from a demolished haunted house.

I open my closet doors and pluck out the white suit farthest to the right. There's a row of matching suits that I obtained in one of Acitok's abandoned stores—all identical—but I always pluck the one on the right. It's a feeling I get. Any other choice feels like terrible luck.

I slip into my suit, soften its cuffs, then zip up my shiny, knee-high red leather heels.

There's a blue bucket of water by my bed with a rag cloth dangling off its top lip. I soak the cloth in the water, twist it with both my hands, then gently dab away the sweat from my forehead and neck.

Some days are easier than others. Some days, I look at what we've accomplished together as women and think to myself, *We won.*

Other days, such as this one, I begin to question our likelihood of surviving. Days blend together, and I lose the drive I once had. I'm drained.

When I was fourteen years old, my mother had me evaluated by a psychiatrist for my mood instability. Some days, I'd come out of my room dancing, while others, I'd lay in bed all day envisioning the afterlife.

This feeling was and still is, unbearable. It

comes out of nowhere.

I think of Dr. Nali, the woman my mother forced me to see, and a faint smile creeps onto my face. When I entered my very first session with my pierced septum and my black-dyed hair, she didn't judge me—not the way most adults did.

She sat across from me and smiled. She was a little Indian woman with a small brown bun fastened at the top of her head and a silky green outfit wrapped around her entire body, almost like a cocoon.

"Have a seat," she said, a small voice accompanied by a thick accent.

I stood there, eyes shifting from side to side, not wanting to move a single muscle. It took time for her to gain my trust, but she was patient every step of the way.

But what I'll never forget about Dr. Nali was the day she dragged her chair in closer to mine. At this point, I still hadn't divulged anything about my personal life. I wasn't ready. She sat still, staring at me from behind narrow charcoal eyes, her knees mere inches away from mine.

"Let's start with the abuse," she said.

Now, I inhale a deep breath and pinch the skin over my right eyebrow—a quirky crutch of mine when I feel an unwanted, heightened sense of emotion. It might have something to do with an old eyebrow ring I used to play with.

The window by my bed is entirely fogged, and the air around me is heavy and humid. If there's one thing worse than not having my medication in Eden while in a depressive state, it's waking up to a rainy day. On such days, most women and children remain indoors, the younger ones running about the corridors, their laughter echoing through iron gates and across the walls.

It drives me mad.

But these women have expectations. I'm expected to be a strong leader—not a pathetic human being whose actions reflect her weak state of mind.

Consistency is what feeds strong leadership. If I'm not consistent, the women will begin to doubt me. They'll see me as a loose cannon—as someone capable of making a wrong decision inspired by *feelings*.

I won't allow it.

I brush my short hair to the side, pull my shoulders back, and make my way in front of my mirror.

You're beautiful—look at you.

These women are lucky to have you.

You're the greatest leader all of Eden could ask for.

My lip curves downward, almost as if capable of identifying the lies I tell myself. But I fight this instinctive reaction and force a wider smile.

You can do this.

I tug at the bottom of my coat and walk out of my room and toward the main hall.

I'm too lost in my thoughts to realize several women sitting on the benches across the main hall, their conversations echoing up and across the high ceiling. The main hall reminds me of a shopping center's food court, only much cleaner and in the shape of an octagon. Glossy yellow and gray tiles cover the floor, and nine entryways every five or six meters—one for each Division, and one for the main entrance. The walls look like they've been painted over a hundred times before someone finally painted them a matte yellow. The color brings life to the room, which is what I'm assuming was the intent given that it was a shared space among prisoners.

The main entrance lies behind Plexiglas, another set of iron gates, and a massive steel door. On the outside of this is another path leading out to the wall's main gates—a barrier constructed of steel and solid wood that lies between our concrete walls.

But the main entrance is rarely used now. Opening the front gates exposes all of Eden to the dangers of the fallen world. Although we used to venture to nearby cities upon first establishing ourselves in Eden, we learned following a series of violent attacks and brutal rapes that we are safest inside the walls.

"Morning, Eve."

My heart skips a beat—I didn't see her.

"Good morning, Agatha," I say, my lip twitching upward.

Smile, damn it.

I try harder, and it feels foreign.

Agatha is probably the eldest of the women in all of Eden, which has earned her a great deal of respect. The journey to this prison was not an easy task, and many women died along the way—especially the elderly.

She smiles up at me, her dry colorless lips stretched on her loose-skinned face.

"How're you today, Agatha?" I ask her.

She shrugs. "Oh, you know, getting by." Her voice almost sounds like a rusted nail turning in wood.

"Still nice and strong, I hope," I say.

Someone bursts out laughing at the opposite end of the room, and I swiftly turn around, prepared to condemn them for their rudeness.

Two women sit on the wooden bench between the entrances to Divisions Four and Five. They're touching hands and leaning into each other as if sharing some of the world's deepest secrets, and I realize their laughter has nothing to do with me or with Agatha.

I hate being on edge like this.

"I'm holding up well," Agatha says. She rubs her veiny, sun-damaged hands together and gently rubs her knees. I can tell she's in pain. "Are you making your way to Lucy's graduation?" she asks.

Then it comes back to me. Lucy. She turns sixteen today.

Children between the ages of five and sixteen attend class every day of the week. Each one of my Specials—the women I brought to Eden who specialize in specific trades—teaches a class of her own. The idea behind this approach is to transfer valuable knowledge to our next generation to not only guarantee their survival but also, to encourage growth and prosperity as we move into the future.

When a child reaches the age of sixteen, she decides which trade she wants to pursue. The idea of male and female roles doesn't exist in Eden. If a girl wants to become a Technician, she's encouraged to follow that path. Every girl obtains knowledge in each area—food preparation, electricity, plumbing, medicine—but she has to choose to specialize in only one of these.

Today, Lucy makes her choice.

"Of course, I'm going," I say, thankful for Agatha's reminder.

"I'd come, but this weather is taking its toll on me." She rubs her knees again and grimaces.

I place a gentle hand on her hard, hunched back that feels like clay. "It's okay, Agatha. I'll let you know what she picks."

Graduation is always held in Division Four because there is a theater room at the very end of the hall. I make my way down Division Four's corridor as fast as I can and enter through the double wooden doors. The room itself is generous in size. Most of the ceiling tiles high above me have turned a dull yellow, and massive windows surround the rectangular-shaped room. Today, the room is filled with a dark gray light, and condensation fogs every window. The blinds remain open most of the time, although I assume these were originally set in place to allow for a dark setting when prisoners were granted the privilege of a movie night. There's an old projection screen at the back of the room, but we have yet to use this.

Fiona, my finest electrician, has recently started working on connecting the projector to our solar panels.

Several women are seated on the metallic, gray-cushioned chairs that are evenly positioned across the room.

I'm met with curious glances, and I do my best to smile at every woman as I make my way to the front stage. How long have they been waiting for me? I can only assume Lucy is waiting in the back room for my call. I wonder if she's changed over the last six months. I haven't taken the time to visit, and I'm sure she's upset about this.

Although I'd never admit it, Lucy is growing up to look like her mother—long, silky red hair and bright green eyes. She has a small pointed nose, like Ophelia, and a spirit stronger than a dozen women combined.

I need to distance myself. It's too hard.

I focus my attention on the audience. Her teachers are sitting in the front row, eyes glued to me like a herd of sheep around Jesus Christ himself. I straighten my posture and readjust my suit.

"Good morning, my beautiful ladies," I say, and the room lights up. "Thank you all for coming to this memorable ceremony—the Graduation of Lucinda Cain."

Eve — Flashback

"You think a sign's gonna get you anywhere?" he says, resting his thumbs on the edge of his leather belt.

I'm holding a red-and-white sign I found on the street near a dumpster that reads "For women's rights, I'll fight." I don't know where it came from, but I figure if I'm going to find my mom, I'd better fit in.

What the hell was I thinking? Coming out here alone? But what else was I supposed to do? I promised Mila I'd find Mom before she did anything she'd regret, like get herself arrested. I didn't want Mila coming out here with me. I couldn't put her in harm's way.

"You'll fight, huh?" he says. He puffs out his chest, his bulletproof vest making him look twice his size. "I've always liked a fighter."

His police cruiser is blocking the end of the alley, and my only way out is to run the opposite way, but his hand hovers over his gun every time I step backward. I shouldn't have cut through here. I thought I'd save some time by avoiding the crowds, but all it did was get me cornered.

"I'm looking for my mom," I say.

He's looking at me like he wants to eat me. He's licking his slobbery, purple lips and breathing hard. He's a pig—I can see it in his eyes. My heart's racing and I debate running the other way. What's he going to do? Shoot me? It might be worth the risk.

"Your mom? How old are you, kid?" he asks.

There's a sick smile under his long, pointed nose, and I know my youth is turning him on. He looks like he's forty-something, like he could be my dad. In fact, he could be my dad, being that he reminds me so much of him: a dirty piece of shit who thinks he's entitled to anything he wants. He'd probably beat my mom the way my dad did, too.

"Fifteen," I lie. If he thinks I'm a minor, perhaps he'll back off. But he's not buying it. He's got an arrogant smirk on his thin, white-edged lips.

His dark beady eyes examine me up-and-down. "You don't look fifteen to me. So I'm gonna ask you again, and if you lie to me, I'll know. How old are you?"

"Eighteen."

The corner of his lips points straight up on one side. "You realize rioting is illegal, don't you?"

"I wasn't—"

He steps closer, and I stiffen. "You have two options here. Either I take you in, and I'll make sure to go into detail about how I saw you throwing rocks through the bank's window on Second Street—"

"But I didn't—"

"Or," he cuts me off, "you be a good little girl and do as you're told."

He grabs me by the shoulder, and I jerk back, but his grip tightens into my nerves and a sharp pain shoots up my neck. He moves even closer—so close I can see up his nostrils. My head is just below his chin, and he's staring down at me like a dog on the verge of eating a bowl of wet food.

I feel like I'm going to pass out. Either that or jump out of my own body. The adrenaline is indescribable. Any moment now, I'll wake up. Any moment. Because a cop wouldn't do this. Cops are meant to uphold the law, not take advantage of young girls.

But I don't wake up. I'm still standing here, and I don't know what to do. I can't fight him; he's a cop. And if I try to run, he'll catch and arrest me.

I stand with trembling legs, praying for the nightmare to end.

"What are you—" I try, but he sticks a cold finger over my lips. It smells like stale cigarettes and alcohol.

He unbuttons my jeans with his right hand and pulls down my panties, his hot booze breath hitting me hard in the face. I'm shaking so bad, I don't understand how I'm still standing.

Run, Eve, just run.

But I can't. I can't move. Why can't I move?

He flips me around like I weigh five pounds and my face cracks against the brick wall. I can't think. Make it stop. Make it stop. This can't be real.

I hear him unbuckle his belt and unzip his pants, and all I want to do is scream. But I can't talk—I can't do anything. Why am I so fucking helpless? It's like the sensation you get when you're in a nightmare, and all you want to do is run, but you're melting into the ground.

I want to wake up.

Please.

He bends me over, his hand wrapped around my

hair. His fingertips touch my vagina like he's mapping it out. He kicks my legs apart with his steel-toe boot and lets out an excited grunt.

"Please, sto—" I try, but my voice cracks and tears stream down my face. "Please."

"This won't take long, sweetheart."

And then all I feel is excruciating pain and pressure as he forces himself inside of me.

CHAPTER 8 – GABRIEL

Gabriel – Present Day

Adam's acting like nothing happened. Like he didn't see hundreds of dead kids in the cafeteria. How does he do it? How is he so goddamn heartless?

"Check the lockers, boys," he says. "Might be some lunches left behind." He throws his shaved head back and laughs, and the blue veins on his neck pop out.

Did I miss the punchline?

He catches me glaring at him and waves his AK-47 toward the lockers. "You too, Gabby. Let's go."

The last person I want to take orders from is Adam, but he's holding a gun, and he's got a temper hotter than the Grinch's fireplace on Christmas Eve. I do what he says, and I start opening and closing lockers down the hall, along with the other guys, who are scavenging through everything they find.

"Looks like no one came back for their kids' things!" Jefferson shouts out, his annoying, multitoned voice echoing throughout the school.

Jefferson's exactly like the rest of them: macho, arrogant, and full of delusional entitlement. He's holding up an empty school bag that looks like it has dinosaur claws sticking out of it, and a pile of chocolate bars and individually-wrapped jujubes start forming a pile at his feet.

"This one probably belongs to a fatty," he says,

laughing, and I have to consciously remind myself that killing him won't get me anywhere. I slam the empty locker I searched, and I sense a few eyes on me.

"Problem, Gabby?" Adam asks.

"None here," I say.

It's only a matter of time before Adam kicks me out of the gang. The only problem with that is—if I'm not one of them, I'm an enemy. He'd kick me out all right, only, permanently. I'd have a bullet between both eyes... well, after he wastes a few dozen rounds because of his shitty aim.

Part of me wants him to kick me out. I know that if they turn on me, it leaves me an opportunity to fight back, to take as many out as I can. I need a reason to fight, and defending my life is reason enough. All I need is to get my hands on that gun.

He catches me eyeing it, and I quickly look away. He may be a moron in some ways, but he's not completely stupid. He knows I hate him, which means he also knows I'm a threat.

The only advantage I have over him is that he thinks I used to work as a pizza delivery guy. He thinks I'm a joke, and I'm fine with that. I'd rather he believe I know nothing about combat or guns, that I didn't spend eight years of my life working covert operations as a Black Marine.

I freeze when I see a Swiss Army knife sticking out of a blue-and-gray backpack in locker #281. A pocketknife? Why the hell would a kid in elementary carry a pocketknife? I look back, and when I see that the boys are busy eating chocolate bars, I tuck the knife in my pocket.

The kid might have used it while camping or fishing with his parents, for all I know. Or, maybe, the kid was smart and knew something bad was coming. A true soldier. I wonder which one he is in the cafeteria. I prefer not to think about it, so I keep searching through the lockers.

I find a container full of mold and brown liquid. I wonder what used to be inside it. A sandwich? A hot meal? Some leftover lasagna?

I toss it back inside the locker and move on to the next. I'm about to unzip the top pocket of a little girl's pink butterfly bag when a single gunshot blows loud against every locker in the hall. I instinctively drop to a crouched position and pull out my knife.

Adam looks as confused as me, which means he isn't the one who shot it. Jefferson's fallen to the floor, his back up against a row of lockers and his hand over his shoulder, which is soaked in blood. His face is contorted, and he's breathing hard through clenched teeth.

I'm about to start giving orders because no one's moving. They don't know what to do. But then I remember that Adam's in charge. Why not let him screw this up? Why not let him get killed? For all I know, I'll become friends with our unknown shooter.

Adam makes some sort of hand gesture that I can only assume means, *let's move*, and the men follow close behind, their boots squeaking in the corridor.

One gunshot? Most likely a lone shooter. But why shoot at a dozen men? I look at Jefferson, who's wincing behind that curly brown beard of his. He keeps smashing his head back against the locker with his teeth bared in pain. I think back to when I heard the gunshot. Adam was standing right next to him, I remember.

The shooter was probably aiming at Adam because he's the only one with a gun. But why? I scan the area, trying to replay the scenario in my head when I realize that he, or she, was trying to protect something. Whoever shot at us didn't want us scavenging through the lockers. They didn't want us taking all the food. And whoever fired the shot isn't too experienced with a gun, either.

I walk a bit faster because there's a good chance the shooter's a kid or a teenager. A scared kid who panicked when they thought we were taking all their food.

My mind races. What if there are survivors in this school? What if some kids are still around, living in the only place they feel safe? The only place they know? No one came back for these kids. No police, no ambulances, no parents. The bodies were left behind. The shooting might have happened before the mass bombings started, destroying the entire city and everyone in it.

I hop into a full-blown sprint, picturing a young kid's terrified face. But Adam suddenly yells something from around the corner of the hall, his voice as harsh as thorns from a rosebush. Then, at least a dozen shots are fired, and metal shells clang against the hallway's tiles before another sound is heard—the sound of a body collapsing.

Gabriel – Flashback

"So, this is Area 82," I say, taking it all in.

It looks like a prison when you first see it. Several concrete buildings are positioned behind massive barbed-wire fences. Military trucks and combat vehicles are parked inside the compound, and hundreds of uniformed men are moving around like a bunch of ants. Most of them are wearing the typical Army Combat Uniform or ACU while others are wearing dress suits, dark sunglasses, and shoes so shiny they look like they're made of metal.

Four big black SUVs with tinted windows are parked in a straight row, and behind these are three brand-new crossover combat drones that look like something you'd see in a science fiction movie— onyx black, sharp edges, and windows tinted darker than the body paint. There are small silver studs around every sharp angle, and if I were to guess, I'd say the blades are hiding underneath their bellies.

"Never thought you'd end up here, did you?" James asks, beaming.

He looks like a rich kid who's giving his poor friend a tour of his mansion. Like he's been here many times before.

"Why are we here? I thought this place was for personnel with security clearances even higher than top secret," I say.

I've only ever heard about Area 82 through some of the guys during our training program. It's something everyone talks about, but only the best of the best ever get to step foot inside.

"This is where we're being trained for GENESIS," he says. He's gazing out through the fogged window, and his freckled face is inches from mine.

It must be nice to know everything in advance—to have friends inside of Area 82. We turn toward the front entrance, and two massive iron gates slowly draw open. The shuttle stops before we enter and its brakes make a high-pitched noise.

The driver opens his side window, and it looks like he's talking to a soldier or a guard. Then, the shuttle's side door opens and a uniformed man holding a blue laser-powered assault rifle steps in. He's wearing goggle-like sunglasses that don't suit his square, butt-chinned jaw at all.

Although I can't see the soldier's eyes, he seems to be inspecting the shuttle. He takes a few steps forward, looking down at the first newbie sitting at the front of the bus.

"Identification," he says, and his voice resonates throughout the metallic cylinder.

The guy at the front pulls out a leather wallet from his pants pocket and extracts his military ID card. I follow suit, even though the soldier hasn't reached me yet. The uniformed soldier does this for each man in the shuttle. When he gets to me, I try to smile at him, but it almost looks like he's disgusted with me.

What's his problem?

He snatches the ID out of my hand, bows his head further, then looks back up at me. He hands me back my card without a word.

Are they all this cold? I'd hoped that military

staff aggression was only part of the training program—you know, for intimidation purposes. What if all soldiers are like this?

Will I lose sight of myself and become like this, too?

When the soldier finally steps off the shuttle, his heavy walk moving the whole vehicle from side to side, the driver brings us farther into the compound.

"Hey, check it out!" someone says.

A few guys jump out of their seats and move to my side of the bus. I follow their gaze, and my jaw drops.

There's a huge dome-like building at the back of the compound. It's made entirely of dark glass and metal support beams. The sun reflects off it at every angle, almost blinding me. Out of this dome comes an F-94 Eagle—one of the newest fighter jets to be designed—slowly taxiing out on the runway.

It's black and red, and its nose is twice the length of any fighter jet I've ever seen before. If rumors are true, this thing flies at a speed of Mach 8.5 and contains a self-charging laser-gun system. Again, I've only heard about this, so I have no idea if it's true.

Then I see the other planes. Three more Eagles sit at the base of the runway, and beside them is a massive Z-149 Hercules that makes the jets look small. It looks like an ancient artifact next to the new jets.

"Holy shit," James mutters.

At the opposite end of the runway, which seems

to be over several miles long, is a landing pad—or at least, it looks like it. Around this are a bunch of camo-colored 2048 Iroquois helicopters.

I feel at home.

The bus comes to a sudden stop, and everyone jumps back into their seats. The driver, who's also wearing a military uniform, stands up and says, "Head to door A-2 and wait there with the new recruits."

When we step off the bus, the air is hot and dry. I feel like I'm stepping foot into a desert. I drop my bag and stretch my back and legs, feeling a pop, and I wonder how long we've been driving. Three or four hours most likely.

The sound of squeaking brakes fills the air behind us. I turn around and see another shuttle bus—a long black vehicle with tinted windows—pull up beside ours. And then another, and another, until there appears to be well over twelve shuttle buses on the premises.

I lean in toward James. "These all new marines, too?"

He pulls out a cigarette, lights the tip, and nods as the smoke comes blowing out in my face. He then turns to me, his green eyes almost yellow as the sun comes shining through them. "Shoulda watched the news."

CHAPTER 9 – LUCY

Lucy — Present Day

Nola looks back at me and smiles—an excited grin that stretches the middle-aged skin of her face.

"It's time," she says.

I know it's time. I heard Eve call my name. I stand up and brush my dress down to get rid of its wrinkles. Nola opens the door for me, and I walk out, suddenly feeling like I'm all the way back in fourth grade walking out into a crowd of parents who are waiting to watch their kid participate in the school play.

Eve is standing onstage. Her bright red boots are the first thing I see. They have a sharp heel at the back, and they make her look much taller than she is. They look like a combination of plastic and leather, and she's wearing the same white dress suit she always does. It's like she has dozens of matching outfits in her closet that she wears on a rotational basis. I don't understand how she keeps them so white. We don't exactly live in luxury. I also don't like looking at her in that outfit. This isn't the Eve I know. The Eve I know would be wearing a pair of jeans, a nice zip-up hoodie, and some Nike sneakers or something. And she'd have long wavy hair all the way down her back, like her little sister, Mila—not some short, perfectly combed doo.

She's smiling at me, and although it looks

genuine, I don't trust her. Aunt Eve's changed. She doesn't even visit me anymore. Am I supposed to smile back? Is that the rule? I force my lips into a grin and feel like a complete idiot.

My eyes shift down to the women sitting on rows of cushioned, metal chairs. They all look like clones, with their glossy eyes wide and bright and their lips pulled back in exaggerated grins.

"Lucy," she says softly, reaching out an open hand.

Am I supposed to grab it? I catch it with mine and shake it gently. It's what my mom always taught me to do. If someone gives you their hand, you shake it.

But she's staring at me, and the room is silent. Someone clears their throat, and I glance back, realizing it's Nola. She's poking her head out of the room I came from, motioning a kiss-like gesture.

I look up at Aunt Eve, whose bright blue eyes are glued to mine. It's like she's not even in there anymore... like she's dead. She smirks, but it looks like she's annoyed, even though her eyes are crinkled as though she's smiling.

I bow my head and kiss the back of her hand, and all at once, the crowd says, "To a new start."

My eyes go wide, but I don't mean for them to. I'm a bit freaked out. I've never actually been to a graduation before. Only the adults are allowed. There are a lot of events that only the adults go to. What the heck do they do? Get brainwashed? They look like a bunch of zombies right now.

I feel like I'm back at The Holy Temple of

Christ—a church on Second Street my mom brought me to five years ago, but only once. She was never much of a religious person, but her mom, my grandma, was. I remember her rolling her eyes when my grandma walked into our apartment with a bunch of crucifixes. She said it would clean out all the negative spirits in the home. After that, she said she was taking us to church.

So, my mom got me all dressed and said, "Pretend you're watching a movie in your head, okay sweetheart? I'm sorry about this, but it'll make Grandma happy."

She said I couldn't bring the H-Cap, either. It was the most boring thing I ever did. And that's exactly what it feels like today. Like I'm at church or something.

After I kiss her hand, Eve doesn't let go. Instead, she pulls it up over my head and turns toward the crowd.

"Today, Lucinda Cain announces her destiny," she says, and everyone's smiles stretch even farther, almost like they've been told to do it.

I look over at my teachers, hoping for comfort, but they're smiling and nodding like everyone else.

Aunt Eve lets go of my hand and takes a step back, leaving me alone at the front of the stage. It's my turn, now, like Nola told me it would be. I look at the ceiling, searching for the lines I've been practicing with Nola every day for the last week.

I, Lucinda Cain...

I pledge...

Eden... I pledge...

Why aren't they coming to me? My heart's racing, and if I don't get this right, I worry I'll be punished for it. I turn left a bit. Nola is now standing in the room with me, right beside my teachers. She doesn't look like the rest of them, and I find comfort in that. She looks sincere. Her brows are close together in the middle of her forehead, and her tight lips form a straight line. She's nodding slowly, like a basketball coach watching his players on the court.

As though she's saying, "You've got this."

I nod back slowly, raise my head, and take a deep breath.

"I, Lucinda Cain"—I hesitate, but I look at Nola again, and I feel calm—"I pledge my allegiance to Eden."

"Lucinda Cain," Eve says from behind me, "today marks the day you decide your role in our society. What trade do you wish to pursue?"

I'm about to say, *Technician*, like I've been telling Nola for weeks. But something suddenly happens. I can't describe it or explain it. Something shifts. I feel like being a technician isn't the job I'm supposed to do. It's not what I'm meant to be.

I glance at Nola one last time, knowing that the answer that's about to come out of my mouth is the last thing she'd expect to hear from me. In fact, it's the last thing anyone in this room would expect, especially my teachers, because it's always been the most discouraged choice of profession in Eden.

"I choose Healer."

Lucy — Flashback

I know Aunty Eve sent me to my room because she doesn't want me to hear what she has to say to my mom. That only makes me want to hear it more.

They think I can't handle it because I'm seven. I'm not a toddler. I can make my own choices. Plus, I'm turning eight next month. I wish my mom and Aunty Eve would treat me more like an adult sometimes.

I turn down the volume on my game, Catch Alfred, and hope they won't notice. And I sit there and listen.

Aunty Eve says something about staying calm. I can hear my mom pacing back and forth in the apartment. Aunty Eve is probably telling her to calm down. She does that a lot. My mom gets stressed out easily sometimes. Okay, often. She's usually rushing through the store, or telling me to be quiet because she thinks someone's following us.

I think someone is following us, too, but I don't know who. I don't know who would even want to follow us. Me and my mom have a pretty boring life. I go to school during the day, and my mom comes to get me and we go home. She makes me supper, helps me with my homework, and lets me play on my H-Cap while she talks on the phone. Sometimes with Grandma, but usually with Aunty Eve.

The last few times, though, she started whispering on the phone. Like she doesn't want me to hear. Like it's some big secret. I know something's wrong. I can see it when she looks at me or tells me to go to my room.

I also know something's wrong with the world. My mom usually has the TV playing after I go to bed. She doesn't know it, but I like to press my ear against the door, so I can listen. I also have a glass in my room that I haven't brought back to the kitchen, and I use it to hear better. I put my ear over the bottom of the glass and put the glass on the door. It works well.

She tries to turn the volume down on the TV, but I still hear it. The TV talks about how the world is all messed up. How there are way more girls than boys. I think this is cool, but I guess the adults don't.

Then, she'll turn the volume down even more when there are explosions or guns being shot. She could turn the volume down as low as possible, and I would still hear some of it. I have good ears. Sometimes, though, if it's really bad, my mom turns off the volume. I know because I can see the TV's blue light under the crack of my door, but I can't hear anything.

There's a lot of fighting going on in the world, and I think soon it will happen here in Arlington. Mom says we're close to where the president lives, and because of that, we have to be careful.

The other night, I thought I heard someone shoot a gun, but my mom told me she didn't hear anything. I don't believe her. I know she heard it, but she doesn't want to scare me. She doesn't want me to know that bad things could happen to us.

I look back at my bed and at my favorite sheets. They're blue, red, and green, with Mario sitting on top of Yoshi. Mario's my favorite game. Every time a new one comes out, my mom buys it for me on the H-Cap. They're like small episodes.

I wonder if any other kid near us has the same sheets. I wonder if any other kid near here has gone through some of the bad things they talk about on TV. They must be so scared. I don't like thinking about it too much because then I get scared. I get scared that something bad will happen to me or my mom. But I try not to be scared because if I'm brave, my mom might be braver.

I get up and look under my bed. There's a bunch of little race cars, action figures, teddy bears, and Disney character Barbies. Some of my friends at school think I'm weird for having *boy* toys. I don't think there's such a thing as *boy* toys. My mom's always told me that toys are toys, and I can pick whatever I want.

Mr. Shilo is taking up the most space. He's a giant panda bear, and I've had him since I was little. I push him over and crawl under the bed. I know I left the glass here somewhere. If I don't hide it, my mom will take it and wash it. But I need that glass to hear through the door.

I wave my arm around, hitting as many toys as I can until I feel something hard and cold. It's hiding in the corner, behind my big yellow Camaro car. I pull it out and hurry back to my spot beside the door.

The only bad part about listening is that if my mom opens my door, she'll catch me sitting right beside it. Sometimes she knocks, but sometimes she doesn't. I once told her that I want some privacy, and she said I'm too young to need privacy, whatever that means.

I put the glass against the door, and I'm careful. Then, I put my ear over it. It's cold on my face, but it'll warm up.

"They won't fucking stop ...." my mom says.

She swears a lot when she thinks I can't hear her. It's funny. But if she knew I was listening, she wouldn't find it so funny.

"O, come on. Talk to me. Sit down and talk to me," Aunty Eve says.

My mom whispers something, and I can't hear it.

But I don't give up. I keep my face pressed hard against the glass. I know it's leaving marks on my skin, but I don't care. If Mom asks, I'll say I fell asleep on one of my toys.

I want to know who's following us. I usually only get to hear Mom when she's talking on the phone. I can't hear the other person. But now Aunty Eve is here, and they're talking about what happened at the store.

If I listen long enough, I'll find out.

CHAPTER 10 – EVE

Eve — Present Day

A Healer? Why on Earth would Lucy choose to become a Healer? The teachers know all too well that this profession is to be heavily discouraged. We already have two highly capable Healers, both of whom report to me directly.

To encourage children to become a Healer is to encourage death and disease. For every light, there is darkness. To become a Healer is considered bad luck in Eden.

Not only that—the idea of having a child meddle with toxic ingredients and potent plants is also not something I condone. But, as with any other profession, it's a choice the child has to make. If we deny them the option altogether, they'll start to question my authority, which is how rebellions begin.

And the truth is, we *do* need some children to train in this domain, but the plan was to select them ourselves—to select a child who's suitable for the position. A child who's moldable and compliant.

But Lucy? She's an overly inquisitive creature by nature. She's the last person I'd want in such a powerful position. I grind my teeth, careful not to let my anger show.

Even though the children are given the choice, they aren't supposed to actually *choose* it.

She's standing onstage, her back facing me, and the women in the audience are staring at her. Their smiles have all vanished, and there's a heavy silence in the room. My lips twitch and I step up beside her.

I grab her hand, a little tighter than intended, and pull it up above her head. She lets out a little whimper as I tug, but the women don't seem to notice.

Just finish the damn ceremony, Eve.

"Lucinda Cain," I say, "a Healer."

The women exchange confused glances, and I can tell they don't know if it's okay to clap.

"Wishing you wealth and prosperity, Lucinda Cain," one woman says choppily, and everyone else repeats her words.

I lean my head back and grin, almost painfully, at the audience before me, before letting go of Lucy's hand. She pulls away and rubs her wrist before rushing by her fake mother's side—Nola.

"Congratulations on your graduation, Lucinda," I say, and she's looking at me like I'm a complete stranger.

But I don't care. It's better this way. I walk off the stage and make my way out the door.

Who does she think she is?

No child has ever selected Healer. What is she trying to prove? Is she trying to sabotage our paradise? Everything I've worked for? Is she trying to attract darkness into Eden?

I rush back to my room. I need to be alone—I need to think. As trivial as it may appear to be, Lucy's decision has opposed everything we teach in

Eden. Her decision has proven her to be defiant. It's proven that she's prone to temptation, to select what's out of reach.

I march down Division Four's hall, careful not to make eye contact with any of the children wandering the halls. On Graduation Day, there are no classes. It is a sacred ritual, and the children are left to enjoy themselves in all of Eden. But the last thing I want to do right now is smile at a child who expects me to be nice to them.

When I reach my room, I gently brush the silver nameplate that hangs to the left of the door. It reads, C-1-354—a plain room number like any other. But this room is mine, and I intend to keep a clean plate.

I admit it's much nicer than any other living quarter in Eden. It's located directly beside my office—my Throne Room—and I'm assuming it used to be the staff room. There's a white, yellow-handled fridge in the corner and on the right wall, an old beige kitchen sink without any running water.

We're still working on obtaining our own water supply being that the prison's pipe system is completely corroded. And even if it wasn't—city water is a thing of the past. For the time being, we have stations set up in each Division to collect rainwater and several wells dug throughout Eden. It supplies enough drinkable and cleansing water for the women. To connect the pipes to the well system is a different story, but Renata, my plumber, has assured me that with the proper equipment, she can do it.

Obtaining the equipment, however, is what's proven most difficult. I've considered letting her use one of the military combat vehicles to explore old cities nearby, but I can't risk losing her. She's the only plumber we have.

I close the massive industrial door and make my way across the room, my heels ticking against the wooden floor. When we first established ourselves in this prison, this room was carpeted with the same ugly gray industrial carpet as found in my Throne Room. But a few of my carpenters volunteered to rebuild the floors with oak. They found some cans of varnish and cherry stain in the basement's supply room and used these to refinish the surface.

I'll admit, my room makes me feel like royalty. Golden-laced curtains hang on either side of my window. Iron bars run horizontally across the Plexiglas, but most of the time, I forget they're even there. I've considered having them removed as a safety measure, but I am less worried about fire hazards than I am about male Rebels attempting to break their way in.

My bed, a queen-sized project constructed of two single mattresses, lies at the very back of the room with its head against the wall. The comforter is thick and of a rich purple, with gold stitches to match my curtains. I found these in Acitok, an abandoned village we crossed before settling here.

There is a large, full-bodied mirror hung up near the window. It's old with its mahogany frame and dust-encrusted corners, but it does the trick.

I step in front of it and straighten my posture. I stare at myself for a minute or so—something I do every day—and attempt to center myself.

I reach a hand to my face and gently brush the tips of my fingers down my fuzzy cheek. Right now, there is no pain. Some days, however, I see my sister in the mirror's reflection—crisp blue eyes, long blond hair, and a light beige skin tone—and my heart breaks. My cheekbones are slightly higher than hers, and my face is narrower. Yet aside from that, she's all I see.

But right now, I don't feel sad—all I feel is anger.

What is she trying to prove?

I inhale a deep breath, my nostrils flaring into pointed pink triangles.

She's a child.

She's not trying to sabotage anything.

But if she does anything to get in the way...

I turn my head to the side, unable to look at my reflection. She's only a child, for God's sake. How could I even think of harming her? Of banishing her?

She's not just a child—she's little Lucy.

O's little Lucy.

I catch a glimpse of my reflection again, and a deep sadness overcomes me.

Ophelia.

My brows come close together. Does Lucy know the truth?

What have you done? This is all your fault. Are you proud of yourself? Of what you've become? Of who you are?

It doesn't matter who I am. What matters is that I continue to guide these women in the right direction and away from mankind's monstrosities.

That's my purpose.

That's why I'm here.

I try to smile, but my lip only twitches and I feel idiotic.

There's no reason to smile.

You don't deserve to smile.

I tug on my white overcoat and pull my shoulders back, creating an arch in my back.

"I'm Eve," I say aloud, "and I will bring these women eternal happiness no matter the cost."

Eve — Flashback

She looks so frantic right now, walking from one end of the apartment to the other.

"O, would you sit down?" I say.

She flicks her hand at me as if she doesn't want to hear what I have to say. Yet, she called me.

"Ophelia!" I say, and her eyes catch mine. It works every time—calling her by her full name. I wonder if her mother does this to her, if that's why she reacts the way she does.

She breathes out sharply, then plops herself down beside me and presses her face into her hands. She peeks at me through a crack in her fingers. "Am I losing it? Do you think I'm crazy?"

It's funny how O turns to me for consolation when I'm the undergrad living with my mom, and she's several years ahead of me, with her own apartment and a kid. I feel much younger than her in so many ways—not only in age—but when it comes to her emotional well-being, I'm always able to center her.

"You're not crazy. I'm sure you *were* followed," I say.

"I was," she says, almost snapping, but she quickly collects herself.

"Was it Jason? Is that ass..." I lower my voice, realizing that Lucy may be able to hear us. "Is that asshole still harassing you?"

Jason's her ex-boyfriend. Well, he wasn't much of a boyfriend at all. He was an acquaintance through friends. O says she doesn't remember what happened, but I think she doesn't *want* to remember. She says her friends found her in the laundry room with her pants down to her ankles seconds after Jason walked out, and there was blood in her panties.

Now he's been harassing her—telling her if she doesn't let him see Lucy, he'll take her to court. But it doesn't end there. He has some macho friends he's been sending out to stalk her. He seems to think that intimidation is the way to get what he wants.

What worries me is that Jason's already threatened to let his guys do whatever they want to her and said if Lucy happens to see them gang-banging her mom, then that's *too bad*.

He's a goddamn lunatic.

She looks like she's about to cry, but she swallows hard and bites down on her bottom lip. "Yeah, he still is. But he's not the problem right now. He knows I've been talking to Laura Stanford—a lawyer I found online. He knows he needs to keep some distance right now. It's his fucking henchmen. If anything happens to me, or my daught"—her voice cuts out—"they'll deny having any connection to Jason."

"And the police? He's harassing you, O."

She rolls her eyes at me. "Did you forget? Jason's in Police Foundations. No one's gonna take my word against a soon-to-be cop. Not to mention, he's already buddy-buddy with a bunch of cops at the station, and they're all men. I can't remember the last time I saw a female cop. No man is gonna take a woman's side—not with everything that's going on."

I let out a long sigh. Although I'd never say it aloud, I wish someone would kill him. He can't be arrested, and she can't sit around and rely on the court system. Murder seems like the only plausible way out.

"What're you thinking?" she asks me.

I must have had my *thinker* look on: a spacey gaze below two furrowed brows.

I'm picturing him lying in gravel beside an alley dumpster. His face is beaten to the point of deformation. His bloody teeth are on the ground, and his lips are a dark gray-blue.

"Nothing," I say. But the truth is, I'm also picturing myself standing over him with a crowbar hanging at my side. Or a big piece of wood. I'm not sure what I'd use. Anything I could find, I suppose.

Where are these thoughts coming from? I know they're wrong, but I can't help myself. He's a piece of shit and he deserves it. In fact, he's more than a piece of shit—he's a sociopath. O's told me some stories about his past that would make anyone want him dead—animal torture, mostly.

I quickly force a smile when I catch her staring at me again. It's only a thought, I tell myself. It doesn't mean anything. Everyone has violent thoughts every now and then. I'm sure O has them, too.

"You have any big guys as friends?" I ask.

She cocks an eyebrow at me.

"You know, to go after these guys. To go after Jason's lapdogs."

She shakes her head. "It's only me and Lucy."

I'm running out of ideas, and I find myself turning back to my original fantasy.

What other way is there?

"You want some noodles? I'm making spaghetti," O says, pulling me out of my barbaric train of thought.

I smile up at her. "Sure."

She goes into the kitchen, and the sound of plates and utensils clanging together echoes throughout the apartment.

"Lucy, honey, food's ready," she shouts out.

Lucy comes bolting out of her room—much faster than I'd have expected. Was she just sitting there? By the door? Listening to everything? I'm glad I didn't talk about killing anyone.

She smirks at me, almost mischievously, and I know she was listening.

"How's your game?" I ask. "How many points are you at?"

She's quick on her feet. "Twenty-three thousand."

I nod slowly even though I know she's bluffing. She's a smart kid, I'll give her that. She gets a bowl of spaghetti with steaming hot tomato sauce and runs back into her room. The whole apartment smells like warm thyme and oregano.

"Here," O says, handing me a kid's plastic bowl with spaghetti inside. It looks like the 2042 holographic version of *Finding Dory*, but I can't tell because most of the blue paint is chipped off.

"Nice dishes," I tease.

She shoves a spoonful of spaghetti into her mouth, pink noodles dangling against her chin. "Dat's—dat's what you get," she tries, "when you 'ave kids."

I wonder if I'll ever have children. But then I think of O and the heartache she's going through, and the idea turns me off entirely.

"Do they know where you live?" I ask.

She takes another bite and looks up at me, this time her mouth too full to even try to speak.

"His goons," I add.

She nods.

I clench my fingers tight around my fork. Poor O. I know exactly how she's feeling—how difficult it is to feel powerless at the hands of a man. I'm suddenly drawn back to that awful night, and I can feel the police officer's breath on the back of my neck before he spreads my legs open and forces himself onto me.

I want to tear off my skin or step into a fountain of acid.

I feel so dirty—so violated. I never told anyone about that night, especially not O. She's already out of touch, devastated, even. I can't add anything to her stress although it's eating me alive.

My eyes are wide, and the fork's metal handle is creating a groove in my palm.

They're animals—all of them. It's no wonder there's a war starting. I want to make this right for her. I lick the spaghetti sauce off my fork, then lean forward and smirk at her.

"Let's kill him," I whisper

I can't explain why I said it, but I did. And there's truth to my words, even though I let them spill from behind a smile.

Her first reaction is to stare at me, eyes wide. Then, the corner of her lips pull up, until finally, she bursts out laughing.

"Yeah, I like that idea," she says, but she's being playful.

I chuckle along with her, but my smile quickly vanishes, and a heavy weight fills the room. I can tell she's picturing it.

It *could* be easy if done right.

CHAPTER 11 – GABRIEL

Gabriel — Present Day

What the fuck did you do?" I snap.

Adam quickly turns around, his face contorted with rage and his rifle pointed straight at my face.

"Back the fuck off, Gabby," he says.

The kid is lying on his back with a pool of dark blood spreading out from under his ribs. He has long brown hair, and he's as scrawny as a praying mantis. He's wearing a ratty orange T-shirt with some dinosaur construction logo that looks like it's too big for him. His eyes roll to the back of his head, and his lips open and close, but nothing comes out.

Under the construction logo is a puncture hole, right where the bullet went—right in his stomach. The kid's sneakers squeak against the floor as his legs slide up and down like he's trying to get away, but he doesn't stand a chance. It's like watching an injured insect attempt to run from some sadist holding a magnifying glass.

"He shot at me!" Adam says. "What the hell does it look like I did? I defended myself."

Masterson steps forward, his big belly jiggling out in front of him. "Chief's right. Almost shot me right here." He points at his shoulder.

My eyes gravitate to the pistol beside the kid's hand. He must have dropped it when he fell.

Adam notices me eyeing it, and he shakes his

rifle that's still pointed at me. "Don't even think about it."

"Are you gonna put him out of his misery, or do I have to?" I say.

Everyone's staring at me, including Adam, who looks as confused as a poodle in a herd of sheep.

"He'll die soon enough," Adam snarls.

He's trying to defend himself. Trying to get out of finishing what he started. He's a goddamn coward. He can shoot at a kid, but when it comes time to actually killing him in cold blood, he can't do it. Even if it's to help him.

I step forward, but Adam tightens his grip on his rifle.

"The kid's suffering, Adam!" I say.

His wheels are turning. He looks down at the kid, who's now gargling massive amounts of blood, then back at me. He eyes Masterson a few times, then the other men. For the first time, Adam doesn't look like a leader. He looks like a scared mouse.

I take another step. "You don't have to be heartless, Adam. What if this was your kid? You shot him in the stomach. He's bleeding internally. He's scared right now, and he's in excruciating pain. We don't have the proper equipment to save him. All we can do is help him move on."

I hate myself for even saying this. I'd never let someone die. In our modern world, he could be saved. A shot to the stomach is treatable if it hasn't punctured any vital organs. But there's no 911 service. There aren't any ambulances or paramedics, and I'm no doctor. If we had a doctor, and a fully-supplied first aid kit, he might stand a chance.

But we don't have any of that.

I can't take it anymore. I can't watch a kid suffer like this.

I move forward, knowing that Adam might shoot me, but it's worth the risk. I pick up the pistol and aim it straight at his heart. Normally, I'd aim for the head, but I can't disfigure a child like that. My stomach tightens, and I clench my jaw. His dark eyes roll toward me, almost pleading, and I fire the shot.

"Drop the gun!" Adam shouts.

He's pointing it at me, even though I'm holding the pistol loosely by my side. I stare at the kid's pale face, and all I can tell myself is that he's in a better place. A better place than this hellhole.

"I said drop the fucking gun!"

I slowly turn toward him, gun down by my side. With my training, I'd have a bullet in between both his eyes before his finger pulled the trigger. But I'm not an idiot. I don't know how many bullets are left in this gun. Certainly, not enough for the rest of the men.

"I'm not gonna hurt anyone, Adam. Relax," I say and drop the gun against the tiled floor.

Adam jerks his chin toward the weapon and makes eye contact with Masterson, who rushes to my side, picks it up, and brings it to Adam like a dog with a stick. He slips it into the side of his belt, his hateful eyes still glued to me.

He's upset that I defied him, but I had no other

choice. I couldn't sit there and watch that.

"Next time," I say, "try to kill him with the first shot."

My mother would be ashamed of me for even speaking those words. He shouldn't have shot at the kid at all. But, like Masterson said, the kid shot at them. It was self-defense. I can't stop Adam from shooting at anyone. The least I can do is hope he kills them on the spot rather than maiming them.

This isn't the first time Adam has fired a shitty shot. I've seen men clasp at their chests or at their throats as we walked away. Adam left them there to suffer. God knows how long it took them to die... if they even died.

He ignores my comment and turns away. "Let's keep moving."

Everyone walks past me, except for Castor, who pats me on the shoulder.

"You okay, Gabe?"

He cringes, and his top lip is pulled back over what remains of his front teeth like I'm going to hit him or something. Like he's scared of me. Or it could be he's not as dumb as he looks and he knows I'm not okay.

He looks up at Adam and the other men, who seem to be making their way to the teachers' lounge, then back at me. He leans in, his hot, rotten breath polluting my nose.

"Ignore Adam. He's a jackass and he'll get what's comin' to him."

Gabriel — Flashback

We're sitting in a giant auditorium, and the room fills with chatter. Uniformed men are everywhere. Some have rifles, others have crossed their arms over their chests. The walls around us are made of gray stone, and the ceiling is abnormally high.

The lighting is dim, with only pod lights illuminating the walkways between each aisle. The stage, however, is lit up. It almost looks like strobe lights are pointed directly at it. A bare microphone stands in the middle of the stage; dark red curtains hang behind it.

Dozens of men with slick, gelled hair and black suits are lined up in front of the stage and several dozen more patrol the walkways. It's as though I'm in a movie. Like any minute, we're going to be given the option to take a blue pill or a red pill.

James nudges me in the ribs. "You ready for this?"

Ready for what? I don't even know what's going on. He can tell I have no idea what to think.

"We finally get to be part of something bigger than us, Gabriel. We're finally going to do something worth being proud of."

But there's an indescribable energy in the air. It doesn't feel prideful at all. It feels dark and loathsome.

A man steps out onto the stage, and the entire auditorium goes disturbingly quiet. He's wearing a black overcoat, black dress pants, black shoes that are shinier than his bald head, and a gold emblem pinned over his heart.

He's a big guy. The kind of guy whose neck is so thick he has rolls at the back of his head. His beard is short and bristly, but I can't make out any of his other features from this distance.

"Who is this guy?" I whisper, but James gives me a stern look that silently tells me to *shut up*.

The man in the suit with the golden emblem walks toward the microphone, the sound of his heels echoing at every step. He clears his throat, a deep rumble that echoes throughout the entire auditorium, then opens his mouth to talk.

"Welcome." His voice is deep and rugged, the sort of voice someone gets when they have a bad cold. But he doesn't have a cold... that's his voice.

"You're here today because you have been hand selected to serve your country."

Silence.

I expect people to applaud, but no one is moving. Everyone's fixated on this man.

"As you all know, things have taken quite a turn for the worse these last few months. Riots have begun erupting throughout the United States, and governments are being overturned."

He plucks the microphone out of its stand and paces across the stage.

"We're at war, gentlemen."

And when he says that, I realize something: there aren't any women in here. At all. I know the military is male dominated, but I didn't expect this. Is this what James was talking about? They're removing women from powerful positions. They're scared that because of this unexplained increase in the female population, women will take over.

But like my mama said to me when we were watching the news before I came here, "Men are so stupid. They think women want to take over the world. Women are nothing like men. We don't want power. We want to live and enjoy life and all of its beauty."

I never take offense when my mom insults men. I know where she's coming from, and deep down, I know she's right. As I look around the room, I'm reminded of exactly how far men will go to maintain control.

What did I get myself into? This wasn't the type of mission I wanted.

The man in the suit clicks down on something, a remote of some kind, and the giant red curtains slide open. A transparent crystal globe is positioned on the stage, and it flickers a few times before a holographic screen appears overhead.

"In the next few days," he goes on, "you'll be witness to some of the most atrocious events that are currently taking place on our home soil."

The video is choppy like something taken with an old cell phone, and it looks like a riot. There's no sound, so it makes it hard to determine what's going on. People are everywhere, both men and women, but mostly women. The camera bounces from left to right, like the person holding the camera is running.

There are bright lights, assumedly gunshots, and then blood splatters on the camera lens. Half the screen is masked with red spots, and the other half fills with images of three women beating down on a police officer with rocks. One woman is hitting him with a chair.

Why is he showing this to us?

He pauses the video.

"As you can see, gentlemen, women have lost control. They're rioting against laws that have been put in place to protect the balance of our population."

I know what he's referring to: the illegalization of aborting male embryos and the enforcing of aborting female embryos. My mama would give him an earful if she heard him bashing women for rioting against President Price.

A few whispers spread through the crowd.

"You may not yet be convinced," he continues. "I know many of you have mothers, wives, children. This is not to say these women are bad people. They have been misled. They are being brainwashed into believing that men are the root of all evil.

I look at James, whose eyes are glued to the man at the front. Is this some sort of joke? I feel like I'm in a cult. Why is everyone entranced by this guy?

He presses play, and the holograph video continues. This time, there are images of women carrying signs that read, "Death to Men," and "Men are Evil."

Where did these images come from, anyway? I've seen the riots, and I've never seen signs like this before.

"The next few weeks of your life will be spent

attending intensive training—nothing like you've endured during your thirteen weeks on a military base and nothing like any mission undertaken."

He walks to the opposite end of the stage, his eyes scanning the soldiers in the first few rows at the front.

"You will begin to question those you love most..."

He turns around.

"As you begin to see the truth in things."

I'd never question Mama. Who does this jerk think he is? But it doesn't matter who he thinks he is. In fact, it doesn't even matter who he *actually* is, because he's obviously a powerful man. I'm not an idiot. I know there's no leaving this mission. And by the looks of this place, I'd probably disappear from the face of the Earth if I attempted to leave.

The man at the front forms a fist and presses it into his chest. "Together, we will save our land."

CHAPTER 12 – LUCY

Lucy – Present Day

"Lucy, honey, talk to me."

There's nothing to talk about. I march my way down the corridor, turn slightly, and head back into Division Five. I want to be left alone.

Why didn't she talk to me? Why did Aunt Eve leave like that after hurting my wrist? What's her problem, anyway?

"Lucy!"

I know Nola means well—she's only looking out for me. But I'm not in the mood to talk right now. I turn around, and she almost bumps into me with eyes round and full of surprise. I wrap my arms around her waist, rest my head on her shoulder, and squeeze.

She's hesitant at first, but she squeezes back and doesn't let go. I can't remember the last time I hugged Nola. She deserves more than what I give her. She's always been there for me, and all I ever try to do is run from her.

"Thank you," I say. "For everything."

She pulls back, her light hazel eyes staring into me. "What's going on, sweetheart? Are you okay?"

I smile up at her, even though smiling is the last thing I want to do. I'm devastated. Aunt Eve is the closest thing I have left to my mom, and she wants nothing to do with me.

I nod to reassure her. "I'm okay, Nola. I'm just overwhelmed. I'd like to be alone for a little bit if that's okay."

She looks carefully at me, one eye at a time like she's trying to understand what's going on in my head. But she won't. She'll never understand because she doesn't even know that I have a connection to Aunt Eve.

When she took care of me, after the war, she asked that I stop calling her Aunty Eve. I think it had something to do with the image it would give her, given that she's the leader of so many women. She didn't want to be someone's "aunty"—she wanted to be her own independent woman.

Nola gently pecks me on the forehead with her lips, offers me a big smile, and says, "Of course, sweetheart. Anything you need."

And with that, she turns around and makes her way back to the main hall. Her long, green cotton dress drags on the ground, almost slithering behind her, and I feel guilty watching her leave.

I make my way into my room. Well, my cell. It's a prison decorated to look like a room. There's no door, either. Only blue curtains for privacy. I take off my silly dress, careful not to rip it because it isn't mine. I'll have to hand it back to Nola, who will return it to the Preparation Room. I fold it four times and place it on the hand-carved night table by my bed. It's a soft slab of cedar wood standing on four unevenly shaped legs.

Some girls have modern furniture that was in the prison before we got here, but others, like me, prefer furniture made in Eden. The wood makes me feel like I'm outside when I'm locked away on rainy days like this.

I wish my bed were made of cedar, but it's an old prison bed made of metal. It squeaks when I lie in it, and it isn't very comfortable.

I have a big dracaena plant sitting under my window. It's probably the most colorful thing in this room, aside from a small painting I found in a dumpster (a painting of a fluffy white cat). I brush the tips of my fingers along its leaves, thankful to Perula for having given it to me. She's one of Eden's Healers. I'll be working with her from now on. I'm happy about that even though I'm not so sure she'll be happy about it.

Perula and Mavis are the two Healers in Eden. They're twin sisters, and they're a little weird, with their long scraggly black-and-silver hair and red tribal-like tattoos on both arms. Perula is the calm sister, and Mavis is the loud one. That's always how it seems to work with siblings. They balance each other out. I wonder if Aunt Eve would still be the same Aunt Eve I knew if her little sister Mila were here with us. Maybe she'd balance her out because Mila was always the more impulsive one. Maybe Eve would go back to being the sweet one.

Perula's always been nice to the kids, but Mavis seems to be impatient. She walks past us in a hurry most of the time without making any eye contact. I hope we'll get along.

I slip into my regular clothes which is an old pair of blue jeans and a plain white sweater. I have a few outfits from our modern world that Nola grabbed for me in nearby villages, but at this point, they're getting worn out, and some are becoming tight on me. Soon, I know I'll have to wear clothing made by the women of Eden: beige dresses with no designs whatsoever. They're pretty ugly if you ask me. And I don't like wearing dresses. So, until that day comes, I'll wear my clothes for as long as I can.

I plop myself down onto my bed, an old mattress with hay tucked underneath the bedsheet for extra padding. I stare at the ceiling. There's nothing but gray everywhere. The walls are the exact same color, and so is the floor. But the walls look like water's been dripping down them for years, and big brown stains stretch from the ceiling to the floor.

It's funny how on the outside, Eden looks like paradise, but on the inside, it's ugly. Well, our rooms, anyways. Someone once told me they saw Aunt Eve's room, and that it's been completely renovated. Why can't they find fresh paint and fix up our rooms? Why does she get the nice room? Because she's in charge?

I stand up on my bed and press my face against the window's metallic cage. The sound of heavy rainfall fills my cell, and droplets of water slide down the thick glass of the little window. I'd do anything to stand out there... to tilt my head back and dance in the rain.

But they don't let us. When it rains, we're not allowed out. I think it has to do with getting sick or something, even though my mom always told me a little rain never hurt anybody.

I wish my H-Cap was working. I brought it with me to Eden, but ever since the war, it hasn't been able to turn on. At least tomorrow, Perula and Mavis will start training me. Hopefully, the weather is nicer, but then again, I've heard that the twins work outside in their greenhouse, even when it's storming.

One more sleep, and then maybe, just maybe... I won't feel like a prisoner anymore.

Lucy — Flashback

I must have imagined it. All of it. I pull away from my door and stare at the carpet in my room. Why would Aunty Eve talk about killing someone? And is it true? Is someone following us? Is this Jason guy trying to hurt us?

Who is he, anyway? I didn't catch everything mom and Aunty Eve were saying, but I heard enough to know that *Jason*, whoever he is, is trying to hurt us, and that Aunty Eve said something about killing him. She tried to whisper, but I heard her.

Maybe she was joking.

I heard Mom laugh, so Aunty Eve must have been joking.

CHAPTER 13 – EVE

Eve — Present Day

There's a knock at my door, and I pinch my eyebrow with my thumb and index finger.

"Come in," I say, although what I would rather say is nothing—pretend I'm not even here. I don't have the patience to deal with anything right now.

The door handle turns, and the first thing I spot is a head full of red-brown hair.

"Nola," I say dully, but I retract and stiffen my posture right away.

Put a smile on, for Christ's sake.

"How are you?" I stand up and extend both arms, almost as a form of invitation. The smile proves a bit more challenging, but I manage to curl my lips slightly.

"Good day, Eve," she says, bowing that big head of hers. "I don't mean to interrupt..." Her pathetic puppylike eyes scan my room, and I feel violated. This is my space, and the women of Eden know better than to waltz in without being called upon.

"What is it, Nola?" It must be urgent if she's come in here to bother me.

"It's Lucy, Your Majesty."

I raise my chin and gaze down at her. Majesty—I like it. It puts a genuine smile on my face.

"I'm worried about her. I don't understand why she chose to become a *Healer*."

I don't understand either, but I would have assumed Nola to be in a better position to decipher Lucy's view on the position. Why is she asking me? Does she know of my past? Does she know about Lucy's relationship with me, despite me telling Lucy to keep quiet about it?

My gaze unintentionally becomes a glare, and I only realize it when she raises two hands up by her face and says, "I didn't mean to bother you—I just know you always have eyes around Eden. I was wondering if you knew something I didn't. I don't know what to do."

"My dear Nola." I step forward and brush my fingertips against her oily cheek, instantly regretting doing so. "She's a child"—I wipe my fingers against the back of my pants—"she's exploring."

Nola doesn't know that I'm as confused as she is, if not more.

"But I have a task for you," I say.

Her eyes light up. It's like talking to a dog awaiting her master's command.

"Keep your eyes on her, would you? I'm worried she may get hurt on this path she's chosen. If anything strikes you as odd, or unlike her usual self, report back to me."

She nods quickly. "Of course, Your Majesty."

I smirk and wonder if this new term will spread among the women. I could get used to being referred to as *Majesty*.

"I'm lucky to have such a loyal friend like you, Nola." I squint my eyes with a pretentious look of love.

She nods again, and an uncertain smile creeps on her lips.

"I will. I will. Thank you," she mumbles and exits my room, walking backward.

The moment she leaves, I turn to my mirror.

Well played.

Now you have someone watching over her every minute of every day.

Which is precisely what I need. Lucy is trouble—I can feel it. She's too curious, too willing to challenge orders for the sake of discovery. With Nola's help, I may be able to find out what it is she's up to. I may be able to stop her.

You're being paranoid.

She's a kid.

A kid you once took care of.

My smirk transforms into a grimace, and I clench my fists.

I'm not paranoid—I'm cautious. This is what leaders do for their people; they anticipate danger and take preventative measures.

These women are lucky to have you.

The top button of my overcoat is undone. I clip it back in place, brush my short hair to the side, and stand tall.

Look at you.

Your Majesty.

I twirl around, analyzing every corner of my room, and I envision marble floors and silk bedding.

Your Majesty.

After everything I've done for these women, is it

so much to ask for? Is it wrong of me to desire a sense of royalty? A sense of importance? I know the women of Eden already view me as their savior for everything I've done, but how long will that last? Will my stature remain over the years, or will their appreciation slowly fade?

What must I do to ensure these women continue to love me?

I want them to worship me.

Eve — Flashback

My phone lights up and a notification appears in the air:

Someone's following me again. I think it's him.

Poor Ophelia. She says she'll get it sorted out, but I'm not too sure she will. Jason's a sociopath and an asshole. He won't leave her alone. I wonder if our last chat resonated with her.

Hundreds of riots are taking place in the country right now; hundreds of lives have been taken. How bad would it be to rid the world of one prick?

I tuck my pillow under my neck and stare at my windowsill. How would I do it, anyway? It's easy to say you'd kill someone, but to go through with it is a different story.

I'm not a killer.

But then I remember the police officer, and I'm taken back to that horrific night. A sharp pain radiates from my groin, all the way up into my stomach.

My nostrils flare, and although all I want to do is cry, I can't shake this indescribable urge to attack a man. Any man. I can understand why there are feminists in this world—why my mom is so passionate about this revolution.

It's because of men. Goddamn men. All they do is take what they want with no regard for consequences. They're entitled animals who think they can control the world because they're bigger than us.

I think back to Jason.

I could find poison somewhere—I could look it up on the Web Database. But then again, that wouldn't satisfy me enough. And how would I get him to take the poison? I bite down on my lip. I could push him down a flight of stairs. Also too uncertain. What if he survives?

I could find a gun, perhaps. A gun would be the easiest way. I'm sure there are tons of weapons on the streets right now. All I have to do is find the right person and give them the right amount of cash. No one would ever trace it back to me. Or, I'd put a mask on, kill that sociopath son of a bitch, and run into a crowd.

It would work, wouldn't it?

Am I crazy?

"Eve!"

I roll over and face my bedroom door.

"Eve!" Mila calls out again.

There's a panic in her voice.

I jump out of bed and run down the stairs.

She's standing in front of the TV, a stiff finger pointed at the screen, her round eyes glued to mine.

"It's—it's mom," she says.

"What? What're you—"

The TV is turned on to the news channel. I can tell because there's a big blue banner at the top that reads TNN and a black bar at the bottom that is forever scrolling white headlines. But the footage in between these two strips is what causes my stomach to sink.

"That's where she was," Mila says, her voice trembling. "That's where mom went. She told me. That's where she went."

There's smoke everywhere, and people are running around like hungry zombies in a postapocalyptic world. It's hard to make out what's going on. My heart's beating so hard I can feel it in my throat.

The screen switches over to a news anchor—a young brunette with soft features. She presses her fingers against her ear, nods at the camera, then says, "Thirty-nine now confirmed dead in today's attack in downtown Washington DC."

The room spins around me.

The footage switches to a helicopter view of the disaster. There is thick black smoke everywhere, and the sound of gunshots still echoes through the screen.

The screen switches over to a man standing in Washington DC near the attack. People scream and cars honk in the background.

"It looks like the attack was led by one of Washington's most notorious feminist groups. We do have the suspected leader in custody, and special forces are coming in now to control the situation."

The woman appears back on screen. "Control the situation? John, what's going on over there? Why is the military shooting at civilians? The internet is blowing up with images of women getting shot at by special forces. Is this true? Is this really happening?"

The screen goes bright blue, with white font that reads:

We are currently experiencing technical difficulties and are working to resolve the issue. We thank you for your patience.

"Are you fucking kidding me?" Mila shouts, her voice cracking. She grabs at her hair and paces the room. Her wet eyes meet mine. "She's out there, Eve. Mom's there right now." And her lower lip begins to tremble.

The news channel suddenly comes back to life, but the female anchor is nowhere to be seen. Instead, a man wearing a gray suit is sitting behind the news desk. He doesn't even mention the previous anchor or why she's been removed from the studio.

"John, can you tell us a bit about what's going on? Have they found any other ties to this feminist group?"

The screen switches back to John. He shakes his overly combed head. "Nothing yet. Police are still investigating, and we have a team of specialized forces coming in to sweep the area. There were threats of two, possibly three other bombs positioned throughout the city."

"We need to go to her," Mila starts. We need—"

"Mila!" I say, but she won't listen. She's walking to the foyer to slip on her sneakers.

I rush to her side to reason with her, but she won't have it. She reaches for the door handle, but I push all of my weight into the door.

"You're not going anywhere," I say, making the

same face my mom does when she tells us to clean our dishes—when she's around to tell us, that is.

"Mom's out there!" she says. "She needs our help!"

"And what if she isn't, Mila?" I snap. I don't mean to be cold, but I'm scared, terrified beyond belief and on the verge of passing out. "What if she's dead? Huh? What if she died in the attack? I can't lose you, too!"

CHAPTER 14 – GABRIEL

Gabriel – Present Day

I'm not sure how much more of this bullshit I can take.

What's the point in a life like this, anyway? Why do I even bother? All I do is follow a prick of a leader and his herd of sheep around a nation that doesn't exist anymore. I couldn't even tell you what state I'm in.

The last sign I saw was some big blue sign with a giant sunflower that read Welcome to Kansas. God knows where we are. We could have traveled across two or three states by now.

There's nothing left. Nothing but abandoned houses, commercial stores, and beat-up cars sitting in the middle of highways. I don't understand how things got this bad. How things got so out of control.

I watch Adam as he kicks over a table in the teachers' lounge. The sound echoes across the walls and a few of the men step back.

"Fuck!" Adam shouts.

He's pissed off because he can't find enough food. And probably because he hasn't had sex in over five years. What did he think was going to happen? Did he honestly think that we'd march our way to a school that was abandoned over a year ago, only to find a ton of nonperishable food?

That's ridiculous. We aren't the only survivors left. Others have probably scavenged through this school many times over. I'm suddenly reminded of the knife I found—the one tucked away in my pocket—and I'm thankful it was left behind.

"What about you twats? Did you find anything good in the lockers?" Adam asks.

Everything he's pulled out of the fridge so far has layers and layers of green and brown muck around it, or it's turned into soup or is now rock hard. There's nothing left that hasn't spoiled.

Steven, one of Adam's sheep, drops a pile of chocolate-coated granola bars on the kitchenette's counter. Adam jumps on it like a dog on a piece of raw meat. He picks it up, examines it by squeezing it in between the tips of his fingers and sliding his nose back and forth over the wrapper, then whips it straight at Steven's face.

"It's as hard as a fucking rock!"

Steven picks up his pile of bars, including the one that hit him in the face, and slips them back into this bag. It's still food, so I'm sure he'll eat it later, even if he has to break his teeth doing it.

"Why don't we grab a truck outside? Get out of here? We'll cover more ground," McGaver says. If anyone else were to be in charge, it would be him. He looks like Adam, only he's even bigger, has way more facial hair, and has more tattoos—one of them a poorly drawn skull on the back of his neck.

Adam glares at him and stretches his neck until two loud *cracks* bounce off the walls. "You think one truck will carry twelve grown men?"

McGaver shrugs. "Why not? One driver, four passengers, and the rest can sit in the cargo."

"And you think someone left the keys in the truck?" Adam sneers. "That it'll start up? God knows how long that thing's been sitting there."

"Lionell here's a mechanic," McGaver says, throwing his chin out at the bearded man beside him. He's been with us for about four months and he's barely said one word to anyone.

Lionell nods but doesn't say anything, as usual. Adam sniffles, the way a guy does when he tries to look tough, then turns his head away. He's always been against driving. I don't know what his problem is. I think it's his need to have control all the time and to do that, he'd have to drive. To drive, he'd have to put his gun down.

The bastard even sleeps with his gun. What kind of leader does that make him? If he can't trust his crew, how does he expect us to trust him? I'm looking forward to the day he runs out of ammo. It's not every day you find bullets for an AK-47 in a postapocalyptic world.

If he keeps firing the way he does—like at kids, for example—he'll run out. It's only a matter of time.

Adam looks at me, and I stare back. It's like he reads my mind sometimes. Could be I'm the one he doesn't trust and with good reason.

His eyes shift over to McGaver, who's waiting expectantly with big brown eyes like a kid who just asked his mom to stay an extra hour at the park. It doesn't suit him at all. I can tell he's not a fan of being a follower—of taking orders.

"Doesn't mean it's even gonna start," Adam says, and that's enough for McGaver to throw an excited fist in the air.

"We can try," McGaver says, and his attention turns to Lionell. "You think you can fix her if she doesn't start?"

Lionell's one of the younger ones here. A French guy in his late twenties, early thirties. He's wearing a green baseball cap and has a pointed chin with about an inch of golden beard grown out. He looks like a nice guy—the type who'd open a car door for a lady—but he doesn't talk much, and he follows every command given to him. I can't read him, so I assume he's an asshole deep down like the rest of them.

He shrugs at McGaver. "I'll do my best. Depends on what's wrong wid it. If dere's a part missing—"

"If there's a part missing, we walk," Adam says, storming past everyone and out of the teacher's lounge.

It's obvious he doesn't want to take the truck. He knows if we don't start covering land at a faster rate, our chances of survival go down. We can't keep walking around pointlessly, hoping to find food. We're burning too many calories. Besides, I think he's hoping we'll come across a military base or some drug dealer's abandoned house so he can scavenge for more weapons.

The guys follow him, and I stay at the back of the crew like I always do. I prefer to have a clear view of everything and to be honest, I don't trust any single one of these pricks in front of me.

I'm about to walk out of the lounge when I hear

a faint *click* sound behind me. I turn around and notice that one of the kitchenette's cabinet doors is cracked open. They were all closed when we got in here. I pay attention to these things—to every detail of my surroundings.

I glance back toward Adam and the crew. They're marching their way down the school corridor, their heavy boots thudding and squeaking. So I move toward the cabinet and pull it open.

The kid lets out a sharp gasp, but quickly covers the mouth of a little girl in front of him. His little sister, I'm assuming. She's sitting in between his legs, and he has his scrawny arms wrapped around her so they can fit under the sink together. The molded sink pipe is hanging in front of their faces, creating a shadow across the little girl's forehead.

The boy must be eleven or twelve, and the little girl, around seven. How is a seven-year-old living in this school? She would have been two years old when everything went to shit in this country. He must have carried her all the way here from wherever he came from.

He's staring at me and looks like a cartoon character, his eyebrows up high on his face and his red lips forming a dark hole. He's terrified. I quickly glance back at the lounge entrance to make sure no one came back looking for me, then back at the kid, who's completely frozen. The little girl's eyes look like her brother's over his white-knuckled hand—huge and glass-like.

"You guys okay?" I whisper.

The boy nods but doesn't say anything.

"Got enough food?"

He doesn't say anything. Smart boy.

"I'm one of the good guys," I say. "Just want to make sure you'll survive."

He nods again.

I reach into my pocket and pull out the pocket knife I found in one of the kids' lockers.

The boy still has his hand tight over his sister's mouth, like they've been through this countless times before.

I slowly hand him the pocket knife. "Here."

It may be stupid of me to give up my only weapon, but I'm a grown man. I can handle myself. These two are kids. They can use it for hunting, gutting, or even to defend themselves if it ever comes to that.

"The men I'm with are leaving now," I say. "If there's more of you, keep hiding for a little while longer, okay?"

For a moment, I tell myself that I'll come back for them; I'll come back, and I'll take care of them. But deep down, I know I'm lying to myself. God knows where I'll be tomorrow. Once I get on that truck, I'll be miles away from here. All I can do is hope they survive.

I close the cabinet door just on time because Castor's half-toothed face pops out into the lounge.

"Gabe! What're you doing? Lionell is fixing the truck right now. We have to move."

"Sorry," I say. "Thought I'd check one last time for some food."

He shrugs like he always does, and I follow him

out of the lounge.

God, I hope they survive.

Gabriel — Flashback

I lie in my bed—the bottom bunk in a room that looks like a science lab—and read my new curriculum. Everything in this room is white. Everything. Even the bedroom door, which is electronic and lets out a high-pitched beeping noise when it's opened.

There's even a holographic screen facing down from the top corner of the room. In front of a diamond-shaped hologram, there's a 3-D man with no hair and weird gray eyes. At first, I thought it was a projection of a real man. But if you look close enough, you can see some pixelation along the edges of his face.

His name, apparently, is Olix, and he's here to serve our needs. He reminds me of a live version of Siri. My mom showed it to me once with one of her old iPhones. She thinks one day it'll be worth a lot of money because it's in mint condition. We'll see. And same as Siri, you can ask Olix anything and he answers you. Only he's more intelligent. Way more intelligent. The only creepy thing is that he makes eye contact with you. How's that even possible unless they're watching us? And why are they watching us?

Right now, his eyes are closed and his face is set to the lowest dimness possible. The bedroom window is sealed with a black panel, which means there's barely any light in here whatsoever. It's electronic, too, so I don't have any way of opening it.

Welcome to Area 82, I think to myself.

I know I should be excited… thrilled that I'm standing inside Area 82. Only a small fraction of military men ever step foot in here. So why do I feel like there's a dark cloud around me? Like this place isn't all it's cracked up to be?

I sigh and look back down at my curriculum. It's a small sheet of metal, or aluminum, the size of a typical tablet. Only, the blue-green text is floating up a few millimeters. If I swipe my finger through the letters for fun, they jumble up before bouncing back into place.

It might seem menial, but it makes me smile. I do this a few times, before reading what's been written out for us.

5:00 a.m. – Room verification

5:30 a.m. – Shower

5:45 a.m. – Breakfast

6:00 a.m. – Aerobic exercise

7:00 a.m. – Shower

7:15 a.m. – Information session

11: 00 a.m. – Lunch

I stop and my finger hovers over the information session line, its letters dancing slightly. Information session? For what? For over three hours? And this is supposed to be a daily routine? What sort of information session takes nearly four hours? I feel like I'm in training all over again, only this time, there is zero room for error.

The room suddenly lights up in a blue hue, and Olix's soothing voice jumps out at me.

"I sense you are experiencing difficulties

sleeping, Gabriel. Do you require assistance?"

I drop my curriculum flat against my chest and shut my eyes.

There's movement above me, followed by deep sleep grunting. The last thing I want to do is wake up my new roommate, Alex. I wish I'd been bunked with James instead, but I had no say in the decision. They split us all up into teams of two. Alex is now my new partner, and I'll be working with him in the field, too. So I don't want to get on his bad side.

He's hard to read, and I don't even know how well we'll get along. But I'm a pretty easy-going guy, so there shouldn't be any issues on my end. My mom always taught me that conflict never resolves anything. She's also put me in my place more times than I can count, so I've learned that mouthing off gets me nowhere.

I peek through my closed eyelid.

Olix is still staring at me with those creepy pixilated eyes of his. Hopefully, if I don't respond to him and stop moving, he'll go back to sleep. It takes a minute or two, but he does eventually dim in color until all I can see is blackness.

I let out a soft sigh. Did I make the right decision when I joined the Black Marines? It seems like I'm about to get involved in something terribly messed up. I was okay fighting in North Korea—I managed to keep myself together because I knew that in the end, it was to protect the citizens of my country. But this... This is something else entirely, and I have a nasty feeling in my stomach. I close my eyes, hoping that if I lie here long enough, I'll fall asleep.

Tomorrow's the first big day of training for Project GENESIS, whatever that is.

CHAPTER 15 – LUCY

Lucy — Present Day

Perula's sitting at the back corner of the shack with a sweet smile on her wrinkled face. She keeps looking up at me from behind a pair of green metallic glasses that sit on a cherry-shaped nose. Her pepper hair is tied up into a loose bun behind her head, and a few strands of scraggly hair dangle over the rims of her glasses.

When she isn't looking at me, she looks down and plucks dead leaves from a plant that's sitting on her lap. She's wearing a pair of jean overalls over a gray undershirt, which is something she seems to like wearing all the time. A lot of women in Eden wear the same clothes over and over again—whether it be a valuable outfit they've held onto for years, or one of Eden's standard hemp dresses.

I wonder if those green-rimmed glasses are her original glasses, or if she had to take them out of our supply room. Apparently, there's so much stuff down there it's hard to cross the room. I'd love to see what's in there one day, but for now, only a few select people are allowed to go.

Then, I look at Mavis, her twin sister. It's hard to believe they're twins. They look nothing alike until you look at their faces. On top of it, their personalities are completely different, so sometimes, I forget they're twins.

Mavis has more of a round shape than Perula, and she tends to wear dresses instead of pants. Most of her dresses look like something you'd find in a Halloween store, too. They're usually orange, yellow, and red and have a lot of black lace on them. She also likes to wear her hair down a lot. That's the fastest way I can tell them apart, aside from Mavis's funky dresses.

Mavis, the total opposite of her sister, keeps grunting while she rummages through cabinets and buckets around the room like she's looking for something. Every so often, she stands up and stretches her slender body, wipes the sweat off her face, and throws her long pepper-colored locks behind her back. Now that I think of it, her hair looks like an accumulation of dust and animal hair you'd find in a vacuum canister. If I knew what she was looking for, I'd offer to help, but I can already tell that Mavis doesn't want me to be here. She was happy working as a Healer alongside her twin sister and nobody else.

"I have to ask," Perula says, breaking the awkward silence, "why Healer?" She crinkles her eyes in an affectionate way.

I shrug. "I'm not sure," I say. "A feeling." I wish I could offer more of an explanation.

She smirks and nods her head like she knows something I don't.

"You have energy surrounding you," she says. Her voice is so soothing, that for a second, I'm able to block out Mavis's grunting and banging.

What's that supposed to mean, anyway? What

energy?

"Someone you care deeply for," she says. "They're with you."

My throat swells. Is she talking about my mom?

"Oh, frog on a stick!" Mavis slaps the table in front of her. "Stop feedin' the poor lass your ghost stories!" She rolls her eyes up at the ceiling and shakes her thick head. Then, her eyes meet mine, and she glares at me. "Don't you be listenin' to my sister's nonsense."

But Perula is sitting there, her lips still curved upward. She doesn't seem annoyed or degraded in any way. How does she remain so calm all the time?

"Just because you aren't connected to the spirit realm, Mavis—"

Mavis lets out a loud cackle. "Perula tends to overindulge in the poppy tea."

"Poppy tea?" I ask.

Mavis bends down, then pops back up again, her face now level with the wooden island in the middle of the room. I can only see her greasy forehead, her wirelike hair, and her eyes.

But she doesn't say anything. Have I already questioned too much? Am I not allowed to ask questions? Or is she the one who's said too much?

"Papaver somniferum," Perula says, looking sideways at her sister. "It's a natural pain reliever."

"Oh," is all that comes out of my mouth. Was that even English? Papav—something.

Mavis scoffs. "Does more than relieve pain."

Perula smiles at me. "Opium poppies."

I still don't know what she's talking about.

Mavis lets out an annoyed sigh the way someone does when they think a person's stupid. "They're basically drugs." She then looks over at Perula. "And this is why kids aren't supposed to become Healers."

Perula flicks her wrist at her sister. "She's sixteen. She can handle it."

I like Perula. For once, an adult is treating me like an adult and not like some snotty little kid who doesn't know any better.

"Why do you drink it?" I ask. "Are you in pain?"

"Always," Perula says. "I got shot during the revolution." She pulls the neck collar of her black dress down, revealing pink scarring on her collarbone. "It caused nerve damage."

I grimace. "I... I'm sorry."

"Don't be," she says. "That's all in the past now."

"Got you!" Mavis shouts out, and my shoulders jerk forward.

She pulls an ugly, beige-colored root out of a bucket of dirt and raises it at eye level.

"What's that?" I ask.

Instead of lowering the root, she tilts her head and looks at me, but she doesn't say anything. She turns around and carries it over to what appears to be a cutting counter underneath the shack's window.

"It's ginger," Perula says. "Helps calm the stomach."

I nod slowly. Ginger for stomach problems, poppy seeds...no, poppy flowers...poppy something for pain relief.

I stand up and slowly make my way around the cabin. Plants are everywhere, and it smells like moist earth. Some kind of watering system that's made out of vines looks like it's connected to the outside of the cabin. I assume it waters the plants using rainwater. The room is hot and humid, and if it wasn't hot enough already, the sun is beating down on us through the glass ceiling. I wonder where they got the materials to build this place

Then, on a shelf, in between two bushes of giant green leaves, is the weirdest plant I've ever seen. It looks like a little red tree full of eyeballs.

"What's this?" I ask, reaching toward it.

"Don't!" Mavis shouts, and I jump.

"Please don't touch anything without asking," Perula says. She gets up from her chair, and it almost looks like she's in pain simply doing that. She winces and grabs her shoulder.

"This," she says, now standing directly beside me, "is a Doll's Eyes plant. The berries are poisonous." She hovers a finger over the black pupil of the white ball, then looks down at me. "If eaten raw, there's enough poison to stop your heart."

I swallow hard.

"But if prepared correctly," she continues, "these berries can be used to create medicine."

"Where did you learn all of this?" I ask. "Did you work with plants before coming to Eden?"

I ask because her hair is dark with white streaks throughout. I was never good at guessing someone's age, but I know she's old enough to be my grandmother. And that means she had a long life before coming to Eden.

She throws her head back and laughs. "Oh, goodness, no. We collected many books before coming to Eden." She points at a shelf behind Mavis. Thick spider webs are spread across the very top corner of a row of books. From what I can see, the books are all about plants and natural medicine. "Mavis and I worked together at Little Blue's Aquatic Wildlife Rehabilitation Center."

"What's that?" I ask.

"It was a rehabilitation center for aquatic animals. Whales, dolphins, fish..." she says.

She eyes Mavis for a brief second, and they exchange a look. They are twins, after all. It's almost like they can read each other's minds.

Mavis rolls her eyes. "Yeah, until they barricaded us from entering."

"Barricaded?" I ask.

Perula nods. "After the big riot started around the White House, men came together to prevent us from returning to work."

I wasn't following.

"A bunch o' purple loons!" Mavis cries out. "They thought that by denying us work, we'd eventually give up on the whole rebellion. That without money, we were nothing. Men are so stupid"—she's gripping a spoon or a spatula and her knuckles are all white— "and they think everything revolves around money and power. Women didn't want power. We didn't want money, either. We just didn't want governmental knives shoved up our cahoochees and killin' our babies."

"Mavis," Perula warns.

"It's okay," I say. "I used to listen to the news in my bedroom then. My mom thought I wasn't listening, but I was. I know all about everything. About how they made it illegal and then wanted to start forcing women to have abortions if the baby was a girl."

There's a silence in the room, and I think they're surprised that I even understand what an abortion is.

Perula steps closer and rests a nurturing hand on my shoulder.

"Lucy?" she asks.

I look up.

"Whatever happened to your mother? Am I allowed to ask?"

No one's ever asked me that before. Not even Nola. My throat swells at the thought of my mother, but I swallow down my sadness and replace it with anger.

"Someone killed her," I say.

Lucy — Flashback

"Come on, sweetheart, hurry up," my mom says through my door.

I don't understand why she's doing this. What are we running from? I look at Mr. Shilo, my giant panda bear, and I want to cry. He's too big to take with me. So instead, I grab Stripes and stick him in my backpack. He's a little tiger the size of my hand with yellow eyes and big brown stripes.

My bag's almost too full to close, but I think I have everything: my toothbrush, pajamas, clothes, socks, my H-Cap ... I think that's everything.

"Lucy!"

"I'm coming, Mom!"

I throw my bag over my shoulder and glance back at my bedroom one last time. I look at the purple star stickers above my bed and at my collection of action heroes on my dresser. I thought about taking them with me, but I don't have room.

The scary part is that I don't think I'm coming back here ever again. I can't explain it. It's a feeling I have. Like I'm saying goodbye forever. I have no idea where my mom's taking me, or why we're even leaving in the first place. I think it's because of *Jason*.

My mom reaches for my hand when I step out into the living room, and she pulls me close beside her.

"You got everything, honey? We're taking a little trip, okay? So make sure you have everything."

I start counting my clothes in my head, and I

think of Stripes, my toothbrush, and my H-Cap.

"I have everything," I say.

"Good." She rushes out of our apartment and closes the door without even locking it. That's not like her. Mom always locks the door.

"Where are we going?" I look up at her, but she's walking fast, and her eyes stare straight ahead. It's like she doesn't hear me.

Inside the elevator we take down to the main floor, an old lady stands beside us and smiles down at me like I'm the cutest thing she's ever seen. I should smile back; I always smile back at strangers, but I'm too scared. Too worried about what's going on right now, and I can't think.

We rush out of the elevator's big silver doors, and I have a hard time keeping up. If Mom wasn't holding my hand, I'd probably be way behind.

"Mom?" I say.

She doesn't say anything.

"Mom, where are we going?"

Nothing.

She pulls my bag off my back and puts it in the trunk of the jeep, then tells me to get in the car. I clip my seat belt together and wait quietly. If I don't say anything at all, she might tell me what's going on.

So I wait.

She gets in, starts the car, and takes off like she did the other day at the grocery store. Like she's running away from something.

I look at the clock in the car. At the small blue numbers. It's been seven minutes since we got in.

She still isn't talking to me.

Nine minutes.

Ten minutes.

I try to be patient, but I can't.

"Mom?"

She reaches over, squeezes my thigh, and smiles big at me.

"Everything's okay, honey. We're going to stay at Grandma's for a little while, okay?"

"Grandma's? Why Grandma's?"

Why is she being so weird? Mom and Grandma barely get along. Why would she want us to live there?

"I'll explain everything later, okay?" she says, looking at me.

I sigh and press my face against the window, and my breath makes a cool gray circle in front of my lips. I don't believe her. She won't tell me what's going on. She thinks I'm too young to understand, and she wants to protect me.

"Goddamn it," my mom says quietly.

I follow her eyes. She's looking at a group of women who are running across the street. They're holding signs and punching upward. What's going on? We come to a full stop in the middle of the road. I think we're stuck in traffic.

"What are they doing?" I ask.

My mom lets out another big sigh. "They're rioting."

"Because of the abortion law?" I ask.

Her eyes get big and she looks at me like I just told her I saw an alien.

"How do you know about that?"

"I know more than you think, Mom."

She nods, and I think she understands me. I think she realizes that I'm not a little kid anymore.

"Yes," she says, "it's about the abortion law, and other things, too."

"What other things?" I ask.

She looks at me, her eyes glossy, and her lips curving down. What is she sad about?

"Sweetheart, the world is falling apart. Women are outnumbering men, and men don't like it. Men can be very dangerous sometimes."

"Because they're stronger than us?"

She smiles at me. "They can be, yes. But only with their bodies."

"What do you mean?" I ask.

"Women are strong with their minds." She pokes me in the forehead. "That's why all these women are out here. They don't agree with the laws men are putting in place. They know it's unfair, and they're fighting for their rights."

I watch as three women chase a man back into his car. I think he was trying to tell them to shut up, and they didn't like it.

"So it's okay?" I ask.

"What's okay?" my mom asks.

"What they're doing," I say. "This... rioting. Is it okay?"

She squeezes the steering wheel a few times, then turns her head toward me and bites down on her lip. She always does that when she's about to have a serious talk with me.

"All I know is that men shouldn't have a say in what happens inside of a woman's body. I can't tell you that it's okay to riot because people get hurt in riots. But I can tell you that even though I don't like it, I do support it. I think it's the only choice we have... It's the only way to fight for our rights."

CHAPTER 16 – EVE

Eve – Present Day

I watch Lauren from behind my Dolce & Gabbana sunglasses—a pair of big brown lenses that I found on a sidewalk in Washington DC before I fled. There's a chip on the bottom lens, but it's not very noticeable. I also realize that these sunglasses carry no monetary value in Eden, but they still make me feel, in a sense, like royalty.

Lauren laughs with the other women with one hand on her belly, the other pulling loose strands of golden hair that keep dancing with the wind out of her mouth. Eight months, I think, trying to calculate the amount of time that's passed since the rape outside of Eden's walls.

This isn't the first time a woman in Eden is pregnant. When women first started arriving inside the walls, a few of them were already pregnant. They all, however, lost their children to miscarriages and stillbirths. Mavis and Perula disagree on the reasoning behind this. Mavis, being as stubborn as she always is, says that all the stress from the revolution is to blame. Perula, on the other hand, believes the miscarriages are the result of malnutrition and dehydration.

I can't argue with either one of them, and as terrible as it may sound, I'm relieved that children weren't brought into this horrid world.

Furthermore, what if a child had been born male? I know it's incredibly rare these days, but it could happen. What then? How am I supposed to tell a mother that her son isn't allowed in Eden?

Or do I allow young boys into Eden? Will raising them in a society of women make them worthy of this place? I pinch the bridge of my nose, thankful that I've never had to make such a difficult decision. But as I watch Lauren, I can't help but wonder: what if it's a boy?

I tilt my head, analyzing the size of her belly, attempting to guess its gender.

A little girl, I keep telling myself.

She catches me watching her, and she quickly averts her gaze. A few of her friends timidly wave a hand in my direction but walk away, their footsteps short and rapid. Do I intimidate them?

A shadow suddenly covers my boots and legs.

"Hey, stranger."

I glance up and spot Freyda who's sitting atop Pearl, her Akhal-Teke—a breed of horse known as a supermodel horse. It has an astounding silky pearl-like coat and beautiful golden-blond hair. Mind you, she's a lot of maintenance and can sometimes fill Division Three's garden with a farm-like smell, especially on top of our livestock, but Pearl provides Eden with fertilizer.

"What're you doing out here?" Freyda asks me.

The one thing I admire most about Freyda is that she doesn't treat me like a goddess—she treats me as an equal. Most women in Eden believe me to be their savior for having guided them through the revolution. Although I appreciate the admiration, being in a position of such power can become lonely. I look back at Lauren and the group of women, who have fled over to the back gardens and as far away from me as possible.

I raise a hand above my eyes to block the sun. "Getting some air."

She grins—a stunning, magazine-worthy smile that would have forced any man to his knees in our old world. Her long dark hair is pulled back into a tight ponytail, and there's a thick stripe of black chalk across her hazel eyes. Her strong, square-shaped jaw gives her a bit of a badass appearance, and she is wearing her usual combat attire—a bulletproof vest and army pants salvaged from the remains of our old world. Two semiautomatic pistols are holstered on the side of her belt, but she never uses them—at least, not since I've locked the gates of Eden, not since Lauren's rape. But she enjoys dressing in combat attire, so I allow it. Behind her shoulders, two sword hilts point upward, forming an X. An entire Olympic pool could be filled with the blood of the men Freyda has killed with these swords since the revolution began.

I can't imagine Eden without her.

She smirks, almost tauntingly. "Some air? Something bothering you?"

I cock an eyebrow and cross my arms over my chest. "How could anything be bothering me?" I lie. "Look at this place."

It's hard to smile up at her when I feel like I'm losing control.

She shrugs, and her heavy combat gear makes a chafing sound. "It may look like paradise, but we're still surrounded by danger."

I avert my gaze toward Alpa's highest point. We've come so far, but I know there's still a long road ahead of us.

She climbs off Pearl and sits down beside me, her hips touching mine. "Still haven't changed your mind?"

Her persistence is admirable. I know precisely what she's talking about—training women for combat. Although I do believe that our women should be trained in combat, I also believe it's a bad omen. I've tried explaining this to Freyda countless times. Eden is a place of peace—a place where war is nonexistent and only beauty surrounds us.

Why train women for battle if we have no intention of fighting?

She catches me smirking at her. "I know, I know. You don't want to attract any negativity."

I let out a sigh and gaze around Division Three's courtyard—at all the beauty surrounding us. I make an effort to visit different courtyards throughout the week. It's important that the women of Eden know I'm as much a part of this place as they are. I want the same things they do.

She tries again. "Being prepared doesn't mean anything is going to happen."

I rest my chin in the palm of my hand and turn my head toward her. "You don't give up, do you?"

She grins, and I look away. Her smile always weakens me.

"No, I don't," she says smoothly. "And think about it, Eve. What're you gonna do if a handful of men show up at the gates of Eden with pistols or rifles? With trucks? With machine guns? They'll wipe us all out. Sure, the gates may be locked, but they'll find a way in. And they won't be coming in here to kill us, either."

I bite down hard. The last thing I want to picture is a bunch of men forcing their way into my paradise and onto my women.

"Please," she continues. "Think about it. I could have a dozen archers trained. We could make bows and arrows. We could protect our wall at all times."

"We don't even know how many males survived," I try.

"No, we don't," she says. "But isn't it better safe than sorry? And what's going to happen when we start running out of resources? The women can't survive on fruits and vegetables forever. Plus, what if our livestock die? It's a possibility—they could carry a disease."

She pauses because she knows I'm getting irritated.

"Look," she says softly, "you and I both know that eventually, we'll have to open those gates. I only want Eden—this magical place you've brought us to—to be safe. For all of us to be safe."

I look over at Eden's wall—a massive construction of concrete covered in moss, green vines, and purple flowers. The thought of men climbing over the wall or blasting their way through it sickens me beyond belief.

"Ten," I say.

Freyda stares at me. "Ten what?"

"When winter comes, you can pick ten women in Eden to train."

Eve — Flashback

"You! Get over here! Help me!"

I freeze. I don't know what to do. I'm terrified, but I know I have to be the big sister Mila needs me to be. I need to find my mom. I didn't expect things to be this bad. Or, perhaps I did, but I wasn't ready to step foot inside the chaos.

This suddenly feels like a mistake. Maybe leaving the house wasn't the best idea. Mom would find her way back to us. Why go looking for her?

But then I remember Mila's glossy eyes and her quivering bottom lip. She begged me to let her go downtown—to look for Mom after we heard about the explosion on the news. She kept repeating, "She could be hurt."

Even though she wanted to leave the house, I wouldn't let her. I put all my weight against the front door until finally, I agreed to look for Mom if Mila promised to stay indoors. She was reluctant at first, but she agreed. And now here I am, standing under a flickering streetlight, surrounded by the sound of war.

People scream, glass shatters, gunshots ricochet through alleyways, and the persistent and nasally sound of a car alarm echoes in the distance. Farther ahead, blue and red lights bounce off apartment windows and across the wet asphalt and cobblestone.

It only stopped raining when I got off the bus. Fortunately, the bus driver agreed to drop people off on the border of downtown but refused to drive his regular route into the downtown core.

I don't blame him. But where am I even supposed to start looking? My mom could be anywhere. And what if she was injured? What if she's transported to a hospital? What if they're not even treating the injured because they're rioters?

I want to cry.

I want to scream.

"Are you listening?" the voice shouts again.

There's a woman crouched low to the ground, and my mind immediately shifts when I see a little girl's body in her arms.

"Please!" she shouts.

There's no one around. All I hear are people screaming and rioting a few streets away. More glass shatters, and then a loud bang goes off. I rush to the woman's side.

"What's wrong with you?" the woman snaps. "I need help!"

"Wh... who is..." I try, but something catches my attention. A few meters away, beside an overfilled garbage dump, is a woman lying on the sidewalk, her eyes wide open. Her entire torso is drenched in blood, and her skin is as white as the collar of her shirt.

I throw a hand over my mouth.

"Do you want this little girl ending up like her mother?" the woman shouts.

The girl she's holding must be four or five years old. She's pale as a ghost, and her skin looks cold and clammy. Her hair is so light it almost looks transparent, and it's sticking to her sweaty forehead. I can't tell if she's hot or cold.

"Wh... what can I do?" I ask.

What am I supposed to do? I don't know what's going on. I don't know what happened. All I did was decide to cross this road to get away from a group of women with firelit T-shirts attached at the ends of street signs.

I notice the woman's hand pressed firmly on the little girl's neck. There's dark blood spilling through the cracks of her fingers, and it's clear that she's doing everything in her power to stop the bleeding.

"Give me your shirt," the woman orders. "It's okay, baby, it's okay," she says softly. She kisses the little girl's forehead, but the girl is barely responsive. Her lips are parted open, and her jaw is loose.

I don't put any thought into it. A little girl is on the verge of dying. I'd remove all my clothes if I had to.

I tear off my shirt—a plain white T-shirt I habitually wear—and hand it to the woman. Her hands are shaking, and she quickly wraps my shirt around the girl's fragile neck. The little girl's body bounces like a ragdoll as the woman fastens the material around the wound, and her little arm falls to the side.

The woman starts applying pressure when a long breath—a perturbing sound almost capable of stopping time itself—comes out of the little girl's lungs.

CHAPTER 17 – GABRIEL

Gabriel — Present Day

Adam's leaned back against a 2027 Chevy pickup truck. It's rusted red, although right now, it looks black under the moonlight. He's wearing a baseball cap over his eyes, and his mouth is parted open. He's been out for about an hour or so, but he's still holding on to his rifle like it's attached to him.

The other men are lying around the campfire, which is nothing but red cinder now, and the sound of snoring almost blocks out the crickets singing around us.

I look at Castor, who's standing stiffly against the back of the truck, his arms crossed over his chest. His head keeps nodding forward because he's fighting so hard to stay awake. It's his turn to stand watch tonight.

I gaze out into the open field, and I wonder how far I'd have to run before finding shelter or before getting myself killed. The longer I stay with these men, the more disgusted I am with myself. I know there's strength in numbers, but these men have no morals.

The idea of being alone in this world right now is suddenly more appealing than the idea of staying here with them. If Adam catches me running, he'll shoot. Then again, he's a terrible shot. I'd probably be fine.

I gaze up at the stars and think of my mother. What would she want me to do? She'd likely pull my ear and tell me how ashamed she is of me for associating with such animals. It wouldn't be the first time she's done that. When I was thirteen, I made friends with a guy named Romelio, who introduced me to pot. When my mom found out, she dragged me across the house by the ear, threw me into the bathtub with my clothes on, and turned on the shower.

She then said, with her thick Spanish accent, "Gabriel, if you touch poisonous leaves, what happens to you? You itch. You hurt. That boy Romelio is poison, and he will make you hurt. And if he doesn't, I will make you hurt!"

I smile at the memory. Mama was always strict, yet I always had such respect for her. I stopped talking to Romelio after that. He thought I was a coward for not standing up to my mom, but I thought he was an asshole for talking about my mom like she was a monster when she was the best thing in my life.

So, what now? What do I do? Adam suddenly slaps himself on the chin, shooing away a loud buzz around his head, but he dozes off again.

Would it be better if I ran back toward the school we came from? But then I remember the rotting bodies in the school cafeteria and the foul stench floating through the corridors, and I feel sick to my stomach. I'd rather be anywhere but there.

I just need to get out of here. I'll figure out the rest later.

Castor nods off again, so I quietly get up and make my way over to him. He looks like a kid who doesn't want to get in trouble. He keeps nervously shifting his weight and his eyes are rolling around in every direction.

"You look tired," I whisper.

He nods.

"Get some rest, I'll cover you," I say.

His eyebrows come together. "Why?"

I don't blame him for being paranoid. No one in this group of men ever offers to help someone *just because*. Especially me. I keep to myself, and I like it that way.

"I'm trying to be nice," I say.

He's not buying it. He's staring at me with that same stupid look he always has—the kind that makes me wonder if he's actually thinking, or if his brain has stopped working.

"Castor," I say, hopeful that my honesty won't be the death of me, "I'm out of here."

He stares at me and opens his big mouth, but nothing comes out.

"If I leave while you're on watch duty, you'll be blamed for it," I say.

Someone grunts and rolls over, and I slip around the other side of the truck to hide. When the silence returns, I lean against the cab of the truck and whisper, "If I take over watch duty, you won't be blamed."

"So, you're gonna take off?" Castor hisses, his bearded face wrinkling so much he looks like a chow chow.

Why is he upset? What does he have to be so angry about? His untrimmed eyebrows are nearly touching, and his half-toothed mouth is open. If there's one person I hoped would understand me wanting to get the hell out of here, it was Castor, but now I'm beginning to think I made a mistake trusting him.

"Is that a problem?" I ask, careful to remain calm. If I wanted, I could knock him out without making a peep. But I don't want any trouble, and I especially don't want to hurt Castor unless I have to.

"Yeah, it is," he says.

I grind my teeth. Why is he making this so difficult?

"What's the problem?" I ask slowly.

He shoots another glance toward the group of men sleeping like babies and throws his chin out at them. "I'm coming with you, but my bag's over there"—he points—"beside McGaver."

Gabriel — Flashback

"What is this?" I ask, twirling my spoon in the bowl of beige mush in front of me.

"Cream of Wheat," says one of the men sitting across the table.

He looks like the rest of us—a gray uniform, a shaved head, and a posture so straight you'd think he has a piece of wood holding him up.

I look around the cafeteria. Men in black stand at each entrance, their rifles in hand, their eyes on all of us. What is this, anyway? Prison? I thought we were soldiers. Why are they treating us like cattle?

"Scooch."

James is suddenly standing behind me, and he squishes his way in between me and Alex, my bunkmate.

"First big day," he says, plopping his bowl of mush in front of him.

No one says anything.

"What's the matter, boys? Not what you expected?" he asks.

I look up and make eye contact with the guy in front of me, and I can tell he's thinking the same thing—wondering what the hell we're doing in this place.

James leans forward on his elbows. "This place is all about standards and discipline. Might feel a little weird right now, but you'll see. They'll make something out of us."

"You!" shouts one of the guards, loosely pointing his AK-47 at James. He jerks his head sideways as if to say, "Stop talking," and James pulls back in his chair with a crooked smirk on his face.

He takes a spoonful of Cream of Wheat, swallows hard, then says in a whisper, "You'll see."

So apparently, there's no talking, either. When breakfast is over, the guards split us into small groups and lead us into separate rooms. The moment I walk in, I'm overwhelmed by a calming sense of relief. The ceiling above us is made of glass, revealing a beautiful cloudless blue sky, and the walls are covered in art—paintings of the ocean, a jungle, mountains. There's even a fountain at the back of the room with water trickling into a massive bowl made of glass.

What the heck is this place?

"Welcome," someone says. A man stands at the front of the room, or the class. He has golden-blond hair pulled back into a ponytail and a fancy suit like the rest of the men in charge around here.

"Have a seat," he says gently, extending his arm out toward the chairs in front of him.

There are about twenty of us in this group, and I don't know a single person. Both James and my new roommate, Alex, were sent to different groups. I sit at the front of the class, observing the man with the ponytail as he paces back and forth, smiling at everyone.

He looks like a genuine guy—the type who'd hold a door open for a lady or who'd stop on the side of the highway to help someone with a flat tire.

"You're probably wondering what you're doing here," he says. "What these so-called 'Information

Sessions' are all about."

No one responds, and it's obvious by the heavy silence in the room that we're all curious about this place.

"I'm Mr. Sinclair," he says, pressing a firm hand on his chest. "But that's not important, because tomorrow, you won't be here."

Everyone shifts in their seats. What the hell is that supposed to mean?

Mr. Sinclair lets out a lighthearted laugh.

"You won't be in my classroom tomorrow," he clarifies. "These sessions are rotational. Every day, you'll be placed in a new environment. It's a learning strategy. So tomorrow, you'll be entering a different environment altogether." He looks up at the glass ceiling and breathes in. "Some will be peaceful, like this one, and others, frightening."

He makes eye contact with me, and I look away.

He claps his hands together, then extends both arms on either side of his body. "So why are we here today?"

Silence.

"Anyone?"

Someone clears their throat. "To learn about our mission."

Mr. Sinclair searches the back of the room with almond-shaped eyes, and the man who spoke raises his hand.

"Ah! Stand up, please," Mr. Sinclair says. "What's your name, son?"

"Brian."

"Brian!" Mr. Sinclair says. "In time, you will most

definitely be learning about your mission"—he turns on his heels and walks across the room—"but before that happens, we're here to *prepare* you for your mission."

"So, you aren't going to tell us what we're doing here?" Brian asks.

Mr. Sinclair lets out a chuckle—an arrogant sneer, almost. "What you're doing here is simple, Brian. You're here to serve your country. That's what being a marine is all about. Now I know you didn't accidentally fall onto our doorstep. You have experience, and you were handpicked to be a part of something bigger. Over the next few weeks, you'll all be challenged in different ways. Some of you will succeed, while others will be sent home. Only once we have our remaining men will you be assigned your mission."

Sent home? That doesn't sound like a bad idea. But as I watch Mr. Sinclair go on about how they need to ensure they have the *right men* for the job, I can't help shake this nasty feeling in my stomach. He says that those who fail will be sent home.

The problem is, I don't believe him. There's something off about this place, and if I were to take a wild guess, I'd say no one ever actually gets to leave—alive.

CHAPTER 18 – LUCY

Lucy — Present Day

I breeze through the pages of *Magical Herbs*, by Fiona Lynch, completely oblivious to the people walking by my room. Perula handed it to me at the end of the day and told me to get started by reading up on all the different herbs, what they look like, and what they do.

"Lucy!" I hear.

It's Emily, a girl I used to go to class with. I wouldn't exactly call her my friend, but I guess she's the closest thing I have to one. She holds a math binder under her elbow and it's pressed up against her chest. She's leaning on the iron bars of my room.

I don't invite her in, but she comes in anyway and sits down at the foot of my bed. She's smiling ear to ear under that button nose of hers, and her long honey-brown locks are all wavy now because of the humidity in here. If I had one word to describe Emily, it would be, *porcelain doll*. Okay, that's two words. Looking at her, you would think she was the sweetest girl you've ever seen. Her skin always looks as white as cream, and her dark eyebrows are shaped into perfect little half-moons. She's pretty much always smiling, and if she isn't, it's because she's working on her homework. In the old world, she'd probably have turned out to be a model.

"Do you like it?" she asks. "Healer?"

I look out toward the corridor of Division Five to make sure no one's around, like being a Healer is some big secret or something. I can't tell her how much I'm enjoying it. Emily's fourteen and she's graduating in two years. The last thing I need is to be blamed for encouraging someone else to take on this position.

"It's okay," I lie. "There isn't much to do, though. Perula and Mavis do all the work. I probably shouldn't have chosen Healer, because now, there's too many of us."

She squeezes her binder harder against her chest and shrugs. "That's too bad. I'm sorry to hear that."

"It's okay," I say. I force a smile and show her the cover of my newly gifted book. "At least I get to read a lot."

She giggles. "Then I wouldn't like it. I hate reading."

A weight lifts off my shoulders when she says that.

"So, what're you gonna pick?" I ask. "What do you want to be?"

She rubs her sticky forehead and shakes her head. "I don't know. I can't decide."

"Why don't you talk to Mrs. Greensmith? She's nice. Maybe she can help you make a decision."

Mrs. Greensmith is our English teacher, and she's the oldest teacher in all of Eden. Her last birthday, which was a few months ago, had candles with the number "68" on them. She's always been my favorite teacher. She's so sweet and patient with all her students, and I've never seen her get upset. Even though she has a hard time walking because of a knee problem in her left leg, she still takes students around all of Eden to show them each job available.

Emily nods slowly. "Yeah, I guess I could do that."

Something's up. It's like she doesn't want to leave my room, even though there's nothing left to say.

I gently tap her shoe with mine. "What's wrong?"

She shrugs.

"Emily, you can tell me."

She shrugs again, but this time, she parts her lips and lets out a short breath. "I miss my dad."

My heart skips a beat and I sit up straight, watching the entrance to my room. "Emily..."

"I know, I know," she whispers. "I'm not supposed to talk about it."

"No, you're not," I say. I'm not trying to be mean, but rules are rules, and Eve's made it clear that our old life is behind us, and we're not to speak of men. She says they're not worth talking about because all they do is bring pain and destruction.

She could be right, I think, watching Emily's face. Her eyes are fixed on the floor, and her posture is slouched. It looks like she's about to cry.

I slide over to her end of the bed and put an arm around her shoulder. I'm not sure how to comfort her about her dad, especially since I never knew mine and everything I've ever heard about men is that they're monsters.

"Why do you miss him?" I ask, confused about how anyone could miss a male figure after the things I've heard.

Her dark, wet eyes roll up at me.

"He was so nice, Lucy."

I'm not sure whether to believe her or not. A man being nice? It sounds like she's imagining her past or making stuff up because she isn't happy here.

"I know what people say about men, but my dad wasn't like that," she whispers. "He used to take me to the park all the time. I'd sit on his shoulders, and he'd run around pretending to be a horse. Whenever I got sick, he'd make me chicken soup and brush my hair back and kiss me on the forehead."

Her eyes are filling with tears and her chin is popping out because she's pouting so much.

"What about your mom?" I ask. "Where is she?"

She shakes her head. "My mom left us when I was five. It was my dad who took care of me."

A man raising a child on his own? I suddenly remember a few of my friends in third grade, and their dads, who would pick them up from school or bring them to soccer. They didn't look like monsters. They looked like people. I'd forgotten about that until now.

"They're not all bad," Emily says, her voice cracking. "I was only seven when they took him away from me." Her quivering voice turns into a sob, and she throws both hands over her face.

"Who did?" I ask. "Who took him away? What happened?"

But a loud alarm suddenly goes off throughout all of Eden and I block my ears. Although I've only ever been told about this alarm, I know what to do. I jump off my bed and quickly close the gate to my room.

Lucy — Flashback

"Oh, come here, sweetheart," Grandma says, her fingers dancing in front of my face. I hate it when she does that. Her nails are long, and I'm scared she'll poke me in the eyeballs.

She squeezes her arms around me like I'm a pet or something and kisses my forehead and pinches my cheeks. I'm embarrassed.

"You're growing every day," she says.

Her mouth is stretched so wide she looks like a bug with her blond hair and her bright red lipstick. Grandma likes to dye her hair a lot. I wish she wouldn't. She looks better with her red hair, same as Mom and me, but she keeps putting blond in it. It doesn't suit her, especially because she's old. Her eyes are green too, like Mom's and mine, but hers look more brown than green most of the time. She has some wrinkles around her eyes and her hands always look dry.

I guess she isn't that old. I shouldn't say that. Mom tells me not to say that. She says it's rude, and then she tells me Grandma isn't old because Grandma doesn't walk with a cane or anything. I think she's fifty-something. But fifty sounds old to me. That's way older than me.

I don't know what to say to Grandma. I don't remember the last time we came to her house. I think I was pretty young then. Might have been a baby. I don't know.

It smells like perfume and chocolate-chip cookies. I don't know if I like the smell, but I have a feeling I'm going to have to get used to it.

"Honey, I'm going to grab the rest of our things," my mom says. "Stay here with Grandma, okay?"

She walks out the front door and to the jeep. My Grandma is talking about all the "crazy people" running around in the streets, but I'm not exactly listening. I'm too distracted by all the decorations in her house.

Crosses are everywhere. Even a big gold one around her neck. On her coffee table is a statue of Jesus with some fluffy sheep around him. It looks like they're made with cotton balls. I wonder if she made them. She likes anything that has to do with Jesus.

I don't get why she goes to church so much. She should stay here instead. Her house looks like a church.

She even has those weird long necklaces with all the beads or balls on them and with a big cross at the end of it. I think Mom told me they're used for praying. I hope Grandma doesn't think I'm going to start praying every day with her. It's weird, and I don't like it.

Whenever she comes over for a visit, she makes me pray before I eat. She says I should be thankful for my food, and I should thank God for giving it to me. She then prays, too, and asks God to bless the food.

Sometimes I think Grandma is crazy. Or else she's just old. Not a lot of people talk about God, so when Grandma does, I get a little weird about it.

There's a loud bang sound, and my mom is

standing at the front door with a big suitcase in front of her feet. She rubs her forehead with her arm to dry her face because it's raining, and then she smiles at me through the screen door.

"Almost done," she says.

"Have you ever heard of..." my grandma starts, but I run toward my mom.

"I'll help you!" I say, and I swing the screen door wide open.

Anything to get away from my grandma. I love her, but she talks too much.

I run outside and stand by my mom, waiting for her to give me something small I can take in. The rain is cold on my neck, but it feels nice. My mom's reaching inside the trunk, and I don't think she even knows I'm standing here.

She pulls hard on a suitcase, and when she stands up straight, she sees me beside her and lets out a little scream. It makes me laugh. It's so funny when I scare my mom.

"I didn't see you!" she says.

I'm still laughing, and I think I'm making her laugh, too.

"Here, you rascal," she says, and she gives me a backpack.

I throw it over my shoulder, but I don't leave her side.

"Mom?"

She's still digging inside the trunk looking for something, and all I can see are her blue jeans. The rest of her is all mixed up with all the stuff we have.

"Yes, honey?" she says, and I can't even tell

where her head is anymore.

"Are we running away?" I ask.

She pulls out of the trunk and stands up tall. It's like she's surprised to hear me ask her that.

"What do you mean?" she asks.

"Are we running from something? Is it from Jason?"

She leans toward me and puts her hands on her knees, so her face is close to mine.

"Yes, we are," she says.

I'm shocked because, for the first time in a long time, she's completely honest with me. "Jason's a bad man, and he's trying to hurt us. So, we need to get away awhile until it's taken care of."

Taken care of, I think. I know I should be thinking about police officers when she says this, but all I can think about is Aunty Eve and how she talked about "killing someone."

CHAPTER 19 – EVE

Eve – Present Day

I march my way to the very front of Eden as women and children return to their rooms, locking themselves inside for safety. The intermittent alarm is bouncing off every wall and giving me a migraine. There are numerous alarms in Eden. This one, particularly, doesn't signify an attack of any sort, which is a relief.

"Eve!"

It's Freyda. She's running down the main corridor to catch up to me. Her cheeks are pink and her lips look like rose petals—soft, silky, and a vivid red.

"What's the meaning of this?" I ask. "Who sounded the alarm?"

"I did," she says, and I'm taken aback.

If Freyda sounded the alarm, she had good reason to. I trust her more than anyone.

"There are survivors standing outside the gate," she says through rapid breathing. "They were shouting over the wall, and some women in one of the courtyards heard them."

"And how do we know this isn't a trap?" I ask, opening the locked door to the main entrance.

Freyda smirks. "There's a guard tower beside the gate, and if you give me some time, I'll check for myself."

I open the front industrial door to the prison, revealing dry soil and yellow grass surrounding the exterior of the building. It looks nothing like the inside of Eden. Everything out here is dead—like the rest of the country, assumedly.

"When you give me the signal," I say, "I'll open the main gates."

There is always a part of me that hesitates when new survivors find their way to my doorstep. The problem with allowing new women inside Eden is the risk of spreading contagious disease, which is why they're immediately taken into the basement and held in isolation until Mavis and Perula can perform a full inspection—well, Mavis, Perula, and Lucy, now.

I grind my teeth at the thought of a child taking part in such matters.

I shake away these thoughts when Freyda whistles at me from the guard tower. Grimacing, she shields her eyes from the sun with one hand on her forehead. She makes a slicing motion across her neck with all four fingers, as if to say, "Don't do it."

My hand has been hovering over the door switch, so I step away and meet Freyda at the bottom of the guard tower.

"What is it?" I ask. "Who's out there?"

Freyda places her hands on her gun belt like she always does when she means business. I can tell she used to be a police officer.

"There's a woman and a teenager," she says.

"So, what's the problem?" I ask.

She makes both of her eyebrows bounce once,

then gazes off into the dead grass. "The teenager's a boy."

Without another thought, I rush to the guard tower to see for myself. A boy? Is it finally happening? Am I finally being cornered into making a decision I'm not ready to make? What am I supposed to do? Let them die? But rules are rules, I remind myself—males are forbidden in Eden. My mind is running a mile a minute as I climb the cool, rusted ladder.

When I reach the top, I peer over the wall in time for the woman's eyes to catch mine.

Her head thrown back, she pleads at the top of her lungs. "Please! Let us in! We haven't eaten in days!"

But her begging isn't what destroys me—it's her.

I know her.

"Eve?" she shouts out.

She recognizes me. What am I supposed to do now? I pull back, the skin of my palms scraping against the concrete, and drop into a crouched position with my head in my hands and my eyes sealed tight as if this will somehow help me devise a plan.

"Fuck, fuck, fuck," I mutter.

It's Madelaine. Sweet Madelaine. I met her in one of the underground rebellion groups when I first started getting involved in the rebellion. She used to talk about her boy all the time—Kevin, I think his name was. He must be at least fourteen years old now because he was four or five when she spoke about him. He's grown taller than her, but he looks like a replica of her: curly brown hair that almost looks red in the sun, eyes as dark as moist soil, and a tanned olive-like complexion.

What the fuck am I supposed to do? Madelaine won't abandon her son, and if I deny them entry, they'll both die.

"Eve!" she cries out again.

I can hear her pacing back and forth through the dry dirt.

She's desperate.

I don't know what to do, but what I do know is that I can't let them sit out there to die. I stand up and give Freyda the go-ahead to open the gates. I can feel the vibrations in the ladder as the gates open, and I rush down to greet Madelaine at the front.

"Oh, Eve!" She throws her arms around my neck, and I stiffen.

"Madelaine, I can't believe it," I say, pulling back. "And who's this?"

I don't mean to grimace at him, but it's instinctual. In my eyes, all men are scum, even if they're young. It's only a matter of time before he turns out like the rest of them.

"This is Zack, my boy," she says.

Zack—not Kevin, I think.

"How old are you?" I ask him.

"Fifteen," he says.

Madelaine nudges her son in the ribs.

"Fifteen, ma'am."

"That's better," she says under her breath.

At least she's teaching him manners, which is

more than I can say about most mothers from my previous life.

"Come with me," I say, turning toward the main building.

Freyda rushes to my side and leans in. "What're you doing?" she hisses.

I give her a look, one strong enough to tell her to keep her mouth shut unless instructed otherwise, and she stares straight ahead as the gates behind us close.

"Right this way," I tell them, opening the gate to the prison's basement.

I have no idea what I'm doing. All I can hope is that with time, a decision will come to me, that after a good night's rest, I'll be better equipped to handle this situation.

"So, this is Eden?" Madelaine asks, her skeptical eyes scanning the prison walls. "I've heard so much about it, but I wasn't sure it was true."

"You'll see it all soon enough," I say.

I lead them to a holding cell, although upon first glance, you wouldn't know it's a holding cell. There's a bookshelf in the corner and a nonfunctional TV hooked up to the wall. It looks like a basic entertainment room.

The light above is flickering, and I give Freyda a quick glance. She'll have someone do the repair.

The moment they're inside, I step back with Freyda and close the gate. A loud *clunk* sound echoes across the basement, and Madelaine swiftly turns around in a panic.

"Eve? What're you doing?"

She rushes to the gate and wraps her fingers around the metal. "What're you doing?" she repeats.

"It's only temporary," I say. "I'll come back for you in the morning."

I ignore her shouts and kicks against the metal gate as I exit the basement, then turn to Freyda and say, "Don't tell anyone about this."

Eve — Flashback

I scan the discolored brick walls—a soft pink that was assumedly once a vivid red. The white mortar in between the bricks has turned a urine yellow, and in some areas, pieces of it are missing.

"Come on, this way," I hear.

"She's coming," someone else whispers.

Everyone is gathering at the far back of the room. The only reason I came here was because I didn't want Mila coming alone. She's been following some secret forum online ever since we located my mom at Glengarry Hospital with two gunshot wounds in her left thigh. One would think that finding their mother injured following a violent riot would be enough to deter them from following that same path, but Mila's as hardheaded as my mom, if not more.

I glance over at my sister, who looks like a kid at a carnival. She's inspecting every face, every décor, every light fixture. If she didn't look so young, I'd tell her to stop because someone might think she's an undercover cop trying to scope the place out.

I find it hard to believe that this place used to be a comedy club. A few stools are positioned at the bar where old wineglasses hang upside down, but for the most part, seating is unavailable.

At the back of the room, there's a stage, and above it, an old lightbulb dangles on a wire. The light it casts makes the red brick look orange. Then, at the very center of the wood-paneled stage, an old corded microphone stands, covered in webs.

How old is this place, anyway?

A middle-aged woman with dark golden skin and a long black braid hanging down her back brushes past the two of us, glancing back only briefly to apologize for the contact. There's a certain presence about her that I can't quite put my finger on.

Who is this woman, and why is she walking up on the stage?

Clad in a leather vest, she grabs the microphone, pulls the cobwebs off with her thumb and index finger, then tugs at the cord to locate its plug. When it comes slithering toward her, she changes her mind and pushes aside the microphone. She then claps two hands together and looks down at everyone, welcoming them with her lively smile.

I can't believe my sister wanted to come to this place. These types of underground rebel groups only worsen the conflict. This isn't some organization gathering to prepare for a peaceful rally—I can feel it in the atmosphere. The tension is so pronounced, the air is almost heavy; these women want to fight.

Women of all shapes and sizes and levels of femininity and masculinity fill the room. A short woman stands nearby, her arms as thick as a man's, a black-inked tattoo covering her entire right shoulder. I can't tell what it is, but if I had to guess, I'd say it's a muscle car encased with vines. Her short, wet-looking blond hair sticks straight up, and I can see more gum than tooth as she smiles up at the woman onstage. But it seems this enthusiasm isn't brought on by actual happiness—rather, she's thrilled to be a part of something so important.

Mila pushes her glasses up the bridge of her nose, fixated on the woman with the long black braid. She looks just as entranced as everyone else in the room. I cock an eyebrow at her, but she's too distracted to even notice. I can't hear anything the woman is saying, but I don't think it matters—it looks like she's chatting with the women at the front of the crowd, like she's catching up with old friends.

"You look new," someone says.

The woman standing beside me has dark cocoa hair that encases her face like a helmet. She's clad in a frilly beige tunic that looks like it was made in someone's backyard, and her skin is the color of wet sand. The corners of her lips point up and she seems nice, but it almost looks like she's assessing me—judging me.

"Yeah," I say, hesitant. "This is my first time here."

She extends an open hand. "I'm Madelaine."

"Eve," I say, shaking her hand.

Someone bumps into her and she jerks forward, her head bobbing back and forth. She lets out a cute laugh and dismisses the whole thing. Obviously, that happens a lot in a crowd like this.

"Don't mind the crowd," she says. "More and more of us are waking up."

"Waking up?" I ask.

She tilts her head to the side, her helmet hair

following. "You know—realizing what's going on in this world. Realizing that men have lost control, and it's time for women to finally take a stand. Now that we're outnumbering them, we're in a position to do it."

I nod slowly. I'm not sure what to say. I've never been to one of these underground meetings before. But I do agree with her—I agree that men are the cause of destruction in this world. That could be enough to warrant my being here.

"My son won't be like the men you see these days," she says. "He'll know who runs the household, and if he ever steps out of line—" But the chaotic sound of a microphone turning on silences her.

I turn toward the stage.

"Thank you for coming," says the woman with the long black braid.

Someone must have plugged in the microphone.

"I see many of you got word of our new location tonight." Her voice is soft and captivating. She searches the crowd, taking a moment to make eye contact with as many women as she can.

"There are a few new faces around the room today," she says, and my stomach sinks.

Are we standing out? I feel like an imposter.

"For those of you who may not know me, my name is Bethany Lee."

Someone whistles and she shakes her head, a modest smile on her face. "I have been organizing these meetings for seven months, as many of you already know."

Another whistle, but this time, she doesn't smile. She walks across the stage, then paces back and raises her square chin. "If you're standing here tonight, it's because you've said to yourself, 'Enough is enough.'"

There's a sudden uproar with women clapping and cheering.

"Enough inequality," she continues, leaning toward the crowd.

Loud cheering erupts.

She punches a fist through the air. "Enough dominance."

Someone whistles again.

"Enough being subjected to laws, words, and images that brainwash you into believing you're less because you're a woman!" she shouts, her last word almost a growl.

"If you're here tonight..." she pauses, staring intently into the crowd, "you're saying No to male superiority."

Everyone cheers so loud that the walls around us shake. I stare at Bethany in absolute awe. How does she generate so much energy? So much passion?

My ears are ringing and people are bumping into me as they jump up and down, but for some reason—and despite my hatred of being touched—it doesn't bother me.

I want to be here.

CHAPTER 20 – GABRIEL

Gabriel — Present Day

"I can't see a damn thing," Castor says, searching through the grass on his hands and knees. His butt crack is showing under the moonlight, and he's crawling around like a homeless person trying to find cigarette butts.

What he's really looking for, though, is a keychain he dropped when his backpack snapped off his shoulder. He says it used to belong to his little girl and that he's not going anywhere until he finds it.

I wish I had a flashlight to help him out, but I don't carry anything with me. I prefer to travel without equipment. Maybe it's stupid. Maybe I should be getting myself a bag and loading it with food or weapons, but I haven't come around to doing it.

"What's it look like?" I ask him. I brush through the colorless grass with my boot.

"It's a silver circle," he says. "It has the letter 'E' inside of it."

Poor guy sounds so heartbroken. I wonder what happened to his little girl. Was she killed? Taken away? I know a lot of dads had their kids taken from them when the women disappeared. When they decided to band together against men.

"What was her name?" I ask him.

He doesn't answer me. I assume Eliza because ten years ago, that was one of the most popular girl names. Or, Emma. That one was popular, too. I get it, though. He doesn't want to talk about it. I don't blame him. Most days, I'm thankful I didn't have children, but other days, I feel like a part of me is missing. All I ever wanted was to marry a loving woman and have kids with her. I wanted a family.

I get down on my hands and knees and start looking for his daughter's keychain. He turns to me, but he doesn't say a thing. He doesn't have to. I know he's thankful.

The grass is cool and dry. I run my fingers through it, and it tickles my face. God, I miss lawnmowers. Everything is growing so fast out here.

I touch something cold against the tips of my fingers and I scoop it up. In my hand is a silver emblem shining under the moon. On it, there's an E.

"Found it," I say.

Castor squeals like a pig and plucks it out of my hand. He kisses it over and over, before sliding it into his front pocket.

"You hoping to find her?" I ask him.

At first, he doesn't respond, but then, he lets out a long sigh. "Been hopin' to find her for over seven years now after all hell broke loose in this country."

"Wife took her?"

He nods.

What I want to ask him is: *Do you honestly think she's still alive?* But I'm not heartless. I know there's a good chance his daughter's dead. I'd never say it, though. Hope's the only thing keeping this man alive.

I only met Castor six months ago, when I got caught up with Adam's crew. I have no idea how long he was with them before I arrived.

"Any idea where she might be?" I ask.

He stops walking and turns toward me as the sun starts rising in the distance. It makes the sky look like cotton candy: orange, pink, and purple.

"If she's alive," he says, "she's either with her mother or with other women."

I'm surprised to hear him say that. I didn't think he'd be willing to admit there's a chance she's dead.

"Any idea where they might have gone?" I ask.

He shakes his head, but his eyes go huge. I can see his features better now: bushy eyebrows, a nose as round as a clown's, a curly beard, and eyes that look like they're permanently sad. He slowly lifts his hairy arm and points a stiff finger toward the orange horizon.

I follow his finger.

"Right there," he says, but I have no idea what he's pointing at. "Alpa."

He looks like a lunatic with his mouth open like that. What the hell are we staring at? I glance at him and lift an eyebrow. "What's Alpa?"

Gabriel — Flashback

I can't believe this. There's no way this is real. I'm dreaming, right?

Only two hours ago, we were debriefed on a situation in New York City. The streets have been overtaken by female rioters, and they've created a barrier around the entire city.

Anyone of the female gender is to be terminated immediately.

The words keep bouncing around in my head like a song, and I'm sitting quietly in a Black Hawk chopper. We're on our way to New York now, and I feel sick to my stomach.

I look around the helicopter at the men in combat gear. I can't see their faces, but I know the second guy on the left is Alex, my bunkmate. I can't talk to him, though. I haven't been able to get a word through for the last month. He never talks to me. In fact, no one does. It's like they've all had their personalities erased over the last few months. I suppose that's what brainwashing does to people. I still don't understand how I'm still alive or how I've survived any of this. I've had to fake my way to where I am. I've seen countless men in my class *disappear*. They couldn't assimilate. And I don't blame them. The things they've been showing us are enough to traumatize anyone. But the ones who couldn't handle it should have faked it like I did. They should have played along, or at least tried to. Maybe they'd still be alive. I'm not an idiot. I know they were killed. They knew too much. If I'm not careful, they'll do the same to me.

I can see the Statue of Liberty. It looks like a little toy figure. Then, out of the other window, I see a dozen more helicopters closing in on the city.

"Fucking bitches have what's coming to them," says the man sitting across from me.

He's dressed like the rest of us: black swat gear, a helmet, a cloth over the lower part of his face, and a semiautomatic gun on his lap. I'm panicking inside. If I don't shoot my gun, they'll notice. But at the same time, I can't take innocent lives. I can't start killing women.

The moment we've reached our target, the pilot lowers the chopper above a high-rise building, and we're ordered to rappel out. I'm the last man to jump out, and the moment my feet touch the concrete rooftop, an explosion shakes the city.

Preserve the city, I remember General Fletcher telling us. The blast sure as hell didn't come from us.

"Move, move, move!"

Everyone shuffles to the door sitting in the middle of a concrete block, and we go down the building's staircase. The sound of gunshots fills the air outside, and my heart is beating so hard I can feel it against my bulletproof vest.

We reach the main floor, and I realize we're in a hotel. Women are hiding inside the main lobby. They probably didn't want anything to do with this riot. There's a middle-aged woman crouched by the elevators, and one of the men on my squad raises his gun and aims it at her face.

"Please," she cries out, the little red hairs of her head dancing because she's shaking so bad. "I don't want—" and he shoots her square in the face. Blood and brain matter splatters on the gold doors behind her.

I want to kill the son of a bitch. The woman didn't do anything wrong. She was just sitting there. What the fuck is wrong with him? Is that Alex? I can't even tell. I have to take a deep breath because if I don't calm down, I'll shoot him in the back.

Another woman hides behind the reception desk, and she runs as soon as she sees us. Our squad leader shoots her in the ankle. She falls flat on the floor, her hands making a clapping noise against the tiles. She cries out in pain.

"Goddamn bitch," he says and makes his way to her squirming body.

He grabs her by the back of the hair and lifts her up even though she can barely stand because she's in so much pain.

"You think you'll be let off that easy?" he says. He wraps his big gloved hands around her arm and pulls so hard that there's a snap, and she screams out in agony.

I stiffen and tighten my fingers around my gun. What is he doing? The two other men in my squad laugh and join him. I can tell one of those laughs is coming from Alex. He's exactly like the rest of them. A disgusting piece of shit. The tallest of the bunch slowly pushes his steel-toed military boot on her foot and rests his weight.

She yells out again and falls to the ground. Her

face is all wet and shiny because she's crying so much.

"Shouldn't have tried to revolt," the guy says, and I realize it's Alex. He grabs her by the back of the hair and pulls downward so her throat is sticking out.

My heart's racing and my vision's getting fuzzy. Why are they doing this? She hasn't done anything. The marine standing behind her (the one who seems to be helping Alex) sticks his finger in her mouth to and forces it open. She gags a few times, and then Alex unbuttons his pants and pulls out his penis.

I realize that I'm slowly raising my gun because the only thing I want to do right now is shoot the three of them dead—Alex, the other guy, and the squad leader. They're all pieces of shit who deserve to die.

They burst out laughing when Alex starts pissing in her mouth. She gags again, but the squad lead holds her face in place.

I can't. I just can't.

I raise my rifle and fire a dozen rounds at the three of them. The sound of empty shells against tile echoes throughout the lobby and the smell of burning climbs up into my nose.

The woman throws up a pool of stomach acid, then slowly turns my way. Her hair is all over her face, sticking to sweat and pieces of puke. She's shaking like a leaf.

I slowly walk toward her, but she flinches like a wounded animal. I know she must hate me right now. She must think I'm like the rest of them. I don't deserve her kindness, even if I defended her. I take off my helmet and kneel in front of her, right beside Alex's dead body.

She's staring at me from behind moist blue eyes, and her chest is bouncing up and down because she's breathing so hard.

"I know this doesn't mean much," I say, "but... I'm so sorry. You don't deserve this. None of you do."

Her golden eyebrows nearly touch at the middle, and I can't tell if she's upset or confused.

I tear off part of my squad lead's sleeve, and I wrap it around her leg. She yelps out in pain again, but she knows I'm just trying to help. She doesn't push me away.

"You need to apply pressure," I say.

She's staring at me like a caged circus animal. A combination of curiosity and hatred.

"Can I see?" I ask, and I take off my cut-proof gloves. I hold her leg, trying to be as gentle as possible, and it seems to calm her. "You're lucky," I say. "The bullet went clean through."

She wipes bits of yellow vomit off her bottom lip. "Why are you helping me?"

I hesitate. How am I supposed to answer that? But the first thought that comes to my head somehow comes out of my mouth. "Because I'm not a monster."

"They are," she says, glaring at the dead bodies around her.

She's right.

"Keep the pressure on there," I say. "You won't be getting medical care anytime soon, so you'll have to keep an eye on it. Is there any alcohol in this building? Any first aid kits? Anything at all that can disinfect the wound?"

She nods. "In the staff kitchen."

"You work here?" I ask.

She nods again. I notice she's wearing a name tag, and it reads: Josephine Taylor.

"Josephine," I say, and her eyes light up. "I'm Gabriel."

She smirks at me. "Like the angel."

I look down at my clothes. At my big black leather boots and my padded swat gear. "I wouldn't call myself an angel."

She doesn't seem to think my job makes me a bad person.

"Listen," I say, "before you go to the staff room, I'd suggest you take one of their uniforms and lay low. When this is over, you can walk right out of here."

"Pretend to be a man?" she asks.

I shrug. "Yeah. I know it's shitty, but it's your only option. They're killing every woman in sight."

I want to throw up myself. I want to do more, like go outside and fire at every man I see, but I know it won't change anything. I'll have both men and women coming after me.

She nods quickly. "Okay, I'll take his," she says, and she points at the leader because he's the smallest one of the bunch. "But first, I need you to come with me."

I blink.

"To the staff room," she says.

"You need help?" I ask. "I can walk you there."

I get up and I'm about to wrap my arm underneath her, but she shakes her head. "Help would be nice, but no, that's not why. See those?" She points up at every corner in the lobby, where small black cameras are aimed downward. "The main drive is in the security room beside the staff lounge." She pulls out an ID card from her bra. "You'll probably want to wipe that drive after what you've done here."

CHAPTER 21 – LUCY

Lucy — Present Day

With my face pressed up against the iron gate of my room, I stick my nose out into the corridor.

"What's going on?" Emily asks.

I shush her and tell her to stay on my bed. The alarm finally stopped buzzing, but no one's leaving their rooms. Is there a threat that we don't know about? Is it unsafe to step out into the open?

The sound of heels against tiled floor echoes across the walls, and I pull my face away from the bars, my hands still gripped tight around them.

"Who's coming?" Emily whispers.

I shake my head. How am I supposed to know? I can't see that far. But when I hear her familiar voice, I feel calm.

"It's okay, children. Everything is okay," Mrs. Greensmith says.

What follows next is the sound of keys rattling, gates opening, and voices spreading like wildfire. She's unlocking the doors.

"Shhh," Mrs. Greensmith says. "No need to get all excited, now."

I light up when she finally reaches my room. She does a double take when she sees Emily sitting on my bed, her big gray eyes popping out over her glasses that are dangling off the tip of her nose.

"There's two of us, Mrs. Greensmith," I say.

She looks confused... as though she's seeing double, or something.

Then, her eyebrows come together. I know what's she's thinking. She's thinking we broke the rule. When the alarm goes off, everyone is supposed to go back to their rooms and lock themselves in.

"She didn't have time," I say quickly.

Her wrinkled frown disappears and the loose skin of her face stretches like she wants to smile, but she doesn't. "I don't know what you're talking about. I must need new glasses."

I love Mrs. Greensmith. You would think that out of all the teachers, the oldest one would be the most uptight, but Mrs. Greensmith has always been a rule-bender. Her priority is the kids of Eden.

She slides her fat skeleton key into the gate's keyhole and unlatches the lock.

"Is there even a copy of that key?" I ask her, stepping out.

She tilts her head and jiggles the keys in front of me. "Always thinking about every scenario, aren't you, Lucy?"

It seems like common sense to me. What if someday, by some freak accident, the key gets lost? Then what? I know Eve can open all gates electronically, but what if our solar panels stop working? We'd all die in here.

Or, like, worse... what if we're attacked? What if whoever takes over kills all the adults and makes us prisoners?

The thought of being trapped in my room for all eternity makes me claustrophobic, so I move away from it and stand in the middle of the corridor. Sometimes, I blame my mom for my fits of paranoia. Before Eden, we spent years running away from some invisible man. From Jason. Maybe that did something to me and I don't even realize it.

"Don't worry," Mrs. Greensmith says, "There's a—"

"Lucy!"

I turn around. It's Nola. She's running straight toward me with her long green skirt pulled up in both hands, and her flat shoes squeaking on the floor with every step. It sounds like her shoes are wet. As soon as she reaches me, she throws both arms around my neck and I feel a pop.

"Oh, thank goodness you're okay!" she says.

My face is pressed so hard into her chest I can hardly breathe.

I pull away. "I'm fine, Nola. It was a short alarm."

She's freaking out. She keeps brushing her poufy hair back and looking around in every direction possible. Looking at all the kids who are slowly coming out of their rooms, then back at me, then back at the kids.

"What's going on, anyway?" I ask. "Do you know what the alarm was for?"

She leans forward, and Emily suddenly appears beside me to hear the gossip.

"I can't say for sure," Nola says, "but there're rumors that a woman's voice was heard from outside the walls."

"A survivor," Mrs. Greensmith says.

"So where is she now?" Emily asks. "Is she

coming into Eden? It's been so long since we had an outsider come inside."

Mrs. Greensmith and Nola give each other a look. And it's not just any look, either. It means something, but I can't figure out what.

"What?" I ask.

What do they know that we don't? I'm sixteen, for crying out loud. When will adults stop treating me like a friggin kid?

"There's another rumor," Nola says. This time, she hurries inside my cell, and we all follow like a bunch of cats around a can of wet food. "A few women found Eden after we came here. Grace, Anedi, Florence... They were told by Eve not to repeat what had happened, but you know how women are—they like to talk, especially with their friends." She lowers her voice even more and I lean forward, my back curved like an old lady. "Rumor has it that Eve put them in some sort of holding cell in the basement."

"In the basement?" Emily lets out, and Nola slaps a hand over her mouth.

"They were kept prisoners?" I ask.

Nola nods. I look at Mrs. Greensmith. It's obvious that she's heard this rumor too, but she doesn't want to encourage gossip.

Then, I look at Emily, who's probably the spitting image of me with her mouth wide open.

"Aun—Eve's the one doing this?" I ask.

I have to stop thinking of her as Aunt Eve. No one knows about this, and with the things I'm hearing, I'm not so sure I even want that link to her.

Nola nods again.

"Could it be for our own safety?" Emily asks. "Eve's been nothing but good to us. I'm sure there's a reason."

"Three days," Nola says.

Everyone stares at her.

"One of the survivors," she continues, "was kept down there for three days without any food. Grace says it was cold and dark, and that she was only given a liter of water for the three days." She then makes a disgusted face by turning her mouth upside down. "She was forced to go to the bathroom in an old toilet that doesn't even flush."

I can't believe what I'm hearing. Would Aun—would Eve do that? I know she's changed, but I can't imagine her intentionally hurting people. Could someone else have done that, and everyone assumes it's Eve because she's in charge? But then I remember her cold blue eyes and the way she looked down at me when I announced my decision to be a Healer. It was like she wanted to strangle me with her bare hands. Like she hated me.

Nola points a stiff finger in the air and shows her teeth at me and then at Emily. "You can't repeat this to anyone."

I nod and Emily shakes her head, but we both mean the same thing. We won't repeat a word.

"Do you think there's anything else we don't know about?" I ask. "Anything secret that Eve's doing?"

"All right, that's enough," Mrs. Greensmith says. "Come on. Out you go." She brushes air behind our backs. "To the courtyards. Time to stretch those legs and get some exercise."

I quickly shove my book, *Magical Herbs*, under my pillow. I'll have to catch up on some reading later.

We make our way down the corridor and toward the exit door to step out into Division Five's courtyard. The sun is in the middle of the cloudless blue sky and it warms the skin on my head. Kids are playing with balls of hay, and it looks like Ruby found her way to our Division. I friggin love that dog. She's wagging her long, golden-haired tail from side to side and barking at the kids like she's trying to say, "Come on, throw the damn ball!"

The moms and the women are doing their day-to-day jobs: filtering water and plucking berries from bushes. I take Emily against Eden's outer wall, where a long strip of shade is cooling part of the grass. It's too hot to be out in the sun, anyway.

Emily turns around and pulls her long braid over one shoulder. "Do you honestly think Eve would do that?"

I'm about to say, "I don't know," but a short, squat, agitated woman rushes toward a group of women. I know her. I've seen her before. I think she's from Division One, which is the Division located beside the main entrance. I wonder if she knows something we don't. Is she one of the ladies who heard the survivor on the other side of the wall?

I slowly wave a finger at Emily. That's my way of telling her to keep quiet because I can't hear a word the stubby woman is saying. I grab Emily's wrist and rush around some of Division Five's tallest shrubs. They don't serve much of a purpose, but one of the gardeners was real pushy about leaving them there. She said that greenery is important for mental health reasons or something. There's a small opening inside the shrub, so I force us inside, cracking a few of its tiny branches, and place a finger over my lips.

Emily leans sideways and closes her eyes, obviously trying to catch a few words. I do what I'm good at. What I used to do all the time when I was seven: I cup the backs of my ears and pull them forward. I probably look like a rat, but I don't care because it works. I can hear them.

Even though I can't make out every word they're saying, I do catch a few things. A few important things. Did I actually just hear that?

My eyes go big, and I stare at Emily. She didn't hear what I did—that's obvious.

"What?" she mouths.

I lean in and my mouth brushes against her left ear. "Something about a boy on the other side of the wall."

Lucy — Flashback

"Government-regulated abortions? Is this a hoax?" Grandma says.

She's leaning into her laptop, and all I see is the outline of her gray curly hair in front of a bright screen. I'm not sure what's going on, but it sounds like the government wants to start killing babies that are little girls. My mom told me about this. She explained to me what abortion was. She didn't want to, but it was all over the news. She also told me that it was soon going to be against the law to kill a boy inside a mom, but I don't think that's what Grandma's listening to. She sounds so surprised, so I think it's something new that the president did.

"Goddamn it, Mom! Turn that off!" my mom says.

My grandma's jaw drops. She looks insulted. "Ophelia Cain. Thou shalt not take the Lord's name in vain."

My mom rolls her eyes and slams my grandma's laptop closed. "She's eight years old," she says. "She doesn't need to hear all of that."

I'm playing on my H-Cap and pretending that I'm not listening to anything they're saying. But when Grandma was watching the news on her computer, I was watching it, too, but she didn't know. It's not the same type of news they have on TV, either. On TV, it's always a man who talks now. He's always wearing a fancy suit and talking about how the government is doing everything they can to make sure people stay safe during all this fighting. I know he's lying. I can tell. He always blames women, too, like all the men on TV. They're always blaming women for everything.

On my grandma's computer, though, people are posting videos they're taking with their cell phones or G-Cameras (cameras that look like glasses and go on your face). It's a new cool thing. If I wore glasses, I'd want them. Anyways, my grandma tried to turn down the volume when people were shot, but her hearing is bad, and I don't think she realized I could hear it just fine.

Most of the videos were taken in New York City. I guess there's a lot of bad stuff going on over there right now, and the government's hurting people. In one video, I thought the man in the black uniform was trying to help stop the fighting, but he lifted his gun and shot the person taking the video.

I won't lie. I'm scared. I'm really scared. I wish I hadn't seen it. I almost started crying when I saw and heard some of the stuff going on in those videos, but if I cry, Grandma will know I'm watching. And I don't even want to watch, but I can't help it. I don't want to pretend it isn't happening. I know how bad things are. Mom won't even let me go back to school anymore. She said that I could take a break. I miss my friends already. At least I get to play on my H-Cap as much as I want.

"Hey," my mom says, and she sits beside me. The cushion of the couch sinks down a bit.

I try to ignore her and pretend like I'm into my game, but it doesn't work. She knows me too well. She brushes my hair out of my face and kisses my forehead. Her lips are warm and so is her breath. "You okay?"

I nod, but my throat feels tight. It even hurts a bit, because I'm trying to hold everything in.

Don't cry, don't cry, don't cry, I tell myself. Mom is scared, so I need to be strong.

"Sweetheart," she says, and she's playing with the hair behind my neck. I love it when she does that. It tickles, but it feels so good at the same time. "I'm sure you heard some of that."

I'm trying so hard not to cry, but I can't help it. My throat hurts too bad now, and my bottom lip starts to shake, so she wraps her arms around me. "Come here, shhhh, it's okay."

I'm so sad and so mad. Why are men hurting all those women? I know that women are causing some trouble by doing these riots, by that's not a reason to kill them. They're people. They have eyes, noses, and ears like everyone. They have hearts and feelings. They have families who love them. And now they're all being killed. They're all dying. Men are putting bullets through them like they're objects. Like they aren't people.

Why are these men allowed to take someone's life away? It's not fair.

I cry so hard my head starts to hurt, and my mom doesn't let me go. I'm scared to lose her, too. What if she wants to go to a riot? What if the bad men hurt her, too? What if this Jason guy hurts her?

"It's okay, honey," she says. "I'm right here."

I squeeze her tight and don't let go.

"Please don't leave," I say.

CHAPTER 22 – EVE

Eve — Present Day

Freyda's pacing back and forth as if I just told her we were invaded by a group of male Rebels. It's one boy, for God's sake.

She waves a frantic hand in the air, her fingers resembling a panicked spider on the verge of being killed. "What are we supposed to tell the women?"

"The truth," I say.

She wasn't expecting that. Her mouth is half open, and she won't break eye contact.

"The truth?" she repeats. "You want to tell the women of Eden that you've locked up two survivors and that one of them is a boy?"

I get up from my office chair and lean against the window. "Not exactly."

"Eve," she says, "think about this for a minute. You yourself said that the male gender is forbidden in Eden. Do you honestly want to go back on that decision? It'll make you look weak and inconsistent."

"It's not about my image," I say. "It's about our women. The decision should be left to them."

I know what she's thinking—that I'm undermining my own leadership. But, I've sensed some tension in Eden. What better way to regain the women's trust than to provide them an opportunity to make such an important decision? I need them to follow me, and to do that, I need them to trust me.

I'm hoping they make the right decision—I'm hoping they ban him from Eden, but if they don't, eventually, they'll pay the price, and I won't be the one to blame. When that happens, they'll follow me without question; they'll realize I know what's best for them.

"And what if they make the wrong decision?" she asks.

"What *is* the wrong decision, Freyda?"

She cocks an eyebrow at me and rests her hands on her belt. "Is this some kind of test?"

"No," I say. "I mean it. I want to hear your opinion."

She's reluctant, and I don't blame her. But I do want to hear her opinion. If there's one person I admire most in Eden, it's Freyda. I don't think she realizes that.

"I believe that with the right surroundings, a male can be trained to behave properly," she says.

I rub my chin and gaze outside, where two women are crouched and cultivating carrots from their garden. I don't say anything because I don't agree with her. The problem with men is that they're programmed to reproduce and to fight—nothing more. I don't see how any man could ever be stripped of his instinctual sexuality or his anger caused by an abundance of testosterone.

"You don't agree," she says bluntly.

She knows me well. I smirk at her and sigh.

"Unless a man is castrated, I don't think any amount of training will do," I say.

Her eyes nearly lunge out of their sockets and I look away, wondering if I've crossed a line. She has the same look that Ophelia had when I suggested we kill Jason, her abuser—one of shock and confusion.

"What's the matter?" I ask, breaking out into a nervous ramble. "Have you never thought about what it would be like to have a world in which men aren't controlled by their penises?"

Why do I care so much what Freyda thinks? I'm Eve—I don't care what anyone thinks.

She shrugs. "No, not really. I've always pictured a world without men altogether. I guess I never gave much thought to one day coexisting again."

"And what if the women decide to allow the young boy to stay in Eden?" I ask. "What then?"

She tilts her head and makes a twisted face. "Are you suggesting we castrate him?"

I stare at her, searching. Would it be such a terrible idea?

I brush my bangs out of my face and laugh. "Don't be ridiculous. It's only a fantasy."

She smiles at me and I feel at home.

"I'll order a meeting," she says, making her way out of my office.

How Freyda manages to keep her humanity, I don't know. She took countless lives during the war, yet, she's still capable of differentiating right from wrong—something I've been unable to do for the last five years.

I don't believe in right or wrong anymore. I believe in a world of peace without man's corruption, and I believe that this can only be achieved by bold action. If I hadn't made half the decisions I did during the revolution, we wouldn't be here, and Eden wouldn't exist.

Most of these women have no idea what I've done to save us.

They have no idea who I truly am.

Eve – Flashback

I reach for Mila's hand, but she pulls away. I'm as shocked as she is to find out what's happening in New York City, but Mila's taking it a bit harder. She has friends in New York, and right now, they're being massacred by a bunch of men in suits.

The sound of gunfire blares through the television's speaker, bouncing off every wall in our living room. I can't believe this is happening. The last time we spent this long staring at a television screen in disbelief was when we were young—when North Korea launched a nuclear attack on California only to prove a point, killing millions of innocent citizens.

Mila doesn't remember it, but I do. I was eight years old or so, and I remember it like it was yesterday. My mom kept changing the channel, almost as if she thought it was some big hoax—as if it wasn't happening. It's as if she thought she'd land on another news broadcast announcing the whole thing as fake news.

But it wasn't fake and neither is this. It's all over MeFile—or as my mom would say, a glorified version of something called Facebook. I'm scanning through my phone, and to my surprise, everyone is using the hashtag *standourground*. I say everyone, but to be honest, they're all women—women from all over the world.

Goose bumps appear all over my arms. Women around the world should be terrified right now, but they're not. Instead, they're angry. They're fed up, and they aren't going down without a fight. What astonishes me most is the support we're receiving from other countries. Although they're handling the gender imbalance far more gracefully than we are, they're still willing to stand with us in spirit.

Mila's jaw muscles keep popping out, and her eyes are round and unmoving. I can't tell whether she wants to cry or throw the television remote at the wall.

The news anchor—some prick with an overcoat suit and a blue tie—presses his fingers against his ear and nods before looking at the camera.

"Reports are confirming over eight hundred women have died in today's tragic event, however, that number is expected to rise."

He stares into nothingness and nods again.

"The barrier around New York City has been abolished by military forces, and they're sweeping through the city as we speak."

A big red bar scrolls across the bottom of the screen: "Rioters in New York City taken down after President Price approves a kill order."

Mila suddenly jumps up, the remote control held above her head. I grab her by the arm and pull the remote out of her hand.

"I get it!" I say, and my angry voice seems to calm her.

She stares at me, her nostrils flared.

"I'm pissed too," I say, my heart beating so fast I wonder if my shirt is flopping up and down. "Beyond pissed. Livid. If I were standing face-to-face with President Pr—with that piece of shit—I'd fucking kill him. With my bare hands. Okay? I'd kill him. He has no right to do what he's doing. No right at all. He's turning this whole fucking country into a war zone. And the men follow him because they're all a bunch of goddamn dogs. All of them. They're brainless fucking dogs."

I suddenly realize I'm digging my fingernails into Mila's arm. Her eyes are huge and her lips are sealed tight. I quickly release my grip.

"Sorry," I blurt out.

"That's exactly what we need," she says.

I stare at her. What is she talking about?

"That, right there!" She points at me. "That anger. We need more of that fucking anger! Enough is enough!"

I feel like an idiot, having vented out all my anger, but at the same time, I needed the release. I'm so sick of holding everything in—of trying to be the *good* guy who tries to maintain peace or who tries to ignore the topic altogether.

Our country is going to shit, and the women sure as hell don't need a pushover like me to stand in their way. Mila's right—we need this anger. I need this anger. I can't sit on the sidelines and hope for the best because the best isn't going to happen. Things are only going to get worse from here.

"We need guns," Mila says.

I'm a little taken aback by this. I was fine with being angry, but to carry a firearm?

"Don't look at me like that." She throws an open hand toward the TV. "Don't you get it? This is war. This might be happening in New York City, but it's going to start happening everywhere else. What're you gonna do if some guy grabs you in an alley? Huh? Tries to rape you? Haven't you been online? Abuse victims are coming forward by the hour."

I swallow hard and look away. Mila doesn't know, and I don't want her to know. I don't want her to know that a police officer held me down and forced himself inside of me. It'll only hurt her.

"Eve?"

I look up at her. Shit. Did I make a face?

"What happened?" she asks, her tone dropping an octave.

"Nothing," I say quickly.

"I know when you're lying, Eve. Did someone fuckin' touch you?"

She steps forward, her shoulders drawn back and her hands forming fists. If she wasn't my sister, I'd think she was about to hit me.

"It was a cop," I say.

She still looks so angry, but her bright eyes fill with tears.

"When?" she asks. "What—what happened? When was this? Eve? Say something."

I shake my head. "When I went out looking for Mom."

I hate that I brought her into this, but at the same time, a weight lifts off my chest. I can breathe again.

She slaps a hand over her mouth. "Because of me. You went looking for Mom because of—" Her voice cracks.

"Mila," I say. "It's not your fault. It's them. It's all

of them."

She wipes tears from her cheeks and nods.

"You're coming with me," she says, matter-of-factly, as if she's intercepted a direct order from someone with a high pay grade.

"What? Where?"

"Tonight," she says. "Bethany's holding another meeting. I can't talk about it here." Her eyes dart toward her cell phone.

It sounds like something out of a sci-fi story: the government listening in on citizens through their cell phones. But everyone knows they can do it. It's already been exposed. Mila isn't crazy for taking precautions. That's why we're not allowed any electronic devices during these meetings.

Bethany Lee, I remember, the leader of the underground rebellion group. I went to a few meetings, but I haven't been in over six months. Mila's the one who's been keeping in contact with the group.

"Why tonight?" I ask. "What's so important about tonight?"

Her eyes dart toward her phone again, and she bites down on her lip. "They're planning something big—something huge."

CHAPTER 23 – GABRIEL

Gabriel — Present Day

"What're you gonna do?" I ask, staring at the abandoned prison's exterior wall. "Walk right in?"

Castor looks at me with a crooked grin. Like he's the most confident guy in the world. Like he's king shit. "If there's a chance my daughter's in there, then yeah, I'll walk right in."

I pull on the collar of his shirt and look at him square in the face. "Don't be stupid."

He's too impulsive. If Castor's story is true... If women were told to meet by this so-called Alpa mountain after the revolution... Well, chances are, they've been living out here for a while now. Long enough to completely arm the place and collect guns and build solar-powered weapons. And the only habitable thing near Alpa, aside from forest, is this abandoned prison. So that's where they are. I'm sure of it.

I stare at the front gates. How many of them are in there? Are they even in there? What if no one made it? And if some did make it, what if they went wild? Feral. Are they all a bunch of crazies? Or, are they living the life they've always wanted? A life without men?

After everything that's happened to them, I can't imagine them welcoming any man with open arms.

"Let's just hold tight," I say, turning away from

the prison. "We can stay in here for a while... out of sight. We'll keep watch. See if anyone opens those gates. I don't think it's smart to walk up to the place. For all we know, they have snipers watching the walls."

Poor guy. He looks like I just killed his dog. It's like telling a kid about a giant indoor water park, and then telling them that it's going to open in two years. He's so close he can almost taste it. He's licking his lips and blinking over and over the way someone does when they wear contact lenses for too long. There's obviously a lot going on in that big round head of his right now.

I rest a hand on his shoulder. "Hey, come on. We don't even know for sure that there's anyone in there."

Castor nods, lets out a long sigh, and drops his backpack into a pile of leaves.

I want to move closer to the prison. Maybe if we were standing right outside the walls, he'd hear something. But it's too risky. If there truly are women in there who've built an empire, they'll do whatever they need to protect themselves from outside threats. Which essentially translates to killing us where we stand.

"What if they don't open those gates for weeks? Months?" he asks. "What then? We gonna rot here?"

I smirk at him. "Why would we rot? We're in a forest. I'm sure there're animals to hunt."

"I don't hunt," he says.

I laugh. For the first time in months, I laugh. It could be because I'm tired or because of that stupid look he has on his face again.

"Don't worry, princess," I say. "I'll take care of feeding us."

He glares at me but then snatches his daughter's keychain out of his pocket. He runs his filthy thumb across the engraving and bows his head.

"She's a sweet girl," he says.

I notice he's talking about her in the present tense, but I don't say anything.

"She didn't deserve to be a part of this," he continues. "No kid deserves to be born in a world torn by war." He kisses the piece of silver again and looks up at me. "What about you? Did you lose anyone during all of this?"

I look away and clench my jaw.

"Hey, that's cool," he says. "No need to talk about it."

Good, because I don't want to talk about it.

"I *will* find her," he says, now tapping his thumb against the keychain. It's making a ticking noise because his fingernails have grown out so long.

I miss nail clippers. That's what I'll look for in the next town we get to. A pair of good old nail clippers.

I'm envious of him. If only I had that strength. But maybe it isn't strength at all. Could be it's a delusion. Wishful thinking. He wants so badly to believe his daughter's alive that he actually believes it.

There are a lot of things I wish I could pretend never happened, but I can't. It happened, and I'm haunted by the memories of it every damn day. Life isn't some fairy tale that gives you a happy ending because you're *hopeful* or because you're *positive*.

I've been hopeful many times before. Hopeful that tomorrow would be better than today. But every day's only been worse than the last. After the massacre in New York City, everything went to shit. I'm not one to insult a superior, but our president was an idiot.

"So, what're you gonna hunt with?" Castor asks, breaking the silence.

I raise two hands and form claws. Maybe I shouldn't use those nail clippers after all. These bad boys are pretty useful.

He scoffs. "Your hands? And those nails?"

He thinks I'm joking. He has no idea how many lives I've taken with these hands.

"Until I have the time to carve myself a weapon," I say. "Yeah, my hands."

He shrugs and sits down on the forest floor. It crunches underneath him, and it sounds so loud in comparison to the silence around us. "Better get to it," he says, slapping his hard belly. "I'm hungry."

Gabriel — Flashback

James is cleaning his semiautomatic rifle with one knee on the bench and a cigar in his mouth. He's surrounded by six or seven other marines who are sharing a bunch of gruesome stories. I'm trying to block out most of it, but I keep hearing everything. It's disgusting.

"Her head was shot right off," James says, the cigar wiggling up and down. He laughs, puts his gun back together, and makes eye contact with me. "What about you, Gabriel? Any good kills?"

Good kills?

I've spent the last six months trying to take out my own kind without being seen. If I'm caught, they'll tear me apart. Literally. Probably with their hands, too. I've seen some of the men do it. It's like they've reverted to medieval times when they used to tie men up to horses and split them up into four pieces. Only these guys... They team up and use their hands. They pull as hard as they can until things start to snap, pop, and rip. It's the cruelest thing I've ever seen.

The worst part is it isn't enough to kill the woman. Only enough to dislocate her joints, tear tendons and muscles, and cause excruciating pain. I saw this happen in New York City when there was smoke and gray dust everywhere. No one knew what was going on, and men were having a free-for-all. Like it was some kind of party.

I killed the four men I caught doing it, but it wasn't enough. The woman, a middle-aged lady who was in so much pain her face had gone white and she'd passed out, was lying there, her limbs loose and her body looking like a fifty-year-old rag doll

The only thing I could do was offer mercy with a bullet. It's like I'd told Josephine, the woman I saved in the hotel lobby... Help wasn't coming. If the military and special forces received a kill order, there was no way they were sending in paramedics after the attack. The only help they'd be sending would be for our own.

"Come on, Gabe. Let it out," James says.

He's not the James I once knew. He used to be a proud, respectable man who always helped anyone in need. At least, that's the James I met. They'd turned him. Brainwashed him. I stare into those empty marble eyes, wondering how they managed to turn a good man into a monster. I think they used his wife and daughter against him. Made things personal... Made things painful enough for him to get so angry, he'd want revenge on all women.

It would make sense because that's what they did with me. They said if my mom had done her job as a wife, my dad wouldn't have died in battle. I didn't believe it. Not for one second. But I had to pretend I did, which is what killed me. Saying my mom's a worthless excuse for a human being, even if I didn't mean it, destroyed me. But I had to. I had to play along. She's the one person I love most in this world, and I'd do anything to be back home right now.

"Don't worry about me," I say, and I turn away.

The men should know by now that I'm not the type of guy to make conversation in the locker room. One of the men standing beside James, a hefty, six-foot-something guy with a thick black beard, puffs out his monkey chest and unwraps the towel from his waist.

The guy's huge. I didn't mean to look, but he's so damn hairy, I couldn't help it.

A few minutes ago, I watched him bench press nearly 400 pounds. He could easily do damage to someone with his bare hands.

I stare at him, imagining myself pointing a rifle at his face. His muscles can't save him from a bullet. He lets out a deep laugh that resonates across the lockers and claps both of his massive hands together.

"I'm sure you have something to share," he says, his voice so deep it vibrates across the lockers.

I'm about to tell him to piss off, but I'm not suicidal. I know my limits and my weaknesses. I've been through intensive training, and I've fought against some of the most highly trained men this world has to offer, but it isn't enough to take on a dozen men in a locker room... A dozen men who just spent the last hour lifting heavy weights. They're all pumped, with their veins bulging out and their muscles looking hard under their skin.

Sometimes I wonder... Should I try harder to blend in? Should I make up some sick story about something I've never done to a woman? Would this get them off my back? Because they look at me funny sometimes like I'm a liability. Like I'm the guy who's going to fuck everything up.

If only they knew how many of our own I'd killed... They'd tear me to shreds, literally. I stare at the man's curly beard, then down at his chest, where he has so many dark hairs curling around his nipples you can barely see any pink. The man's a beast. He's looking at me, nostrils flared and his bushy eyebrows flat, like he's ready to grab me by the throat and pin me against the locker if I don't answer him.

I can only imagine what he did to women during the New York riot. I wish he'd been a part of my crew. He'd be rotting in a pile of rubble right now.

"Well?" James says.

They're all looking at me like a bunch of hungry hyenas with big smiles on their faces and their tongues practically dangling out. Dozens of ideas run through my head. I have to convince them that I'm as sick as they are.

"Shoved a grenade in one of their mouths," I say. "Blew her head right off."

Who am I becoming?

The bearded man slaps his chest and lets out a laugh so loud, I flinch. "I knew you had it in you," he says. "Sick son of a bitch."

Was it enough? Did my fake story convince them?

"Never even thought of that one," he goes on. "Grenade in the mouth..." He then points a stiff finger toward the industrial ceiling, raises one bushy eyebrow, and leans forward. "Know what'd be even better?"

The men are all hunched forward like kids around a campfire. Only, big kids. Ugly, hairy kids.

He suddenly makes a hook-like movement up in the air and yells, "Grenade in the fucking pussy!"

The entire locker room blows up with *Ohhhs*, and some of the men are punching fists in the air.

Goddamn it. What've I done? I've given these gruesome bastards more ammunition. More imaginative ways for them to murder someone. Because that's what it is. It's murder. The only difference between what they're doing and violent murders in this world is that they've received *approval* from President Price himself.

There's a loud knock on the door, and some man wearing a tightly buttoned blue dress shirt and a long black tie pops into the locker room. I can't tell if he's a sergeant or a messenger. He's probably someone responsible for administrative duties.

He clears his throat. "Gentlemen."

The room goes quiet, and everyone looks at him.

"Master Sergeant Nicholson wants you all in P-04."

P-04. That's one of the large auditoriums here in Area 82. In fact, that's the first auditorium I stepped foot in when I got here. The only time we're brought into P-04 is to be debriefed on our next mission.

"What's this about, Lucas?" one of the guys asks.

Lucas, the man with the tie, smirks at the man who said his name, his light eyes darting from side to side behind his thick-rimmed glasses. For a second, it almost looks like he's flirting with him. He leans forward in a feminine way, his chest pressed against the doorway's frame.

I'm surprised he hasn't been killed yet.

"Something to do with Washington," he says, "but you didn't hear it from me."

CHAPTER 24 – LUCY

Lucy — Present Day

"Where's everyone going?" I ask, looking up at Nola.

All the adults are moving through the corridors, urging the kids to stay in their rooms or to go outside, so long as a sixteen-year-old is present to watch them.

A young girl in the cell across from mine tugs on her mom's dress. "Mommy, where are you going?"

Her mom pulls her little hand away, kisses her on the forehead, and says in a rush, "I'll be back, honey. Mommy has to go talk with the adults."

The little girl is still reaching in the air when her mom turns away, and she bursts into tears. Other adults walk by, ignoring the little girl's cries, and the corridor fills with footsteps and whispers.

"Nothing you need to worry about," Nola says, patting me on the back.

I know when Nola's lying. There's a twitch in her right nostril every time she does. It almost looks like she caught a whiff of something rank.

"Is this about the boy?" I ask.

Nola slaps a finger over her mouth, lets out a long *shhhh*, and pulls me back into my cell. She's hunched over, her finger still over her freckled lips and her candy-green eyes popping out at me.

"You need to keep quiet about that. You aren't even supposed to know," she says.

I know I'm not supposed to know. I overheard it outside a few minutes ago. I'll keep quiet, all right, but I want an answer.

"Well, is it?" I ask.

Nola nods quickly, her eyes shooting toward the now empty corridor. "Go watch the children outside. I'll be back shortly."

She squeezes my shoulders, kisses me on the forehead, and disappears into the main hall. I'm about to head toward the corridor's exit door that leads into the courtyard, when Emily jumps out of nowhere, her hands grasping my cell's iron bars.

"Emily! You scared me," I say.

She laughs. She always loves scaring me even when she doesn't mean to. "Where're you going?"

"Outside," I say. "Nola asked me to watch the kids."

Her braid is splitting all over the place now, but she's still playing with it over her shoulder. I wonder how often she takes it apart and rebraids it. And why the visit? That's twice now that she's come to see me uninvited. She must be lonely.

"Gabriella's already watching the kids," she says, and she retightens the elastic at the end of her braid.

Gabriella's one of Division Five's eldest teenagers, having graduated last year. I stare at her because I'm not sure what it is she wants from me.

She jerks her head sideways, and a sly smile creeps up on her thin little lips. She's trying to tell me something, but I have no clue what it is.

I make my eyes go big as if to say, "Well, spit it

out," and she quick-steps her way into my cell. She drops down on my bed and pushes aside my book, *Magical Herbs*, under my pillow.

"Aren't you curious?" she asks, kicking her feet back and forth.

"About the meeting?" I ask.

She nods and her braid slides up and down on her shoulder. If I didn't know any better, I'd say she was planning something mischievous.

"Of course I'm curious," I say, "but Nola—"

"Nola, schmola." She flicks her wrist in the air.

Since coming to Eden, I've never had the chance to get to know Emily. She's always been so reserved. She's the type of girl who's too shy to talk to anyone in her class, who walks through the corridors with her head bowed and her schoolbooks pressed tight against her chest. And me, having become a major introvert since I lost my mom, well, I never made much of an effort to get to know her, either.

She seems pretty cool, though.

I raise an eyebrow. "Do you know where the meeting's taking place?"

She twirls her braid around her index finger over and over, then lets it go, and it dances on her shoulder. "Doesn't take a rocket scientist to figure it out."

She hops up onto her feet and pokes her head out of my cell. The loose, straggly strands of hair at the top of her head follow her back-and-forth movements.

"Clear," she says, and she waves at me to follow her.

She makes her way down Division Five's corridor, avoiding eye contact with some of the little girls who look up at us from inside their cells. Some are playing with wooden dolls and combing through their hair that's made of grass, some are reading books, and some are playing with their friends.

"Where you going?" one girl asks, but Emily just walks faster.

"Hey, you're not allowed!" someone else says.

A few heads pop out into the open, and they watch us as we make our way to the main hall. During the adult meetings, we're not supposed to leave our Division.

"They're probably in Division Four's theater room," Emily whispers, but her voice carries out across the hall. "That's where I see them go all the time."

All the time? How often do they hold meetings without us around? And why is it for adults only? When will everyone stop treating me like a friggin' kid? I graduated. I'm an adult now. Plain and simple.

"When do you think we'll start going?" I ask. "To the meetings, I mean."

She shrugs. "Can't say… Marylin's eighteen and she still hasn't gone to one. I hear her complain about it a lot."

I know who she's talking about. Marylin was one of the first girls to graduate a few years ago, but I don't know anything about her.

"Come on," Emily says, and she leads me through an office door.

We enter a small office space. "This isn't the theater room," I say.

It's dark, but there's enough light coming through the dust-caked window for me to make out the furniture and décor. There's an old pine desk and a chair that looks like it hasn't been used in decades. An old broom leans in the corner with cobwebs all over it. A few dozen boxes piled up on the back wall look pretty new.

She smirks back at me. "No, it isn't, but it leads to it."

"What is this place?" I ask.

"Storage," she says. "We're not supposed to be in here, and if you talk about this room to anyone, they'll tell you it's haunted. That's something the parents say to keep the kids out."

"What do they store?" I ask, stretching my neck toward one of the boxes.

"I haven't checked," she says.

I avoid the temptation and follow her as she crosses the room. Then, I notice something. I can hear people. The sound of voices filters through the wall.

"Is that them?" I ask.

She nods, and a small-toothed grin stretches her pale face. "We're right beside the theater room. See this door?" She points at a white door with half its paint peeled off. "That leads to the lounge."

"Lounge?" I ask.

"Yeah, the lounge at the back of the theater. That's where the kids get ready for a play, or where you would have been waiting for graduation.

There's a couch to sit on and everything."

I remember the lounge, now. I sat on a sofa while Nola poked her head out through the front door, waiting for my name to be called out. I wonder how often Emily comes to the theater room. She seems to know this place inside and out. I watch her reach for the door, looking excited and sneaky all at the same time. She doesn't look like the shy little Emily I thought I knew.

"This isn't your first time, is it?" I ask.

She goes quiet for a second, then looks back and says, "You can't tell anyone about this."

"I won't," I say. "Promise."

Before she turns the handle, she looks at me, her chocolate eyes almost glowing. "Whatever you do, don't make a sound."

I close an invisible zipper over my lips and pretend to toss away the key. She turns the ancient doorknob and slowly pushes, but only a crack. Only enough for us to see through. A strip of yellow light shines into the office. I stick my head out over Emily's and with one eye, look through the thin crack of the door.

The first thing I see is a table—the type you'd find at a family picnic or a school event. It wasn't there when I was in the room with Nola. It's plastic and foldable, and on top of it are a bunch of small cups. There are dozens of them. It looks like they're filled with something. A drink, perhaps.

"Happy-oh, happy-ah, happy-vanilamalay," someone says.

I'd recognize that crazy, frog-like voice

anywhere. It's Mavis. What's Mavis doing in the theater's Preparation Room?

"Quit your gibberish," comes Perula's voice.

"Only a pinch," Mavis says.

"I know what I'm doing," Perula says.

I see one of their long fingernailed hands, but I'm not sure whose, stretch over the little cups and sprinkle powder, or herbs, into each one.

I look down at Emily, and we exchange a confused look. What the heck is going on? Are they planning on poisoning the adults? Mavis and Perula wouldn't do that, would they?

But then I hear another voice, and it makes me feel like my stomach just dropped to the floor.

"Mavis, Perula... are the drinks ready?" Aunt Eve asks.

Lucy — Flashback

My mom's hunched over my birthday cake and her chin looks like a fuzzy peach over the candles. A big smile spreads across her face, and she's clapping her hands together while singing "Happy Birthday."

I look down at the cake. I know my grandma helped her because my mom can't bake. I also know my grandma helped her because the bright green writing on the cake isn't my mom's. It's in cursive writing, and my mom doesn't know how to write in cursive. It says, "Happy Birthday Little Lucy." That's more of a guess because it's so hard to read.

Other than the writing, there isn't much. It's a plain vanilla cake with creamy vanilla frosting.

My mom looks back at my grandma, who's wearing an old birthday cone hat that's probably twenty years old, and she says, "I know it's not much, honey, but it's the best we could do."

"It's perfect," I say, and I blow out the two mismatched candles.

They worked so hard to make this cake.

"I wanted to get you a present," my mom says, and she looks back at Grandma again, "but you know—"

"I know, Mom," I say. "It's not a big deal."

I know that buying groceries is almost impossible now. From what I saw on the news, *the economy is crashing,* whatever that means, and it's making everything so expensive. The other day, my grandma came home with a loaf of white bread that she says cost her eighty-three dollars. I don't buy groceries, but I know that's expensive. It's usually ten dollars for the cheapest bread.

Most nights, we eat pasta or rice. It's the cheapest thing to buy, and it lasts a long time. We also try to eat fresh fruit and vegetables whenever we can. Grandma has a garden in the backyard, but a lot of the time, her fruits and vegetables go missing overnight. Some kids in the neighborhood must have found out about it, and they're probably stealing our food.

I'm pretty mad about that because Grandma works so hard even to grow one tomato, but maybe these kids don't have any money. They might not be able to buy groceries at all, and Grandma's garden is the only thing keeping them alive.

Then there's a whole other problem. There's the *looters,* as mom calls them. She won't even let me go to town with her anymore. She says it's too dangerous. There's only one grocery store left, and it's surrounded by men with big guns and suits.

All the other stores are being broken into, and no one has control anymore. We're lucky that we're here at Grandma's house. She lives in Bruntonburg, a small town close to Washington DC. It's a historic place, Grandma says, with buildings as old as 400 years.

I've been in town a few times with my mom to buy groceries. There were cobblestone sidewalks and roads so small you can barely fit two cars. There were a lot of people on bikes and a lot of people walking around.

It was really pretty. I loved it. Well, when people

weren't fighting with each other or breaking stuff. A few months ago, Mom said I couldn't go with her anymore. She took a picture on her phone to show Grandma and me, and I wanted to cry. In the picture, there was broken glass everywhere. There was even a car flipped over, with its belly on fire. There were a lot of the old stone and brick buildings covered with spray paint. The words were written in red across doors and over the brick walls. I couldn't read all of it because Mom isn't very good at taking pictures, but I remember a few of them:

Stand Our Ground

Not My President

We Will Not Fall

Mom says the women who are rioting are putting all of that on the buildings, and even though it makes me sad to see such a pretty town get ruined like that, Mom doesn't seem too upset about it. She says this is what happens when the government doesn't listen to its people. I think she's on their side. The rioters, I mean.

And after seeing everything that's happening now, I'm on their side, too.

Mom's been letting me watch the news a bit more. She says there's no use trying to protect me and that it's better if I know what's going on.

I look up at my mom while she cuts me a slice of birthday cake. I'm so thankful for everything she's doing. I'm so scared because I feel like every time she goes out to town, something bad could happen. Ever since all of this started happening, I've been nicer to my mom. I don't disappear to play on my

H-Cap anymore. I'd rather spend time with my mom and Grandma because I'm scared I don't have much time left. I know I shouldn't be thinking like this, especially because I'm only nine, but it's a feeling I have in my stomach and it makes me cry every night.

My mom hands me my piece and I take a big bite full of soft frosting.

"Delicious," I say, and the warm frosting squishes out of my mouth and onto my face.

My mom looks down at me and blinks hard like she's fighting off tears. She's probably having the same feelings as me. I think she's scared something bad will happen to me. She brushes her thumb on my cheek and squints her eyes like she's smiling with them.

"I'm glad," she says. "Next year, though, I'll get you a special gift—could even be a dog."

I laugh because I know Mom will never get me a dog. She's only saying that because she feels so bad right now. And by the look on her face, it almost looks like she's not sure we'll even make it that long. I think she's trying to make herself feel better.

I swallow my bite of cake. I have to try to make her feel better, so I say, "I'd love that."

Mom's about to cut herself a slice, but there's a weird noise coming from outside. It sounds like a deep rumbling. Like a junky old car.

My mom gets up from the table and rushes over to the living room. She moves the blinds a little bit and sticks one eye close to the window. "What is it, Ophelia?" Grandma asks.

But Mom doesn't say anything. She pulls back and slaps a hand over her mouth, and her eyes are big and round.

What's going on?

I drop my fork onto my plate and it makes a loud metal noise. I run to the curtains to see for myself, but Mom holds me back from moving the curtains. That doesn't matter, though, because I can still see what's outside through the little crack.

It's an old red truck. It looks almost yellow in some spots, and there's a bunch of dark gray smoke coming out from the back of it. It's moving slowly, and the guy inside seems to be looking for someone. He's wearing a baseball cap, and it moves from side to side because he's eyeballing every house.

I don't have to ask my mom who that is. I know who it is. I recognize the truck because that's the same truck that's followed us before when my mom started acting funny. And I also heard my mom talking to Aunty Eve on the phone about the *red truck*.

It's Jason, the man who's trying to hurt us.

He found us.

CHAPTER 25 – EVE

Eve – Present Day

Mavis and Perula step out into the theater room carrying silver saucers filled with small foam cups. Fortunately, we have bags of these by the thousand in our basement supply room. I'm not entirely sure what Mavis and Perula concoct when they make these elixirs, but I do know they've mentioned the use of something called scopolamine, which they've also referred to as Devil's Breath.

According to myths, Devil's Breath is capable of removing one's free will, rendering them entirely complacent. I don't believe in the myth, mind you, because these women don't become blank slates after drinking what Mavis and Perula now refer to as Devil's tea.

But, over the last few years, their Devil's tea has time again spread an indescribable euphoria among the women. This became especially useful when we first established Eden because many of these women lost people they cared about and many fell into depressive states. But now, I can see it in their eyes after they drink; there's an indescribable happiness. Every time they drink, their pupils become dilated and they're more receptive, making it easier for me to emphasize Eden's direction without opposition.

Mavis and Perula are the only ones who know

the ingredients to Devil's tea. The women believe it to be a mixture of chamomile flower, alcohol, and cannabis oil. The truth, however, is that the ingredients are far more potent than anyone could ever guess, which is why I did not want any young graduate choosing the path of Healer. I've made it quite clear to the twins that Lucy is to know nothing about Devil's tea. The last thing I need is for her to begin questioning my ways—to doubt my methods.

The twins make their way around the room, bending over as women desperately reach for their tea.

"Welcome," I say, stepping up onto the stage.

The women greet me with glazed eyes and smiles on their faces. Every time I step up here, I feel like royalty. This isn't what I expected when I led the women to Eden, but over the last few years, I've grown to crave their love—to desire their obedience and loyalty.

I wait a few minutes, watching as everyone finishes their drinks.

"Thank you all for coming," I say. I twirl a finger in the air, and Freyda sweeps through the room, picking up the empty cups.

She knows about the tea, but she doesn't drink it; I'd rather have her clearheaded.

"I believe some of you may have heard voices over the wall," I say, and bickering spreads across the room like fruit flies in an abandoned kitchen.

With the click of my fingers, everyone goes quiet.

"We found a mother," I say, and the room lights up. But when I add, "And her son," the women all frown at the same time.

"A boy?" someone says.

"As in, a male?"

"How old?"

"Where are they now?"

I raise a hand, and silence returns. "They're being held in isolation until Mavis and Perula ensure they're not infected with anything from the outside."

They all nod, and I can tell the tea is settling well.

"He's young," I continue. "Fifteen." I pause and clasp my fingers together over my stomach. "But that's not important. What's important is that he's a boy who will soon become a man."

The women are still slowly nodding, and it's as though I'm talking to robots.

"The reason I've brought you here," I continue, "is to allow you all to make an important decision today."

They turn their heads from side to side, eyes wide and lips parted, almost as if the person sitting next to them might know something they don't. I think confusion is also setting in because the women aren't used to having the freedom to make decisions in Eden. I've always been the one to guide them.

"Do you want to allow the boy to stay?" I ask.

Whispered words are exchanged, and women are leaning into each other, their faces nearly touching.

"You know best, Eve," says one woman, standing. "Why don't you decide."

"Yes, you decide, Eve."

"She knows best."

"She's always guided us in the right direction."

I wonder how much backlash I'd have received had the women not drank the Devil's tea. They look happy now with their pathetic smiles and rosy cheeks. They stare at me from behind large sheep-like eyes and wait for me to speak.

I have them right where I want them. They need to be shown that free will is precisely what will destroy them. These women don't know what's best—they make decisions based on their feelings and nurturing instincts. I've heard the late-night meetings held in Division Seven's courtyard. It's directly beside Division Eight, the only isolated Division I often visit by myself. Over the wall, I've listened to the bickering and the frustrations shared regarding their insatiable desire to bring men into Eden. If it isn't their sexual appetite blinding them, it's their motherly instincts. Many of these women— especially the young ones—yearn for a man's touch and want nothing more in life than to be mothers.

You would think that going to war with the male gender would be enough for them to despise men. But it isn't. There's a primal desire that I can't seem to eliminate.

"I've always led you toward a better life," I say, walking across the stage. "But today, I want *you* to decide."

"What do you think is the best decision, Eve?"

I smirk—not intentionally but because this is as easy as taking candy from a kid.

"It isn't up to me," I say. "I wouldn't want my decision affecting your lives in any way." I watch them, tapping the tip of my nose with my index finger. "But do remember that this boy would be surrounded by female influence... by mother figures who could mold him into the ideal man."

They break out into rapid nods again, looking at each other in deep contemplation as if my words stem from heaven itself. It's only a matter of seconds before silence returns, and the most vocal of the women—the one whose voice I've heard gossiping over the wall at night—stands up and presses a hand over her hefty chest.

"We feel that the boy should stay."

Bingo.

"Then I respect your decision," I say. "After all, I'm here to ensure you all are happy and that your needs are being met."

Watching them is like holding a piece of bloody meat in front of a pack of dogs—big eyes, stiff postures, and smiles stretched across their faces.

Some of them reach for each other's hands, excitement filling the room as they bounce their shoulders and grin from ear to ear.

"A boy..."

"The first boy."

"Can you believe it?"

I smile at them.

The boy will fail us—I know it. His primitive

nature will eventually take over, and once it does, the women will come to realize that they're nothing without me.

Eve — Flashback

"All clear, Beth."

Bethany Lee, the leader of one of Washington DC's most influential underground rebel groups, is sitting straight across from me, a glass of water in one hand and a blue gel pen in the other. She's hunched forward, her leather vest rubbing against the table and her rounded shoulders giving her the appearance of a professional boxer. Her hair almost looks dark brown under the light overhead, but anywhere else, it looks jet-black.

The girl who just walked in is Shilo—Bethany's watchdog. She scouts the area every ten minutes, and that's on top of the other five girls Bethany has watching every entrance and exit, including windows, to our current location.

Several weeks ago, Bethany gave up on the underground comedy club—she said something about government officials being on our trail. We've since had to relocate several times.

Tonight, we're sitting in someone's basement apartment. The owner died two nights ago from a drug overdose. A rotten smell still lingers, but apparently, the family won't be coming by until next week to gather his belongings, which makes this place our safest bet for the week.

"The government's losing power," she says, a shadow cast over the upper half of her face, her high cheekbones still prominent. If I didn't know any better, I'd say she had native ancestry.

"Men are losing power," someone says, and

Bethany smirks at them.

She then smacks a fist on top of the coffee table, causing the warm strawberry-scented candle in the middle to dance from side to side. "We're going to hit them where it hurts." She looks up at everyone in the room—a total of approximately twenty people—and stiffens her posture. "Are preparations still in order?"

Mila nods and pulls out a slip of paper.

The crowd is usually much thicker than this. In the comedy club, we reached maximum capacity: a total of 150 women. But I think Bethany is worried that too many women may make it easier for government officials to track us, which is why she limited tonight's crowd to a select few only. I don't blame her—I'd have done the same thing.

"It's getting tough," Mila says. "The White House has already fired all its female staff... Congress is all male. The US military is all male. We're losing our connections."

Everyone stares at her, and for a moment, although I don't like the idea of my little sister involving herself in a rebellion, I'm proud. She's come a long way, and to see her take part in something so big is awe-inspiring in many ways. I know there are dangers to what we're doing, but ever since the riot in New York City, everything's gone to shit. The women of the world are enraged beyond belief.

We can't just sit around.

Instead of listening to his people, President Price signed an executive order to cut health care for women. In a speech he recently gave, he said something along the lines of, "Until women submit themselves and stop rioting, we will continue to treat them as foreign outsiders. They will not be given access to any of our country's benefits or protections."

And what did that do? It made things worse. Homemade explosives go off every hour in various cities across the United States. President Price has even called in all special forces to help fight the rebellion, but the problem is, they don't have enough men—we outnumber them. They might control the government, but we control the cities.

Countless marriages have fallen apart because men are brainwashed by the news, led to believe that without women, none of this would be happening. So, what do they do? They turn on their wives, their girlfriends, their mothers and try to convince them that this entire rebellion has been blown out of proportion.

Schools have been shut down, and traffic is at a standstill with car parts and debris littering the cluttered roads. You wouldn't even know you're in the United States. Aside from city skyscrapers and glass buildings, everything looks like a third-world country.

And all of this could have been avoided had President Price agreed to put an end to government-assisted abortions and let us live as people and not as objects to be controlled by men. He is tearing this country apart by spreading hatred, sexism, racism, and fascism. I never thought

I'd follow in my mother's footsteps—never thought I'd become a feminist—but enough is enough.

I'm at the point where I am prepared to die if it means that somewhere down the road, this country will be salvaged, that peace will return. Because from where I'm standing, this life isn't worth it anymore.

"I think we should reconsider our original plan," Mila says, pointing at her slip of paper. "We can't prepare an attack from the inside if women aren't working there anymore."

There's a vibration in my pocket, and I look up at Bethany.

"Sorry," I say, and I get up to answer the phone, even though I don't recognize the number. I can hear Mila going on in the background, something about taking drastic measures, but the moment I hear Ophelia's voice, everything around me fades.

"O... O... calm down. Talk to me. What's going on?"

I haven't heard from O in over six months. I assumed she got her cell phone plan cut. Her voice is quivering, and she's breathing heavily.

"Eve, he's here. The fucking asshole found me."

"Found you?" I ask. "Where are you? Where have you been this whole time?"

She lets out a long sigh, and it sounds like she dropped her weight against a wall or on a couch.

"I'm at my mom's place with Lucy," she says. "I had to leave—I just had to."

"I wish you'd said something," I hiss into the phone, and several eyes in the basement roll up at me. I turn away and sneak into the bathroom with my hand pressed against my other ear.

"I'm sorry... I didn't have time," she says. "I tossed my phone and came straight here. I thought I was a goddamn lunatic, Eve. A lunatic. I thought I was being completely paranoid and overthinking the whole thing. But he's here! In Bruntonburg. Who the fuck comes to Bruntonburg? There's nothing here!"

"Bruntonburg," I repeat a few times. I've heard the name. "Where is that again?"

"About twenty miles south of Washington," she says. "Goddamn it, Eve. What am I supposed to do? He knows I ran. He's gonna kill me... He's gonna fucking kill me. Why else would he come here?"

The guy's obviously a psychopath, so I believe her when she says he's going to kill her.

"Take a breath," I say, and I fight to catch my own. I sit down on the toilet lid and crane my neck back, my eyes fixated on the yellow-stained ceiling, then down at uncapped needles lying on cracked tiles around the toilet.

What a dump.

I turn my attention to the shower curtains. They're see-through with weird duck-like designs on them that almost look like guns.

That's it.

"O," I say, "give me the address."

"What, why?"

"Just give it to me."

She gives it to me, and I punch the information into my cell.

"Hold tight," I say, "and whatever you do, don't leave the house."

She doesn't even have time to say goodbye because I hang up and slip the phone into my pocket. I open the bathroom door in a full swing, and everyone looks at me. Mila's lips are parted, and her glasses are hanging off the tip of her nose.

"What's up?" she says.

"It's O," I say, and Mila stiffens.

Ophelia's always been a family friend, and Mila loves her like an aunt, the way Lucy thinks of me as her aunt.

"What's wrong?" Mila says.

"Jason found her," I say, and Mila stands up.

"What do you need?" Bethany asks, leaning back in her chair.

I look at her and then at Mila. "A car, and maybe a gun or two."

Bethany nods toward one of her watchdogs, and they move toward the candlelit table. The sound of heavy metal scratches the table's surface, and in front of me are two black pistols—one with a silencer and one without.

"Granger here will show you how to shoot it," Bethany says.

Granger, the girl who handed me the guns, pulls out a set of keys attached to a metal ring. She twirls it around her index finger, then drops it into my palm.

"Black Vexer at the back," she says.

I look at Bethany—I don't know how to thank her. I've come to view her as a mother these last few months. She'd do anything for us. She's been more of a mother than mine's ever been.

"How long are we gonna be gone?" Mila asks.

"Not sure," I say.

"Shouldn't we tell Mom?"

I stare at her. "You mean like she tells us when she disappears for weeks at a time?"

I don't mean to sound so resentful, but my mom's been absent lately. If she isn't coming home with bruises or bloodstains, she doesn't come home at all. We've found her in the hospital about six times now, and with health care recently cut for all women, I'm sick to my stomach every night when she doesn't show.

She refuses to involve us in what she's doing even though we're doing the exact same thing she is. The only difference is we're smart about it—we're thinking things through. Mom goes out and joins any riot she can find. She's so angry, and one day, it's going to get her killed.

"Thank you," I say, and Bethany gives me a gentle nod.

I don't know what I'd do without her.

Mila picks up the pistol from the table and tucks it into the side of her pants.

"When we get back," she says, "we're killing the president of the United States."

CHAPTER 26 – GABRIEL

Gabriel – Present Day

I stare at Castor as he shoves a piece of rat meat into his mouth. His lips, two shiny lines of pink, flap up and down underneath that big red-brown beard of his. He's been letting it grow these last few weeks—not like he has much of a choice because we're running out of water and the razor he has is dull.

"Good?" I ask.

He nods but doesn't answer.

I wonder how long we'll be sitting here waiting. Is it even worth it? Even if his daughter is in there, who's to say we'll ever get close to her? What if these women are so feral they're willing to cut off our penises at the first sight of us? I wouldn't blame them for wanting to, after everything that's happened. But at the same time, how are we supposed to ever reunite in peace if the women are unwilling to see that not all men are the same? That there many of us who are genuine and who wouldn't treat them like garbage.

In all fairness, I've known some pretty cruel women. It's not only men. I wish people wouldn't generalize an entire gender because of the bad ones.

I stare at the prison wall, then up at the overcast sky, wondering how much longer we'll be forced to live like this. Rumor has it that Canada hasn't been affected as badly as we have and that thousands of men and women have sought refuge in the north. And what about other countries? What about Europe? Why isn't anyone trying to help?

The last time I read the newspaper—a torn black-and-white front page—the article went on about how the female population was expanding everywhere incredibly fast. So why is it that we've destroyed ourselves when other countries haven't? Unless they have now... There's no telling because there's no electricity, no internet, nothing.

Maybe the whole world's gone to shit.

Maybe there's no getting out of this at all.

I look back at Castor, who's finished eating and now sits with his head pressed against the bark of a birch tree. He has two hands over his face, and he's rubbing up, down, and through his hair. He's probably thinking about his daughter.

"Have enough to eat?" I ask.

He doesn't look at me, but he nods.

"We need to build shelter," I say. I step over a fallen branch; my boot crunches through leaves and twigs.

His head rolls up and his dark eyes catch mine. He looks disgusted. "You think we'll be here that long?"

What's his problem anyway? Did he prefer following Adam around?

"Got somewhere better to be?" I ask.

He inhales a deep breath through his hairy nostrils and hits the back of his head against the tree. "I can't just sit around, Gabe."

I stare at him, then out through the woods. "So don't. Get up and help me build a shelter."

"That's not what I meant."

I step my other boot over the branch and cross my arms over my chest. "Then what do you mean, Castor? You think I want to sit around, too? Don't you think I'm fed up with just *surviving*? I didn't ask for this. No one did. But sitting around moping about it isn't going to fix anything."

His eyes narrow on me and he squeezes his jaw, and I wonder if I might have overreacted. Maybe I was a bit insensitive. The man has a daughter to worry about after all.

"You don't get it," he snaps, throwing his arms out. He stands up, then starts pacing back and forth, and bits and pieces of dead leaves and sticky dirt fly all over the place. "My baby girl, if she's still even alive, would be twelve years old right now. Twelve!" His eyes go big and he stands there staring at me like he's waiting for it to sink in.

I'm not entirely sure what he's trying to get at, and I think he realizes it because he keeps going. "The last time I saw her, she was seven years old. I'm missing all of her special moments. She'll be a teenager soon, and I'm not even around to help her through it. She's my baby girl, and I have no idea where she is, how she's doing, or if she's even alive. Do you have any idea how hard that is for someone?"

His shoulders are hunched, and his mouth, which is missing several teeth, hangs open.

I feel like a jackass. The poor man is heartbroken, and here I am, basically telling him *suck it up, buttercup.*

"Castor, I'm—" I say, but I don't have time to apologize.

He drops to his knees, both hands over his eyes, and starts sobbing the way I've never seen a grown man sob before. Drool slips out of both sides of his wide-open mouth, and he lets out a loud bellow—wailing like a person who's lost someone they love.

I swallow hard, feeling a tinge of actual emotion for the first time in years, and make my way over to him. I place a hand on his bouncing shoulder, kneel level to his, and say, "Hey, I'm sorry, buddy. I didn't mean to be an asshole."

I'm not entirely sure he heard me over the sounds that are coming out of his lungs because he keeps crying.

"Hey, Castor, listen. We'll find her, okay?" I can't stop the words. They spill out of my mouth. "We won't stop until we do. She might be in there. You know, in the prison. We need to play this right, okay? I'm trying to be strategic about this."

He pulls his hands away from his face. His eyes are completely bloodshot and his mustache and a part of his beard are covered in snot. He sniffles, then breathes in hard to catch his breath. "Y-y-you think she's in there?"

"Maybe," I say. I don't know what I'm doing. I don't want to get his hopes up because realistically, his daughter probably died along with most people back when the war started. It's highly unlikely that she survived, but he doesn't need to know that. The only thing that's keeping this man alive is the hope of finding his daughter. "There's only one way to find out, right? We'll get inside those walls one way or another."

He nods fast the way a kid does when you reassure them that they have no reason to be scared.

"Let's give it a few more days, okay? If your daughter's in there, a few days isn't going to hurt anything. If she's in there, it means she's with women... With adults who're taking care of her."

He nods again, then wipes his mustache and beard with the sleeve of his pink-and-beige flannel shirt. It used to be red and white.

"I'm gonna help," I say, and I pat his shoulder. "Don't worry."

He pulls out his daughter's keychain and rubs his crusty thumb against the soft metal, before spitting out a few bubbles of saliva and letting out one last little cry. But I pat him again, and it seems to help because he doesn't start full-blown crying again.

He looks up at me like an abandoned dog with those big wet puppy eyes of his. "Thanks, Gabe."

I force a smile and stand up.

"How about you come help me out? The walk might do you some good. I need to collect as much wood as I can, and we can build some type of—"

But a sound catches my attention. Something close. My eyes follow it through the hundreds of trees standing as tall as giants. I can't see where it's coming from, but I know what it is.

It's the sound of an engine.

Gabriel — Flashback

"What the fuck do they think they're going to accomplish?" James sneers, resting a hand on his holstered gun.

I stare across the north lawn of the White House and through the fountain, where thousands of women are standing behind barriers waving signs and shouting. Their mouths and eyes are open wide like rabid dogs. They've been standing there for months, rioting against President Price's new bill. The one to illegalize male abortion. There were more before them, but the crowd was way smaller. It's getting big now, and I know why. It's because of the second bill: the one that plans to force women to abort female embryos.

Basically, the government is going to say who gets to keep what.

"Is this how you thought it would be?" James asks, glancing sideways at me.

I cock an eyebrow at him and regrip my E9 energy rifle. I'm pretty lucky to be holding this thing. It's a brand-new design, and it's been given to Black Marines as a pilot. It has unlimited ammo (bursts of compressed energy), but the only downside is that it can overheat.

"Being a marine," he says. "Did you think we'd ever be assigned to the White House? Alongside the Presidential Protection Unit?"

I look at him, then at his dark blond hair he hasn't cut in months and at his unkempt beard that hangs like a rat's nest over his Adam's apple.

I don't know what he wants from me or why he's even talking to me. James isn't the same man I met during our training program. He isn't that same quirky, carefree guy who spends most of his time thinking of ways to *prank* someone. Now, he's thinking of ways to *kill* someone. He's an asshole.

"If I had it my way," he goes on, "I'd nuke 'em. All of them crazy bitches."

I clench my jaw and stare straight ahead. I need to be careful. Careful not to let my anger show.

"It's only a matter of time before they do something extreme. I mean, yeah, they're women, so they're not the smartest, which means it's highly unlikely they could ever build a bomb strong enough to take out the White House, but who knows... They might try." He turns toward the uniformed man standing on the other side of him and laughs. "Maybe they'll throw bloody tampons at us."

"Have some respect," I snap, but I immediately regret opening my mouth.

"Some respect?" James growls, stepping toward me and breaking formation. "Are you fucking kidding me? Do you have any idea what these women are doing to my country?"

"*Your* country?" I sneer. I'm about to crack his nose with the stock of my gun.

"Back in your position, Walsh," someone says, and James backs up, his back facing the White House.

"Careful who's side you're on," James says. His face is all red and blotchy, and the color is spreading down to his neck.

I sense several eyes on me and wonder if I've crossed the line. We've been taught—brainwashed—to hate women, and here I am, defending them.

"I don't agree with what they're doing," I say, trying to fix the mess I've made, "but I'm able to remember that they're still human beings."

James lets out a snort, and I look over at him. He's shaking his head and popping his jaw muscles in and out.

"They're the reason this is happening," he says, his stare fixed on the rioters.

"I get it," I say, even though I don't agree with him. "I have a mom, okay? I still love her."

"I hear you, Gabe. We all have moms." James finally looks at me. "But they *chose* to turn against us."

There's no use trying because I know there's no getting through to him. A few other men bicker, taking James's side. So, I stop talking because I know nothing good will come of it.

Two combat helicopters fly overhead, followed by a fighter jet. For a second, it masks out the sound of women shouting. I can't believe I'm standing at the White House in the middle of a war zone. It's only a matter of time before President Price gives another kill order, and when that happens, all hell will break loose. Because what else is he going to do? That's what he's good at. Creating conflict and worsening situations. And when someone doesn't *obey him*, he needs to show them who's in charge. Especially if that *someone* is a woman.

Hundreds of men are lined up around me holding E9 rifles. All around Lafayette Square are snipers positioned on top of buildings with their guns aimed at the crowds building in the streets.

How is this even happening?

A man wearing a black suit and a tie cuts through the lawn, followed by two heavily armed bodyguards. He's pressing his finger against his ear and talking into his sleeve.

Then, off Pennsylvania Avenue comes a row of beige ground combat vehicles, followed by two massive blacked-out SUVs. They barely make it up to the White House with all the women crowding the road, but dozens of men in army gear point their guns, and the crowd loosens up a bit.

"What's going on?" I ask.

James doesn't answer. He's obviously still pissed off about what I said.

Another helicopter flies overhead, and it's as though I'm in a movie. I don't understand how this is happening. How are we at war with our own kind? With the opposite gender?

Someone fires a multiple-round shot, and women scream at the top of their lungs. The last SUV drives in, and the metal barriers close. Women rush behind the barrier and throw themselves on their hands and knees. I can't see what happened, but it looks like someone was shot at for getting in the way.

I scan the lawn and realize there's no one dressed in riot gear. That ended last week when the riot was small enough to contain. But now it's out of control. Last I heard, women are coming in from all over the country, clogging the streets of Washington and bringing traffic to a complete standstill.

The crowd is getting so big that I wonder if Washington DC might just cave in.

Then a deep voice as smooth as butter comes into my earpiece.

"Hold your positions. We've lost count at two point five million women."

Lucy — Present Day

I rush back into my room with Emily by my side. After everything Eve has told us about boys, I can't believe they're bringing one into Eden. Why would she do that? And why the heck would she give the adults of Eden the choice?

"What're you thinking?" Emily asks, breathing fast to catch her breath.

She should know what I'm thinking. Isn't she thinking the same thing? Isn't she totally confused? What was in those drinks and what were they doing with them? And why was Eve giving the adults a choice? She never does that. She always makes all the decisions in Eden.

I shake my head. "About what? The meeting, or that weird drink?"

She shrugs. "All of it."

All I know is that Aunt Eve isn't who she pretends to be. I don't think she's honest about a lot of things.

Aunt Eve.

I shake my head again.

Eve.

She isn't my aunt, and she isn't family. I don't even know who she is anymore. She even looks different now, with her short blond hair and the dark bags under her eyes. It's like she isn't even the same person I knew when Mom was alive.

"Are you okay?" Emily asks.

She doesn't know that I've known Eve for a long time, so she doesn't understand how betrayed I feel. After Mom died, Eve brought me to Eden. She took care of me like I was her own. But now, she barely even looks at me. It's like I don't exist.

"I'm not sure what to think," I say. "But I don't think the adults are being honest with us."

"About what?" Emily asks.

I shrug. "About a lot of things."

Emily scratches her eyebrow and lies down on my bed, scrunching the pillow under her head.

"Well, most of the teachers seem to think Eve is the best thing that's ever happened to us," she says.

I stare at her. Maybe the adults aren't the problem—it could simply be Eve.

"What about other parents?" I ask. "Have you listened in on other meetings?"

A sneaky smile creeps on her face.

"You can tell me," I say. "I won't tell anyone."

"I've heard a few things," she admits.

"Like?"

"Well, everyone seems pretty happy with how things are around here. I only ever hear the adults complain about one thing."

"And what's that?"

"How they want at least one man in Eden."

I frown. "Why the heck would they want to bring a man in here?"

She makes both her eyebrows bounce up and down and the corner of her lip goes up. "You know..."

I roll my eyes and slap a hand over my face. "For sex?"

She's still smiling, but she doesn't say anything.

"That's disgusting," I say.

"I'm only telling you what I heard."

"You would think after everything men have done to us, the adults would want nothing to do with them. And now you're telling me they want to have sex with one?"

She scrunches her nose, obviously as disgusted as I am. "This is why only the adults go to those meetings."

There's a soft tap on the iron bars to my room, and Nola is standing there, her cheek pressed into the metal.

"You two behaving yourselves?" she asks.

She looks more relaxed than usual, and I think it has something to do with the drink she had.

"So?" I ask. "Is everything okay?"

For a second, it almost looks like she's glaring at me. But not in a mean way. It's like she knows when I know something. She steps into my room, her frilly green dress dragging on the cement, and sits at the foot of my bed.

"You already know about the boy," she says, resting a hand on my thigh. "It looks like they'll be bringing him in."

I try to act surprised by making my eyes go big and by opening my mouth, but Nola quickly sticks a finger to her lips.

"Don't repeat anything just yet," she says.

"You think it's a good idea?" I ask. "Bringing a boy in here?"

She slaps a finger over her mouth again, her emerald eyes growing even bigger. "It doesn't matter what I think."

"I'm just asking, Nola. I'm sixteen now. You can stop treating me like a kid."

She brushes my hair back, leans forward, and kisses my forehead. To her, I'll always be a kid.

"I'm not sure what to think of it, but Eve knows what's best for us," she says.

She smiles down at me, squeezes my shoulder, then gets up. She walks out through the iron bars, then glances back at me and says, "Just have faith," before walking down the corridor of Division Five.

I'm confused. Eve knows what's best? Eve isn't even the one who made the decision. She asked them to make the decision for her. Unless that was her plan. Maybe she wanted them to choose. But why?

The moment she's gone, I look back at Emily who's staring up at the cement ceiling.

"It's like they're being brainwashed or something," I say. "Those drinks might have something to do with it."

"Who?" she asks. "What're you talking about?"

I throw my chin out toward the corridor. "The adults. You saw it, too. You saw those drinks that Mavis and Perula were making. They put something in it. It wasn't alcohol."

"You think Eve's drugging them?" she asks, sitting upright.

"I don't know," I say, "but I'm gonna find out."

Lucy — Flashback

My mom pokes her head into the closet and says, "Don't be scared, honey." She gives me a flashlight, kisses my forehead, then slowly pulls out.

"Mom," I say. I don't want her to leave me alone in here again.

"A little while longer, okay sweetheart?"

"My H-Cap's dead," I say.

She lets out a sigh. She squeaks the closet door open, steps inside, then closes it.

"Come here." She wraps an arm around me.

I press my head against her chest and close my eyes. I'm scared. I know we're hiding from Jason, but I don't know why. I don't understand why he wants to hurt us so bad.

"Is he still out there?" I ask, my head pressed underneath my mom's chin.

She doesn't say anything, but she nods, and I feel it.

"What's he doing?"

She squeezes me tight again. "I'm not sure. I think he's trying to figure out if we're inside. That's why the best thing for us to do is to hide and pretend like we're not here."

"Will he hurt Grandma?"

She rubs her thumb up and down my shoulder. "No, honey, I don't think so. He's after me, not Grandma."

What if she's wrong? What if he knows we're in here, and he knows Grandma's lying about it? Will he hurt her so he can find us? If we're hiding in a closet, it means he's a dangerous man. Why isn't Mom calling the police? Why aren't they protecting us?

"Aren't the police coming?" I ask.

I feel her throat swallow hard against my forehead. "It's not that easy anymore, honey. There's so much going on in the world right now. It's a dangerous place for women. There aren't any female police officers anymore, so if we call, they'll send male officers. And with the way things are going, they'd probably take Jason's side and arrest us."

"For what?" I ask. I'm so frustrated. "We didn't do anything!"

My mom shushes me and warns me to keep my voice down.

"It's not about right or wrong anymore," she says. I can't see her eyes, but I know they're looking down at me. She swallows hard again like she's trying not to cry. "Remember that, okay?"

I nod, even though I'm not sure I understand what she's saying. Why would we get punished for not doing anything? We're the ones who are in danger. If police officers won't save us, who will? Aren't they supposed to protect us? Are we supposed to keep running from this man? And what will happen when he finds us? Is he seriously going to kill us? I don't want to die. I'm so scared my legs are shaking.

"I'm scared," I say for the first time.

My mom wraps her arm around me even tighter and kisses the top of my head. Her hot breath makes me feel warm.

"I'm right here," she says, but I can tell she's scared, too.

"How long do we have to hide in here?" I ask.

"As long as it takes," Mom says. "Until Grandma says we can come out."

"What if he doesn't leave?" I ask. "What if he sits out there and waits for us? Because eventually, we'll run out of food. What if he knows that? And what if I have to pee, Mom?"

She doesn't say anything, and it gets quiet in the closet. The only thing I can hear is the clank of dishes being put away in the kitchen. I wonder if Grandma's scared, too. She didn't ask for any of this. I can picture her moving around the house, cleaning anything she can like she does when she's nervous.

I close my eyes and lay my head on my mom's shoulder while wondering if it would ever be possible to live in a place where boys don't exist. Maybe then, the wars would stop because every time I watch the news or look over my grandma's shoulder when she's on the internet, I see men with guns.

It's always men.

I'm about to ask my mom if she thinks a place like this could ever exist, but something makes an explosion-like sound. My eyes go big, and for a second, I think my heart might stop.

I know that sound. I've heard it before.

It was the sound of a gunshot.

CHAPTER 28 – EVE

Eve – Present Day

Madelaine stands up from the darkness of the basement looking deathly. Her son rushes to her side, his curly brown hair reaching the same height as hers.

"Why are you keeping us here, Eve?" she asks as I enter the room.

I cross my fingers over my stomach and raise my chin. "It was only a precaution," I say. "Bacteria can remain on one's clothing for several hours. You have to understand, Madelaine..." I force a smile, feigning gentility to the best of my abilities. "I need to ensure my women are safe. And now that you've remained isolated for several hours, you are both free to enter Eden, our paradise."

She parts her lips and simply stares at me as if she's unable to comprehend anything I've said.

"Welcome home, Madelaine."

She collapses to her knees and slaps her veiny hands over her eyes, tears streaming down her dark-skinned face. Her son places a hand on her back, and his eyes meet mine with a look of anguish. I stare back at him, seeing nothing but a young animal.

He's fifteen; it's only a matter of time before his primal instincts set in—before he begins feeling emotions such as anger, rage, and jealousy, before he experiences sexual desire.

And when this happens, the women will grovel at my feet like a herd of helpless sheep. Perhaps then they'll probably let go of the ideology that a man is needed inside of Eden's walls. What better way to prove them wrong than to bring in a boy—a boy who does not yet possess the strength of a man.

I grind my teeth and crack my neck before finally stepping forward and brushing the tips of my fingers against her grimy, tearstained face.

"Come," I say, and her wet eyes look up. "Let me show you your new home."

She wipes the tears from her face and sniffles before reaching for her son's hand and rising to her feet.

"There is no war here," I tell her. "No pain, no misery."

She nods, maintaining her balance by holding on to her son.

I open the door, where Freyda is waiting for us at the top of the stairs, and glance back at Madelaine. "There is one thing you should know."

She stares at me, her sunken face barely visible in the darkness.

"Zack is the only male in all of Eden."

She widens her eyes at me and then at Zack, almost as if I've just told her that human beings no longer require oxygen to breathe.

"The women of Eden know about your son," I say, and I turn my attention to Zack, who is staring at me—almost studying me. "You may be followed a lot or looked at strangely. Some of these young girls have never seen a boy before."

I consider telling him to be on his best behavior, but it isn't up to me to save him from his fate.

I turn toward Freyda, but a cold hand reaches for my arm. I look back at Madelaine and nearly grimace. She squeezes my arm, and a faint smile appears on her face.

"Thank you, Eve," she says.

I stretch my lips into a warm smile and place a hand over hers. "Anything for a friend, Madelaine."

I turn toward Freyda, wipe my hand on the leg of my pant, and lead Madelaine and Zack inside of Eden.

I'm not surprised to find the main hall full of women and children as we approach—news travels quickly. Little girls are seen hiding behind their mothers' dresses or pant legs, with only their small heads sticking out into the open.

Voices carry across the hall as the women and children whisper about Zack, the only male to ever step foot inside of Eden.

"That's a boy?"

"Who's that, Mommy?"

"Why is she so tall?"

"That's a boy, honey."

"I thought boys were bad."

"He looks nice."

"Who is that?"

I spot Lucy standing by Nola's side near Division Five's entryway. She's staring at me with small narrowed eyes, not once turning her attention to the boy. What does she want from me?

"Stop it," Zack says, pulling his arm back.

A little girl in a white dress is poking at him, almost as if he were a zoo animal.

"She's only curious," Madelaine says, reassuring her son. "You've seen girls before. Some of these girls have never seen a boy."

Sahana—a middle-aged Indian woman who resides in Division Six—walks up to Zack with a wide yellow-toothed grin on her face.

"What's your name?"

Her accent is as thick as it was the day I met her—the day our battle was won.

Zack pulls back and curls his lip up over his front teeth. "Zack."

I can't help but smile. I can already see the hostility. It won't be long before the women realize they've made a grave mistake.

"Welcome home, Zack," Sahana says, and she bows her head as a form of respect.

He doesn't deserve respect, but it's up to them to learn from their mistakes. An awkward smile is plastered on his face, and he rubs his arm with his hand—a nervous twitch. "Thanks."

There's a hoarseness to his voice—a deep tone that's no doubt only recently developed. He has thin facial hair that looks like nothing more than a shadow on his face and dark bushy eyebrows. He's wearing an old white shirt that now looks transparently brown, and a pair of torn jeans stained with dirt, sweat, and blood.

"Would you like to put on something new?"

Sahana asks him, her orange-brown eyes dancing up and down at his attire.

"Like, clothes?" he asks.

"Yes," she says. "I work well with cotton. I could make you a fresh outfit."

I fight the urge to roll my eyes. It's like watching a group of preteens play dress-up with their Barbie dolls. I can't recall the last time I saw so much excitement among my women, and truth be told it infuriates me.

But I can't let them know how I feel. I step forward and wrap an arm around Zack's shoulder. He tenses, so I pull him even closer, causing his head to rock from side to side.

"Don't be shy, Zack," I say, digging my fingernails into his arm. "This is your family now."

The women and children are all grinning ear to ear, mesmerized by the male presence in Eden's main hall. Perhaps they've forgotten all the monstrosities inflicted by the male species. Or, his youth is blinding them, as would a tiger cub before growing to full size and killing its owner.

"S-sure," Zack says, his voice cracking. "I'd like that."

Sahana lets out an excited laugh, then reaches for his hand. "Come with me."

He looks back at his mom, who nods and smiles as a way of permitting him to go.

"He's in good hands," I tell Madelaine. "You have nothing to worry about here in Eden."

She looks pleased. "Thank you, Eve. For everything."

I look at her and part my lips, but someone interrupts me.

"Eve, do you have a minute?"

I swing around to meet Gretchin's hazel eyes. She's one of my carpenters—someone I rely on heavily for almost everything that's been constructed in the courtyards. I tilt my head and lead her away from the crowd of women who are now circling Zack.

Freyda follows us but only because I signaled her too.

"What is it, Gretchin?" I ask.

"I know we've talked about this before, and you refused—"

"Is this about exploring beyond Eden's walls?"

She nods her freckled face, her bright eyes glued to mine. "I've done all that I can to recycle old materials, but we're running out of supplies. We need a new garden house to maintain enough food for our society, and I don't have enough wood. I know it isn't safe, Eve, but I thought that since you've allowed a boy to enter—"

I wave a hand lightly back and forth. "It's fine, Gretchin. So long as you have three other women accompany you, you can step foot outside of Eden for supplies."

Although I don't like the idea, there are a few things other than wood that I need myself. Mavis and Perula have already warned me that some of their most potent of plants have dried up and they are running low on seedlings. Apparently, there's a forest right outside of Eden's wall filled with numerous herbs and flowers.

Her jaw drops open, shocked that I would agree so quickly to such a demand.

"I want you to speak with Mavis or Perula before you go. There are a few herbs they need," I say.

Although I considered allowing Mavis to go with Gretchin, it's too great a risk. If something happens, I would be losing one of my Healers.

Gretchin bows her head. "Thank you, Eve." She turns on her heels, but I call out her name and she turns back around, prepared to obey any order I give.

"Good luck, Gretchin. You can leave tomorrow morning as soon as the sun rises. And remember—once you step foot outside of Eden, the gates will be closed and only reopened to you if you come back unfollowed."

She gives me a firm nod and walks away.

Freyda leans in, her lips brushing against my ear. "Only four women? If you'd have let me train—"

Impatient, I wave a hand. I don't need a lecture on how I should be managing Eden—on how I should have allowed her to train women to fight *before* winter. Right now, I need all of my women focusing on gathering as many resources as possible before winter, not practicing target shooting.

I turn to her, a ball of anxiety in the pit of my stomach. "It wouldn't even matter if I sent women trained for battle. If they were to encounter male Rebels—especially Rebels with guns—they'd all be as good as dead, and I can't afford to lose more women.”

Eve — Flashback

For a split second, I convince myself that I'm only dreaming. Because that's the only explanation for this—a dream. Everything is spinning, my ears are ringing, and my head keeps telling me that this isn't happening.

This can't be happening.

My hands shake uncontrollably, and I'm staring through the windshield of Bethany's borrowed car at my little sister's body. She's lying in the middle of the road with a pool of dark blood spreading around her head and neck.

This can't be real.

It can't be.

Wake up, Eve. This isn't happening. Wake up.

Please, wake up. Wake the fuck up.

The man who shot her steps out of his red truck and kicks her boot. It dances from side to side, but she doesn't move.

That's my little sister.

That's my Mila.

He killed her.

He killed my fucking sister.

I jump out of the car's driver's seat, and his big eyes roll up at me from underneath his baseball cap like he didn't even know I was there. I nearly fall flat on my face because my legs are shaking so much, and I point the pistol that was given to me at his slanted figure. I can't even see him. I can't look at him. All I see is his shape because my vision is so blurry.

But I know one thing—that son of a bitch fucking killed my sister.

My arm is waving from side to side because of all the adrenaline inside of me, and I can't think straight. Without giving it any thought, I pull the trigger over and over and over as I move toward him, and the sound of multiple gunshots bounces off every house in the neighborhood. I feel the kickback, but it doesn't stop me.

He steps back and slaps a scrawny hand over his stomach, and a silky red fluid slips through the cracks of his fingers. He looks confused, and for a split second, I look him in the eyes—black balls that are sitting in the middle of two dark blue bags. He looks like he's either sick, or he's a drug user. His gun is dangling beside his waist now, and he takes another step back. But then, it almost looks like clarity kicks in, almost as if he's now realized he's been shot. He pulls his upper lip over his crooked front teeth, revealing red bloody gums, and he raises his gun at me.

I start walking toward him and let out the loudest scream my lungs can create and fire again and again and again until my gun makes a clicking sound.

His arms fly upward in a dancing motion, and blood spits out into the air before he collapses flat on his back, his gun bouncing several feet away from him.

I move toward him, still screaming, and bash my boot into this face. The feeling of bones crushing vibrates through my calf and thigh, and his jaw dislocates, but I keep bashing.

"Eve!"

I don't even see a face anymore—it's a mess of broken bone and bloody flesh—but I can't stop stomping. There's cracking and popping and crunching, but all I can think about is how I want to stomp on him until there's nothing left but a puddle of tissue.

"Eve!"

A hand grabs me and I swing back, but Ophelia catches my wrist.

"Jesus Christ, Eve!"

She pulls me in and suddenly, the anger dissipates. I collapse into her arms and my chin lands on her shoulder.

"Eve, what happened?"

I fall to my knees, and she follows me to the ground. A few feet away, Mila is lying on her back with a small hole in the front of her throat. Blood oozes out like water from a fountain, and her black-rimmed glasses rest several feet away from her, one of the lenses shattered.

"Mila," I moan.

That's my sister.

My little sister.

Rapid footsteps sound in the distance, and Ophelia turns her head. "Lucy, get back inside, right now!"

Why did she step out of the car? Why did she go after him like that without thinking?

I squeeze my eyes shut, trying to remember what happened.

The moment we pulled up, she saw him sitting in his truck, and she stepped out... Walked right up and pointed a gun at him through his truck's side window.

Oh, God.

Why did she have to be so impulsive? Why did I even bring her along? This is all my fault.

"Eve, what happened?" Ophelia presses, but her voice sounds like it's being carried through a long tunnel.

I crawl out of her arms and drag myself to Mila's body, my knees scraping against the asphalt.

"Mila, please," I say, shaking her. "Mila, wake up."

This can't be happening. Any second now, I'm going to wake up in my bed with Mila's face floating inches away from mine, and then she'll start venting about President Price—about how he's a complete jackass who deserves to die.

Because this isn't real.

She can't be dead.

"Mila!" I scream, drool dangling from my lips.

I shake her again, and a thick stream of blood squirts out of her throat.

"No, no, no," is all I can say, but it sounds like the words are coming out of someone else's mouth, and everything goes black.

CHAPTER 29 – GABRIEL

Gabriel — Present Day

"Stay low," I warn Castor, and he sinks farther down into the forest's damp earth.

"The fuck is Adam doing here?" he whispers. His moonlit face is aimed at the small campfire up ahead.

"What do you think?" I say, and I look toward the prison.

His mouth goes loose. "You think they'll try to go inside? You think they know about Alpa?"

I smile even though all I want to do is laugh. "They probably do. That's fine. Let them try. They'll be strung up by their balls if they do."

Castor looks at me. "What makes you so sure there are women inside?"

"If you heard rumors about Alpa," I say, "it's because there's truth to it. There's no way that place is empty."

Castor doesn't say anything and breathes heavily through his nostrils. Farther up, I hear Adam laugh, and a familiar rage builds inside me. Someone opens, then closes the truck door. What are they doing, anyway? And why haven't they slept? The sun went down hours ago, and they're still moving around the fire.

Could they be carving weapons, preparing to invade the prison?

I shift my position a few times, trying to get comfortable. I'm exhausted, but I can't take my eyes off them. I need to know what they're doing. I'd ask Castor to keep watch, but he's such a lug, he'd probably fall asleep or sneeze and give us away.

If they find us, we're as good as dead. I know how Adam operates. Any time a man tried to leave his crew, he shot them point-blank. I can only imagine what he'd try to do to us for having *actually* left.

"If you don't follow me, you're against me," he'd say every time he aimed his rifle at a man's face. They'd plead and plead on their knees with their hands tied behind their backs, but Adam wouldn't care. Two of the times, he even laughed at them, before firing his gun and blowing off half their faces.

It took three kills like this for the men in his crew to realize he wasn't dicking around.

I watch the orange-haloed figures walk around their camp for what feels like hours. My eyes are heavy and my muscles are sore from dragging long branches all day to build us a shelter. I'd do almost anything to go back to Area 82 to sleep on my shitty, paper-thin mattress.

Better yet, if I could go back, I'd take my mom someplace far away from here. I'd try our chances with Canada or Mexico.

I'm pulled back to reality the moment my vision changes. The trees become more defined, and a dark blue sky replaces the black one. Nautical twilight's set in. How long have I been sitting here watching them?

I shove Castor in the ribs, and he lets out a grunt, smacks his lips together, then mumbles, "W-what?"

"Wake up."

He shifts his position and groans but stiffens up when he realizes that the sun's slowly coming up.

"How long was I out?" he asks, but I'm too focused on Adam and his men to respond.

It isn't long before nautical dawn starts, and an orange strip emerges on the horizon behind the prison. I blow hot air on my fingers, only realizing then how cold I've been all night. Hopefully, the sun will bring some warmth.

At last, when half the sun has pierced through the sky, a violet color spreads through the clouds like diluted paint on a canvas. Adam shouts something, but then, the whole crew goes quiet and they drop into crouched positions. I do the same, even though I'm far away.

Did they see something? Did they see us, and now, they're trying to hide?

I look at Castor, who's as confused as I am, his bulging eyes and wide nostrils expanding with every quick breath he takes. He rests his hairy hand over the log in front of us, trying to hold himself upright even though he's now lying on his side.

But Adam and his men aren't looking at us. I can see them now, their muscular figures gaining a bit of color—beige cargo pants, blue jeans, multicolored T-shirts, and army-colored sweaters, all scraps they picked up from dead bodies along the road.

Although I can't see their faces, I know they're

not looking this way because a few of them are wearing baseball caps with their brims facing in the same direction… the prison.

I follow their gaze and perch myself up a bit when I see something I thought I wouldn't see for days, weeks, or even months.

The front doors. Two massive gates at the front of the prison are slowly opening.

Gabriel — Flashback

I keep slipping in and out of consciousness with one hand behind my head and one over my belly. I'm lying on a thin piece of foam in the corner of the room filled with dozens of uniformed guys who, like me, want to catch a little shut-eye.

I've spent the last twelve hours on my feet stationed in front of the White House like I've been doing for the last seven months. I don't get it. Why aren't we doing anything? How long are these women going to keep rioting?

Some of our senior officers created temporary sleeping rooms for military personnel so we can recuperate after our shifts. I never thought I'd find myself sleeping in the White House, but if I'd had to imagine it, I wouldn't have pictured myself lying on a piece of foam.

A nice California king mattress, maybe.

Food is supplied throughout the day, and they're bringing it all in by helicopter, the same way they're bringing men out who've been injured by gunshots, stab wounds, or even by rocks thrown over the barrier.

The scary part in all this is that despite the armed forces opening fire a few times to get the women to back off, it hasn't done anything. Dead bodies are piling up, and it's only making things worse. The crowd is getting bigger and bigger. If you look at Washington from an aerial shot of the district (I saw a picture on one of my fellow marine's phones), you can't see any streets at all. All you see are multicolored shirts and small heads around square buildings. It looks like a bunch of Legos.

If we don't do something soon, we're all dead.

Someone beside me sits up in his bed, moves his shaved head from side to side, and cracks his neck, then hunches over his phone. It's a little screen that's barely visible in his two big hands. It looks ancient with its regular glass screen.

"Holy Mother of—" he mumbles with a groggy voice, and a few heads turn his way.

He flips his phone around to show the men who've woken up. A few jaws drop, and one man jumps off his foam mattress and plucks the phone right out of the marine's hands.

He lifts it to his face and his nose almost touches the phone. His eyes look yellow and blue because they're reflecting the screen's glow. He presses two fingers on the screen and wiggles them around, trying to zoom in and out of the picture.

"This can't be real," he says, and a few guys behind him try to grab the phone.

It's passed around the room, waking up the few men who are left, and within seconds, everyone's bickering back and forth. The phone finally ends up on my lap, and several marines huddle behind me to get a second look.

It's a satellite image of Washington DC. The White House looks like a tiny little white square surrounded by black and green dots spread out all over the South Lawn and Lafayette Square.

"Is that us?" I say, but before anyone can

answer, I realize these little dots are military personnel.

"Zoom out!" someone says.

I swipe two fingers toward each other on the screen, zooming out from the aerial view. I can see the little heads and multicolored shirts that are clogging up the streets of the entire district.

"I've already seen this," I say, but someone slaps me on the shoulder.

"No, no, keep zooming."

I zoom out even farther until I can see cities, buildings, and landmarks that go way beyond the district. The words Alexandria, Arlington, and Greenbelt Park show up on the map now, and I nearly drop the phone.

There are no more streets to be seen anywhere. They're all filled with a bunch of colors, and they spread all the way outside of Washington DC. Even the Theodore Roosevelt Bridge, the Arlington Bridge, and the 14th Street Bridge are completely clogged.

I swipe back on the phone to exit the map and it takes me to a news article with a big black title at the top: New Estimated Count of Female Rioters Rises to Thirty-Four Million.

CHAPTER 30 - LUCY

Lucy — Present Day

"D-d-don't touch that, you wart-faced frog!" Mavis shouts.

I flinch and pull away from the purple-leafed plant.

I want to ask her, "why are you always in such a bad mood?" but keep my mouth shut. She's leaning over her cauldron-looking soup pot (something she found in the prison's old kitchen) and stirring a bunch of herbs and water that she threw in there. She looks like a witch with her long salt and pepper hair dangling over one shoulder and her pointed nose hovering over the brew. I almost laugh.

Perula catches me smiling and says, "Don't worry about her, child. Mavis lost her temper a long time ago."

Mavis grumbles something, but I can't make it out. Maybe it's some sort of witch language. She seems to like talking gibberish.

I scan all the herbs with my eyes only, careful not to touch anything. I wonder which one they've been using during Eve's meetings.

"Do you guys make alcohol?" I ask, and Mavis's cold eyes shoot up at me.

"Aren't you a little young to be asking that?" she says.

I shrug. "I'm sixteen. I'll be twenty-one in five

years. What about you guys? What about the adults? Don't you ever drink like you used to before this war happened?"

Mavis squints one eye, then looks at her sister like she's trying to figure out why I'm asking so many questions. I hope they don't realize I'm trying to figure out what they made in those little cups. They don't know I saw them, so there's no way they're onto me. Right?

"The adults will, on occasion, have a glass of wine," Perula says.

I nod and keep making my way around the cabin. "Must feel nice, you know... With all the stress."

"Stress?" Perula asks, and I realize I might've gone too far. Eden is supposed to be a place of paradise without fear, stress, or anxiety. They're probably wondering why I'm talking about stress.

I shrug again. "I don't know. I'm just saying. You know... with the war. A lot of people were killed. Kids died, too."

"That's enough," Mavis says sharply. "The past is behind us."

"Sorry," I say and sit down on the stool beside Perula. I definitely crossed a line. Ever since entering Eden, no one talks about the war. No one talks about people they lost or anything. It's like it never even happened. The only thing Eve wants to talk about is how *bad* men were. How they've destroyed the world. Or how beautiful Eden is.

But no one ever talks about their feelings in Eden. I miss that. I miss having my mom hold me against her and tell me that it's okay to be scared. It's okay to be sad, to feel hurt, and even, to get angry. I've never seen anyone get angry in Eden. I don't understand. Sometimes, I feel crazy. Did I imagine the war? Did I imagine seeing women raped and beaten in the streets? What about when the bombs went off, and I felt Grandma's house shake? Did I imagine that too? What about Eve's little sister, Mila? Did I make the whole thing up in my head? Did I imagine she was shot in the throat and left dead in the street? Or, what about the time I saw a group of shirtless women jump on an old man who didn't even do anything? He'd been walking with his dog, and the three women attacked him, beating him until he died.

Was all of that in my head?

My hands become clammy, and my heart beats fast.

Maybe this is why we don't talk about it. Maybe we're not even supposed to think about it because all it does is make us feel horrible.

"Did you talk with Gretchin?" Perula asks, looking up at her sister. "Eve said she'd come talk to us, and I haven't seen her."

Who's Gretchin? I wonder.

Mavis nods and takes a whiff of her potion or whatever it is she's making.

"You explained to her what it looks like?" Perula presses.

"Yes," Mavis said sharply, saliva splashing into her cauldron.

"I hope she finds it," Perula says. "Our last plant

is succumbing to the same disease."

"What plant?" I ask.

Mavis' eyes roll up toward her sister, almost like she's warning her to keep her mouth shut.

"A plant for my pain, child," Perula says, but she doesn't even make eye contact with me.

I don't believe her.

After a few minutes pass, I get up, pretend to stretch my legs, and start making my way around the cabin again. I can feel Perula's eyes on me, but I don't care. She said the last plant was diseased, which means it should be sitting by itself somewhere, looking sick. This diseased plant might be what they're using during their meetings. Why else would Mavis have looked up at Perula like that? Like she was upset?

I run my fingers along the dusty shelves, and when I pull my finger back, it's covered in gray muck. No wonder it always smells so stuffy in here. They don't clean.

There're dirt and dried up leaves on the floorboards underneath the shelves, and when I reach the end of the cabin, I notice a spider the size of a golf ball weaving its sticky web in the corner of the room. When I'm about to cross behind Mavis to keep looking for the diseased plant, I see it. It's hiding right in the corner behind some orange-flowered plant that's sitting in a clay pot.

This must be the plant they're talking about. It has holes in its green, smooth-edged leaves and a few black balls that look like blueberries. One of the balls looks mushy like it's rotten.

"Lucy, let me show you something," Perula says.

I turn toward her, and she's holding something that looks like a ginger root.

"How about I start showing you what we use this for," she says.

I stare at her because this is the first time since I've become a Healer that Perula wants to show me something without me having to ask. I look back at the dying plant, remembering what it looks like so I can find it in the book the twins gave me: *Magical Herbs*. But Perula clears her throat and starts talking to me again, "Come on now, child. Have a seat."

She pats the stool beside her, her long fingernails clicking against the wood, and I can't help but feel like she's trying to keep me away from that plant.

Lucy — Flashback

My mom has her hand over my eyes, and she's squeezing so hard I can feel my eyeballs moving around against her palm.

"She's almost ten," I hear Aunty Eve say. "She'll be exposed to this sooner or later."

My mom breathes out hard like she always does when she's either annoyed or when she doesn't get her way. She slowly peels her fingers from my eyes, and I look around the room.

I think we're in a warehouse, but it's hard to tell. The windows are all covered with big pieces of wood, and long lights hang from the ceiling—the kind of lights you'd see in a big bulk store. I know this because my mom used to take me to Cosono all the time (according to my mom, it used to be called Cossco, or something). Every time we'd go, I'd sit in the cart, looking up at the gray tubes, and sometimes, if I got lucky, I'd see little birds flying around.

This place looks like an empty Cosono. A bunch of gray plastic tables with black metal legs are spread out everywhere, and as we keep walking, the sound of our footsteps bounces off the walls. It's huge in here.

But I don't pay much attention to the dirty white floor, the walls, or the high ceiling. Instead, I'm focused on all the women sitting at the tables... hunched over a bunch of guns.

They're big guns, too. The kind you'd see in video games. There're a bunch of metal sounds all around me, and I can't tell if they're cleaning the guns or putting bullets in them.

"Most of these women are ex-military," Aunty Eve says, leaning toward my mom.

There's something different about her. Ever since Mila died, and ever since she killed that man, she's been weird. Sometimes I wonder if her heart is broken. She's smiling at my mom, but it doesn't look real. It's not the same smile she used to give her.

And then, whenever I try to talk to her, it's like she doesn't want to hear anything I have to say. She's too busy with all the thoughts in her head. Too busy to care about anything other than revenge. Because that's all she ever wants to talk about: revenge.

After she killed Jason, Mom said we had to leave Grandma's. Probably because if anyone found out, or if any of the neighbors saw it happen, they'd call the police. Aunty Eve says the police won't come chasing us in Arlington because they're too busy with all the riots going on in Washington DC.

But I don't think my mom expected things to get this bad in Arlington, too. The rioters are here now, trying to make their way to the president. And he's so stubborn because all he keeps saying on TV is that he refuses to give in to any demands that the rioters are making. He doesn't want to leave the White House, either, because he says presidents stand their ground.

I think he's being stupid, but that's just me.

"So, what's the plan, here, Eve?" my mom asks. She's staring Aunty Eve right in the face. "I have a daughter. I can't just pick up a machine gun and charge toward the White House."

"We're not going to be stupid about it," Aunty Eve says. "See that woman over there?"

I follow my mom's eyes and Aunty Eve's finger. A woman sits by herself in front of a bunch of wires, metal pieces, and plastic. Her blond hair is tied back in a ponytail, a few wrinkles around her eyes, and big arms full of muscles. She's wearing some kind of military uniform. It looks like she's trying to build something. A bomb, maybe?

"That's Zoey," Eve says, and she's smiling like she's proud of it.

Who's Zoey, anyways?

My mom must be wondering the same thing because she's giving Aunty Eve the stink-eye like she does to me when I'm hiding something. It's a look that says, *Just spit it out already.*

"Zoey's been contracted through the armed forces to assist with dozens of extremely covert operations. She's one of America's most sought-after—"

"What's your point, Eve?" my mom says. "Does she make bombs? Is that it? Are we going to bomb the damn White House?"

Aunty Eve smirks in a way I've never seen her do before. "We have plenty of people who can make bombs, O. This isn't about bombs. She's building a nuclear EMP device."

My mom bursts out laughing but not because she thought Aunty Eve made a joke. She's laughing the way she does when she doesn't know how else to react. A few women across the giant room look at us, and my mom shakes her head and pinches the top of her nose.

"Are you guys insane?" my mom whispers. She's hunched forward, and I can tell she's upset. "You want to build a fucking..." but she looks at me and apologizes for swearing. "You want to build a device that could destroy the entire country?"

Aunty Eve's eyes go flat like she's bored or something. "You need to step outside of the rainbow, O."

My mom points a finger at her face. "Don't you tell me—"

But Aunty Eve points one right back, almost poking my mom in the eye. "No! Don't *you* tell me anything. This is what Mila would've wanted."

My mom nods, and I can tell she's being careful about what she's going to say next. "This isn't about Mila, Eve. I'm devastated about what happened, too. And I don't agree with President Price or any of what's going on—but this is absolute destruction we're talking about."

Aunty Eve lifts her chin, looking like she has no emotion at all, and says, "I'd rather die fighting than stand around doing nothing."

My mom grabs my hand and pulls me away from Aunty Eve.

"Come on, honey," she says, but right before we walk away, some lady with a long black braid down her back almost bumps into us.

She grins from ear to ear. "Oh, I'm sorry. I almost ran into you there." She stares at my mom, then at me, before saying. "I'm Bethany Lee, what's your name, sweetheart?"

"Lucy," I say. I know that name. Aunty Eve's talked about Bethany so many times. She says she's the leader of a huge underground resistance group. I won't lie, I'm a bit intimidated by her. If she's the leader, she must be pretty tough.

"I'm Ophelia," my mom says. She's trying to be nice, but I can tell she's in a bad mood now.

"Ophelia," Bethany repeats, and she shakes my mom's hand. "I've heard so much about you. It's a pleasure to finally meet you."

My mom forces a smile, then grabs my hand again.

"Are you leaving?" Bethany asks. "I was about to talk to Eve, but I think you might want to hear this, too."

Aunty Eve looks at my mom and lifts both her eyebrows.

My mom looks at Eve, then at me, and finally says, "All right, what is it?"

But Bethany Lee doesn't say anything. Instead, she moves her head sideways and starts walking toward the back of the building, so we follow her. She brings us through a big metal door, then down hard gray stairs until we reach the basement.

Instead of a big open space, it's a long hallway with doors all over the place. We walk past a few doors until Bethany Lee turns to the right and opens a door that has the number 9 painted on it. Inside, it looks like the kind of room you'd see on cop shows when they question people. There's a tiny window at the top of the wall, right under the ceiling and a big table in the middle of the room.

There are also four plastic chairs, and on the table, some sort of TV. It's small, and it has an antenna and a bunch of wires around it. Bethany Lee sits at one end of the table, and Aunty Eve sits beside her. So my mom sits down on the other side and taps the chair beside her, telling me to sit down.

"What's going on?" Aunty Eve asks. She almost looks worried. I haven't seen her show any real feeling since Mila died. "Is this about my mom?"

Bethany Lee places a hand over Aunty Eve's and squeezes it. "No."

Eve looks relieved. Since we've been living with her for months now, I know what bothers her the most, and that's her mom. She disappears for weeks at a time without contacting Aunty Eve. Every night, Aunty Eve sleeps by her phone, waiting to either hear from her mom or from the hospital.

She thinks her mom is in Washington DC, with all the women who are going to riot at the White House. I feel bad for her because if my mom were out there, I'd be scared to death. Every day on the news, they talk about how many more people have been killed because of this riot. What if one day her mom gets shot? And if that happens, how will Aunty Eve even know?

Bethany Lee lets out a long breath, and her dark eyes roll up at us. She's about to open her mouth to start talking, but my mom interrupts her. "Is this something a nine-year-old should be hearing?"

Bethany looks at me and smiles warmly. "It's up to you, but if I had a daughter, I wouldn't want to protect her from the truth. Being blind to what's happening is far more dangerous than being aware of it."

My mom nods and squeezes my shoulder, and Bethany Lee continues. "One of our tech teams intercepted communication from the White House."

Aunty Eve's bright blue eyes go twice their size and she leans forward on the table.

"I don't want this getting out yet," Bethany says, "because the women won't react well, and we're not ready. Zoey still needs a few days to finish the EMP."

I hear my mom let out a sharp breath beside me, and I know her bad mood is coming back.

Bethany Lee must sense that my mom wants nothing to do with this because she leans on the table, looking almost sad. "I can tell you're not up for this," she tells my mom. "But believe me when I say that we're already at war. They're slaughtering women left and right, and people are dying of starvation because grocery stores are phasing out. Is that the sort of life you want for your daughter? I'm fully aware that a nuclear EMP will be catastrophic for our country, but if nothing is done, women will continue to be slaughtered at the hands of men until we either submit to their laws or until they regain control of gender population... And you and I both know how they're planning on doing that."

My mom taps her fingers against the plastic of

the table. I can tell she's thinking hard.

"The only advantage they have," Bethany keeps going, "is their advanced military technology. We outnumber them seven to one. We have plenty of brilliant minds who are ready and willing to rebuild a society once America falls."

"What about the guns?" I ask. I know I probably shouldn't be part of the conversation, but I need to know.

"What do you mean, sweetheart?" Bethany asks.

"All the guns upstairs," I say. "Are they gonna be used on men? I mean, what about dads and grandpas who aren't fighting against women?"

Bethany smiles at me, then up at my mom. "You're doing a fine job raising this one." She turns her attention back to me. "We're only going for the White House. We're well aware that there are men who want nothing to do with this war. Most of them are hiding in their homes with their families. They're not the ones causing this."

Aunty Eve rolls her eyes. "Men are men, and in the end, they'll always turn against women."

Bethany doesn't seem to agree with her, but she doesn't say anything. Instead, she pats the top of my hand and says, "We're only going after the bad guys."

She then looks up at my mom and asks, "Are you on board?"

My mom bites her bottom lip, obviously thinking about this for a second, then nods. "Yeah, count me in."

Bethany Lee sits back in her chair, smacks her

thighs with her hands, and breathes out loudly. "The communication we've intercepted... it isn't good."

Both my mom and Aunty Eve slide their chairs closer, prepared to hear the news.

Bethany Lee rubs her forehead hard, leaving a red mark, then finally she says, "President Price has officially declared war on all female rioters." Bethany's staring at all of us, waiting for it to sink in, but it's so quiet in the room, I can hear myself breathing.

"He just gave a kill order," she says.

CHAPTER 31 – EVE

Eve — Present Day

There's a soft knock at my door, and Freyda slips her fingers through the crack, revealing only half of her face.

"Come in," I tell her.

She bows her head, then straightens her posture and repositions her armored vest. "The women have left Eden."

"Thank you, Freyda," I say. "If they don't make it back by sundown, the doors are to remain closed."

Freyda nods, but then pulls her shoulders back. "There's something else."

I stare at her.

"Lauren—you know, the pregna—"

"I know who she is, Freyda."

I don't mean to be so sharp, but her very name aggravates my anxiety. Not only do I not like to be reminded of her rape, but the child she's carrying has been in my dreams for months. Every time I hear her name, my heart races because I don't know what I will do if she gives birth to a boy.

"She had a miscarriage," Freyda says, bowing her head toward the floor.

I'm about to say, *Oh, thank God*, but I bite my tongue, even though I'm rejoicing inside. Instead, I thank her for the information, careful not to show any form of emotion. She's about to turn around when I call out to her. "Freyda?"

"Yes, Eve?" she asks.

I smile at her—the only person I care to smile at. "I don't know what I would do without you."

Her lip curves upward, and she bows her head again as a way of acknowledging the compliment.

"Well, I'm not going anywhere," she says, and I can't help but laugh.

"Have a seat, would you?" I say, extending an open palm toward the chair in front of my office desk.

She hesitates, then closes the door behind her and sits in front of me.

"Can I ask you something?" I say.

She shrugs, her heavy equipment chafing against her clothing. "Anything."

I lean back in my chair, then kick my white-legged pants and red boots up onto the desk. "Do you think they're out there? The Binaries?"

Freyda knows who I'm talking about—in fact, every woman in Eden would know who I am talking about. The Binaries are self-proclaimed experts who publicly announced their future involvement in the rebuilding of our society, should it collapse, which it did. I had the privilege of meeting a few of these women while working alongside Bethany Lee, and they assured me that should the EMP attack be successful in permanently damaging electronic devices throughout the country, they would be the first ones to pull us out of the Dark Ages once the war was over.

But the war has been over for nearly five years,

and no one has heard from them.

Freyda shakes her head and pouts. "I hope so, but there's no way to tell."

"Why not?" I ask, and she laughs at me.

"Because we have no way of communicating with the outside world," she says. "Even if they're out there, we have no way of knowing. For all we know, half the country's running on electricity again."

I scoff. "I don't think so."

"Me neither," she admits, "but there's still no telling what's going on out there. I mean, unless they've been killed, which I doubt given that we outnumbered men ten to one after the war. They're probably settled somewhere remote, working on developing pieces of advanced technology."

Her dark glossy eyes narrow on me, and she tilts her head almost playfully. "Why? Are you starting to miss technology? We still have our solar panels and—"

But I wave a hand to cut her short. "It's not the same."

"No, you're right, but—"

"This place won't hold us forever," I say, "especially if more women find their way to us."

She pinches her chin with her thumb and index finger, evaluating what I've said. "No, it won't. But what else do you have in mind? We're safe here."

"I know," I say, gazing absentmindedly across the room. "But as time passes, we're going to need more resources, which means we will have to keep opening the front gates. If anyone is watching from the outside, they might pay attention to our schedule and coordinate an attack."

"You're still convinced there are a bunch of male Rebels out there?" Freyda asks.

I stare at her, contemplating whether to be respectful or to accuse her of being a complete moron. She shifts uncomfortably as I watch her, then adds, "Well, I'm sure there are *some*."

"Men are like cockroaches," I say. "They survive." I comb my hair with my fingernails. "And the danger in all of this is that most surviving women don't have semiautomatic rifles. They don't carry guns. They're caring for their children and seeking shelter. A few strong men could easily attack a large group of women."

Freyda nods slowly, taking it all in. "So, what are you saying?"

"I'm saying we need the Binaries," I answer. "If we have them, we have technology, and if we have technology, we can travel and communicate across the nation to gain control."

"So, in other words, you want to take over the world," Freyda teases.

I interlock my fingers over my thighs and lean back even farther into my chair, a soft squeak filling the room. "Not the *world*, silly—America."

Eve — Flashback

My head is racing a million miles per minute.

A kill order? I knew it was only a matter of time, but I didn't expect it to happen so soon. We're not ready. We don't have the EMP built yet.

"Eve, are you okay?" Bethany asks, her voice carrying across the small room.

Am I okay? My head is spinning, and I feel like the ground underneath me is melting—as though I'm going to be sucked into the Earth until I reach hell. How could anyone be okay in a situation like this? Millions of women are going to die tonight.

"We can't just sit around," I say.

Bethany reaches for my hand, but I pull away. "No, Bethany. I respect that you're in charge, but you're making a huge mistake if you don't give the order to attack tonight."

Surprisingly, Ophelia cuts in. "I have to agree with Eve."

Bethany pulls away, rolls forming underneath her chin. "The EMP isn't ready yet. This is suicide you're talking about."

What the hell is wrong with her? These are the lives of millions of women we're talking about. EMP or not, we have to do something. I slam my fist against the table and Lucy flinches. "It's going to be a fucking massacre!"

Bethany frowns, looking more worried than frustrated. "What do you propose we do? Gear up and charge toward the White House? First, the crowd's getting so tight we probably won't even be able to get through. And secondly, we'll be the first ones killed. The moment they see women with guns, they'll take us out. They have choppers flying overhead and snipers positioned all over the city. And if we die, what chance do the rest of the women out there have? They don't have the guns. They have sticks and shovels and kitchen knives, which aren't going to do a whole lot against the US military."

"Don't we have snipers?" I ask.

Bethany hesitates. "Y-yeah, I mean, we do—"

"Then tell them to get ready. We can take out their snipers first, then have women prepare to shoot down the choppers. They won't expect it. They think we're merely a bunch of angry women who want to swing our bras in the air."

She looks a bit taken aback by my sudden change in demeanor. I can hear myself talking, and I sound exactly like Mila—stubborn and unwilling to take no for an answer.

"Bombs have gone off, Eve," Bethany says. "It's pretty obvious we're capable of building weapons."

"Bombs," I repeat. "What about grenades? How many do we have?"

Her jaw drops, and she slides her chair back to get a good look at me. I can tell Ophelia is looking at me funny, too, but I don't care. I'm ready to fight even if it means I'm dying tonight. The sudden image of Mila's bloody, lifeless body flashes in my mind, and I clench my fist.

Bethany stands up and places her chair underneath the desk. "I'll talk to the council and see what they have to—"

"We don't have time to talk," I say. "You're in charge—give them the orders."

"Am I?" she asks.

I'm breathing so hard I might start to hyperventilate. "Are you what?" I spew.

"In charge?"

She's staring me cold in the face, and a dangerous rage builds inside me. Why is she doing this? Why is she even debating the option of attacking when so many lives are at stake? I slowly stand, my hands against the table, meeting her eye to eye, and I grind my teeth.

"You can either make the order," I say, enunciating every word, "or I can."

Her mouth drops open and her eyes resemble those of a lost child. A heavy silence fills the room, and even Ophelia is sitting still, her lips parted.

"This isn't personal, Bethany. I'm trying to save lives."

She finally regains some composure, her shoulders drawn back and her long braid reaching her buttocks. "I know," she breathes.

"Well," I say, sounding a bit more impatient than intended. "Let's round up the women and communicate with any and every underground rebel group we know." I glance toward Ophelia, who's holding on to her daughter for dear life and staring at me like she doesn't know who I am. "We attack tonight."

CHAPTER 32 – GABRIEL

Gabriel — Present Day

"Shit, shit, shit, shit, shit," Castor says, pacing back and forth.

"Take it easy, big guy," I try, but he's not listening.

I watch through the tall birch trees as four women make their way toward the forest and straight to where Adam and his crew are hiding. There's a redhead who appears to be leading the group. She's wearing khaki pants and a white shirt, and the three women behind her are wearing beige dresses that are dragging in the crispy grass. What are they doing? Looking for resources? I don't see why else they'd leave the safety of their walls.

The sun's sitting behind a bunch of chunky white clouds, and the air is warm and humid. The redhead's eyes appear to be darting from left to right, up and down, like she's on the lookout for danger.

Why doesn't she see them? I look toward where the campfire sat all night, and all I see are a few baseball capped heads hovering close to the ground. The red truck's gone because Adam put it in reverse and drove it out of sight the minute he saw the women.

One girl behind the redhead looks young, early twenties, and she's clutching onto her dress, lifting it from the ground so she doesn't get it dirty.

"They're gonna catch them," Castor blurts out, throwing a hand toward the women.

I grab his arm and tug hard. He needs to stay close to the ground.

"They're going to do a lot more than just catch them," I say.

Castor looks at me with big bug eyes, and I tilt my head, signaling him to follow me. I head south, away from Adam and his crew, and make my way toward them at an angle.

"Stay low," I say.

"What're you gonna do? Get involved?" Castor whispers.

He's obviously scared, and I don't blame him. But I can't sit around and watch Adam, the piece of shit that he is, and his disgusting dogs gang bang a bunch of women.

"He has a gun," Castor whispers. "A big one."

I'm about to tell him to shut up when he steps on a thick dry branch, and a loud snap spreads through the forest. I grab him by the collar and pull him down onto his stomach.

"Ow, fuck," he whispers, and I elbow him in the ribs.

My eyes are sealed shut and I'm lying on my back, praying to God that Adam didn't see us. "Don't move."

I raise my head a bit, enough to see over the fallen branch and toward Adam's crew. They're all staring at the women like a bunch of starved hyenas. If I were closer, I'd probably see them panting, too.

At last, the women come into view. Their curved figures sway from side to side as they walk. The leader of the women, the redhead, has frizzy orange hair and a freckled face that makes her look sweet. Two of them have beautiful, creamy white skin and long blond hair. And the last one who's walking behind the three of them has dark skin that's shining in the sun and shoulder-length brown hair. I can't remember the last time I saw a woman. I've been surrounded by a bunch of hairy, stinky men for the last five years. My jaw loosens, and I stare in awe, almost hypnotized by their beauty. It's almost like I'm staring at goddesses.

Castor nudges me when he realizes that I'm in some sort of trance.

I'm afraid to get up to keep moving because I'm lying on the broken branch that made a loud snap earlier. If I get up the wrong way, I might make it snap again. I slowly roll to my side and wince, scared that I'll make that one wrong move and Adam will be shooting bullets my way.

But I don't have time to overthink anything because a loud scream suddenly blocks out all other sound.

I throw my head up to find Adam's men bolting out of the forest, and the four women are running in the field, back toward the prison and tripping over their dresses.

"Fuck," I mutter.

The men are laughing and grunting as they run out into the open, and the women are screaming hysterically.

"Now!" I say, and I make a run toward the field as fast as I can.

With the women screaming and the men laughing, they can't hear me coming. Adam's jogging behind them with his rifle in both hands. It's almost like he sent off a bunch of bloodhounds to hunt. Almost like he's waiting for his boys to catch his prize for him.

The tallest blonde is the first to be taken by one of the men. He grabs her by her long hair, and she flies straight to the ground on her back. I hear the impact from where I am. He climbs on top of her, pinning her hands over her head, and grins back at Adam while she screams.

Adam's men catch the other three women within seconds and slam them to the ground.

The first woman they caught is now being held by her wrists and ankles by none other than McGaver, the biggest guy in the group. I hate that son of a bitch. She tries to slap him and screams through a waterfall of tears, but she doesn't stand a chance. McGaver pulls her dress up and it rips. He then spreads her legs apart and looks back at Adam, who's slowly walking up to her, his thick shoulders pulled back and his rifle over his shoulder.

My heart's beating so hard, and my back is drenched with sweat. Everything is happening too fast. Jesus Christ, Gabe, run faster.

The other three women are held down and forced to watch as Adam pulls out his dick and mounts the blond woman. She's screaming so hard that her voice breaks and she's trying to squirm her way out, but McGaver's grip is so hard I'm scared he'll snap her limbs. Adam spreads her legs even farther and forces himself inside, and she screams again, but this time, it's more of a cry. He then thrusts hard, his glutes clenching through his pants and his arm muscles bulging on either side of her. McGaver's face is all red from holding her so tight, and he just sits there, laughing.

Adam thrusts again, and the woman cries in pain. But then, McGaver's eyes nearly pop out of his head when he sees me coming. And then all the men see me, and they look like a bunch of fucking meerkats. McGaver doesn't even have time to warn Adam, because I reach a hand around Adam's head, fasten a grip so hard around his chin that I feel his teeth through his skin, and I snap his neck.

He collapses on top of both the woman and McGaver.

I yank his rifle off his lifeless shoulder and fire two clean shots into McGaver's head. I'm about to shoot at the rest of the men when the whole crew grabs the four women and yank them up to be used as human shields. I have Adam's gun aimed straight at Masterson's face, the fat slob who always managed to eat everyone's food. But he keeps ducking behind the dark-skinned girl, only popping out every few seconds to see if I'm still aiming my gun at him.

"Throw me the gun!" shouts one of the men. It's O'Connor. I don't know the prick, but I know his name. He has a veiny hand wrapped around the redhead's neck, ready to crush her throat.

"Let them go!" Castor shouts. He's hiding a few feet behind me, but he means well.

O'Connor squeezes his hand, and the woman reaches for her throat. Her mouth's wide open as she's making weird noises trying to catch her breath. "I said throw me the gun!"

My eyes scan the situation. Eight men remain now that Adam and McGaver are dead. Two are having a hard time hiding, so I quickly lift my gun and fire another two rounds.

Bang, bang.

They both collapse, grabbing at their bloody chests, and O'Connor's eyes go wild. He digs his fingers so hard into the redhead's throat that her eyes bulge and the veins on her forehead pop out like little worms.

Down to six.

I can handle six.

"Okay, okay!" I shout. I raise an open palm, hold the rifle in one hand.

"Toss it!" O'Connor says.

I listen and throw the gun a few feet away from him. And he does exactly what I expected. He lunges for it like a man at a puddle of water in the desert.

And I charge for him.

Right as he pulls himself back up with the rifle in his hands, I punch a tight fist directly at his nose in an upward movement. There's a loud crack, which I know is the sound of his nose breaking and cartilage crushing. If I'm lucky, I might have sent the fracture up toward the brain and did some permanent damage. Either way, he's out cold, because his eyes roll back and he falls flat on his back with the gun still in his hands.

Down to five.

But I don't have time to reach for the gun because the five men jump on me.

I feel a crack in my ribs and a knock against my face. I swing back as hard as I can. Something snaps at the end of my fist, and I kick sideways—another snap. Someone lets out a pained cry and falls to the ground, clutching his leg.

Down to four.

There's another hard blow to the side of my ribs, and a shooting pain brings me to my knees. I look up in time to see Castor's hairy, openmouthed face. He's yelling something, but I can't hear anything because my ears are ringing. He swings his massive fist at one man's jaw, and it dislocates with a loud crack. It dangles there by the skin, and Castor knocks him again right in the ear.

The guy with the dislocated jaw falls on his side, out cold.

Down to three.

A surge of adrenaline pumps through me because, for a second, I think I might just win this fight. I'm about to smash my elbow into someone's eye when I see Castor's face go flush. He breathes so loud it sounds like he's trying to purposely fill his lungs with air. He then slaps a hand over his heart, and dark red fluid fills up and around the grooves of his fingernails.

The man beside him is holding a pocket knife covered in blood. He's smiling at me and gooey black liquid slips through the cracks of his rotten teeth. It almost looks like he's thinking, *You're next, asshole.*

I shouldn't have looked at him. I shouldn't have let my guard down.

My arms are suddenly locked on either side of me. I realize I'm being held by the other of Adam's guys. I kick and pull, but they dance with me, holding me in place.

The man with the knife takes one step closer, ready to slit me open like a pig. He's so cocky about it, too. Wiggling the knife around like he's going to enjoy it. Like he's about to teach me the biggest lesson of my life. The only thing is, I won't remember it because I'll be dead.

His knuckles go white around the knife's handle, and his face looks like it's melting now that his smile's turned upside down. He lifts it up, ready to stab me right in the neck when part of his face is blown off.

Pieces of flesh splatter on my face and bottom lip, and I turn my head away.

What the fuck.

The redhead is standing a few meters away, holding the gun in her hands. It's shaking from side to side, and her legs are trembling. The skin on her forehead is wrinkled, and she's letting out loud grunts and shaking the gun at us.

It's like she's too traumatized by everything to talk. Instead, she keeps poking her gun in the air and yelling at us.

What does she want?

"Let him go!" she manages to shout.

The two men who were holding me must realize she's completely nuts because they raise their hands in the air and slowly step back.

"Look, lady, we didn't mean—"

Bang, bang, bang.

She's thrown back a few steps because of the gun, and I duck, because I know she doesn't have full control of the weapon. One of her bullets skims my shoulder and a hot burning spreads down my arm. I can tell she's never fired a gun before. The women behind her cover their ears and turn away.

The man she shot grabs at his stomach, falls to his knees, then lands flat on his face. The other guy beside me is shaking his head from side to side, pleading for her to have mercy.

Serves him fucking right.

Bang, bang, bang.

He dances backward a few steps and his arms flap on either side of him before he lands on his back.

I realize she might shoot me, too, but all I can think about is Castor. He's lying in the grass, his knees up to his chest, and wincing in pain. I run to his side and press a hand on his scruffy neck.

"Oh, Castor," I say. "Hang in there."

The stab wound's right over his heart. I know he won't make it.

He reaches a bloody hand into his loose-threaded pocket, wiggles his fingers around, and pulls out his daughter's keychain. He brings it to his lips and kisses it, then presses it into the palm of my hand and forces my fingers over it.

I flinch at the sound of another gunshot and look back to see the redhead. She's walking through the bodies toward me with her gun pointed toward the ground.

Bang, bang.

She shoots one of them point-blank in the face, blowing off his entire head. It looks like she's killing off the ones who survived.

"Please find—" Castor says, but he loses all color in his face, and his eyes glaze over.

"No, no, Castor." I shake him. "Castor!"

My throat swells, and I clench my jaw, but the sound of a body falling to the ground catches my attention. I twist my head and see the redhead on her back. What happened? The three other women are huddled around her like cheerleaders around an injured sports player.

I rush to her side and slide the gun out of her hands just in case. I'm worried she might wake up and shoot me in the face.

"Gretchin?" one of the women asks, and they all start panicking.

"Gretchin!"

"What's wrong with her?"

"She's in shock," I say. I tap her gently on the face, but she doesn't wake up, so I scoop her in my arms. Her arms dangle beside her, and her frizzy orange head falls back.

The women hop around me. Their heads are

barely level with my chest, and they're reaching for their friend, Gretchin, as I move toward the prison. I realize that I'm taking a huge risk walking toward a colony of women, but I don't care. She needs to rest, and I don't know if she has any other wounds that I can't see.

"Y-you saved us!" one of the women says.

"I told you," one of them whispers, "not all men are evil."

"Don't let Eve hear you say that!"

Eve, I repeat in my head. The way they're talking about it, it sounds like she's the leader. I wonder if the rumors are true. If there's only one woman leading an entire society of females.

"What's your name?" the dark-skinned beauty asks me.

I stop walking for a moment to look down at her. She's staring at me with such tenderness in her eyes. I never imagined I'd receive a look like this from a woman after the revolution. I expected to have my testicles cut off.

"G-Gabriel," I say.

"Gabriel," she repeats, and she reaches a warm hand against the scruff of my beard, "like the angel."

Gabriel — Flashback

I feel like I'm in a movie. I put on my equipment and prepare my gun. I can't get President Price's face out of my head. A video of him circulated around the room after he declared America in a state of emergency. In the video, he was sitting in the Oval Office, his jet-black hair combed to one side. He was wearing a gray suit with a red tie and sat calmly while talking to the camera.

"I understand this is a hard time for all of my fellow Americans. For months, we've tried, and tried, and tried to get these women to see things from a scientific standpoint—to realize that all we're trying to do is save this beautiful country. But we can't go on living in a world where the gender ratio is out of balance." He then shook his head, stood up, and leaned his body weight against his oval desk. "But the president of the United States stands for his people and with his people. Today, twelve of our soldiers were murdered at the hands of these rioters when a bomb went off right behind the White House's South Lawn." He stood up tall and fixed his tie. "America will not back down. These women are a threat to our nation, which makes them our enemy."

He bent over his desk, slipped a pen out of his chest pocket, and signed a piece of paper.

"Today marks the day that the United States of America becomes at war with itself."

A few voices are bouncing around the room, and I think everyone's as panicked as I am.

"Are we seriously at war with women? Officially?"

"You heard the president."

"It serves them fucking right. They killed twelve of our men!"

"They killed more than that."

I want to say, "And how many women have we killed?" but I keep my mouth shut. The last time I tried to play devil's advocate, James and a few other men turned against me.

It's hard to believe it's official. We're at war with our own people. Because they are our people. They're just angry. They're outraged. That's not a reason to kill them. But this isn't some riot gone bad anymore. This is America crumbling, and I'm standing on the other side, fighting for a cause I don't believe in.

A loud bang suddenly shakes the White House and the floor trembles. I stiffen my legs so I don't fall.

"The fuck was that?" someone says.

Everyone rushes to the window, where we can see a massive hole in the ground out at the edge of Lafayette Square. Gray smoke clouds the air all around it, but as it starts to dissipate, all I see is blood and body parts.

The sound of a fighter jet roars above. They must've shot a missile at a group of women. Hundreds of them scatter, rushing away from the horrific scene, but others lose their minds and hop over the barricade, then charge full force toward the White House with arms above their heads and mouths open so wide they look like black holes.

Hundreds of rounds are fired and a gray layer of smoke floats in the air. Women collapse before even making it to the White House's fountain. Why are they even trying? They don't stand a chance. Why are they killing themselves?

My throat swells at the sight of the massacre, but the voice of a superior vibrates in the room.

"Out of bed, soldiers. You're needed downstairs."

We're urged to finish gearing up and led down through the White House's front doors.

"Guard the House with your life," says one of the commanders. "If the women get close enough, shoot to kill."

Everything around me is pulsating like I've been injected with drugs. Shoot to kill? I've been ordered to assassinate American citizens. My eyes dart from left to right, and I watch in horror as millions of women march forward, screaming at the top of their lungs. The sound is indescribable. It doesn't even sound human... more like the Earth is shattering from its core.

Blood splatters in every direction as soldiers shoot into the crowd, and women keep hopping over bodies, moving closer and closer. It looks like a mudslide.

Some of the guys beside me start shooting their energy bullets. It fills the air with a piercing noise, and a quick *clunk* follows after every shot because the guns are reenergizing.

Then, the fighter jet comes back.

For a second, the sound of gunshots is masked because of a sharp, whistle-like noise that gets louder and louder until finally, there's impact. Everything trembles as hard as an earthquake and hundreds of body parts fly into the air.

But it doesn't stop them. They're not stopping. Why aren't the women stopping? My heart's pounding so hard and all I want to do is vomit. I watch, mortified, as the rioters run forward with shovels, sticks, knives, and swords, sacrificing their lives to move their rebel army one step closer toward the White House.

CHAPTER 33 – LUCY

Lucy — Present Day

I glide my finger across the pages, searching for a green plant with weird blueberry-looking balls on it. It's like I'm pulling at straws. Then again, the saying might be *grasping at straws*. My mom used to say that all the time.

I have no idea if this plant is what Eve's using, but I find it a bit weird that she'd finally let women step outside of Eden after always telling us how dangerous it is. Obviously, she wants something, which is why she asked Gretchin to talk to the twins. She wants Gretchin to pick something up for her that only the twins know about.

I flip through hundreds of pages, going through all kinds of alien-looking plants until I finally land on page 379 – Atropa Belladonna. I turn my head sideways and analyze the picture from top to bottom. Unless my memory is really bad, it looks exactly like the plant in the corner of Mavis and Perula's greenhouse.

This is it.

I slide my finger along the faded ink underneath the word Belladonna, then make my way to the first paragraph, where a title in bold black ink reads: *Deadly Nightshade.*

I swallow hard. That doesn't sound good, and it definitely doesn't sound like medicine. Could it be

I'm actually onto something? I start reading the text, feeling like words are literally jumping out at me from the pages: *toxic, hallucinations, delirium...*

These are all side effects of ingestion. I don't know what to think. Why would anyone want something so dangerous? Maybe if it's prepared properly, it's safe. It wouldn't be the first time Perula made some kind of elixir and said to me, "If done incorrectly, this plant can cause..."

The book then lists all the dangerous side effects. It's usually something along the lines of upset stomach or heart palpitations, which isn't all that bad. Especially compared to the words toxic, hallucinations, and delirium.

I sigh. I'm about ready to give up on the whole thing because I don't know enough about using herbs as medicine. The twins haven't taught me much yet, which is frustrating. But then, I see another title at the bottom: *Devil's Breath.*

Some people believe Devil's Breath, also known as scopolamine, to be the most dangerous drug in the world. Although evidence is limited, victims of Devil's Breath are coming forward to describe their experiences.

"I felt like a complete zombie. It's like I lost all willpower and obeyed any order given to me," says Matilda Lauren, a victim of the drug, which she states was blown directly in her face.

I don't even bother reading the rest because this is it... This is the answer—it has to be. Now it all makes perfect sense. If there's one thing Eve would want to do to people, it would be to have them obey her. Right? I slam my book closed and slip it under my pillow. I'm about to get up and find Emily, when Nola slips into my room, looking like she usually does when she catches me rushing around: suspicious.

She narrows her eyes and little wrinkles form at the corners. Mom used to look at me like that, too, only she didn't have wrinkles. Mom always had such soft-looking skin. It must be where I get it from.

"Whoa," she says, sticking out a straight arm to block my path. "Where are you running off to?"

I stand on my tiptoes and look over her shoulder. "N-nowhere."

But she crosses her arm over her belly and leans back into the bars of my room. She's obviously not buying it. She knows me better than anyone... and sometimes better than I know myself.

"Spit it out," she says. "Is this about Zack?"

"Zack?" What the heck is she talking about? "Who's Zack?"

"The boy," Nola says. "A lot of girls are lining up to meet him."

I roll my eyes and laugh. I'm not trying to be rude, but the last thing anyone will find me doing is lining up to see a boy. I have better things to do, like figure out what the heck Eve is up to. And the last thing I want to do is be anywhere near a male. I push my tongue against the inside of my cheek, debating whether I should ask Nola about her adult meetings.

"Well?" she asks, her eyes shining over her big doughy cheeks.

She's almost always smiling, even when she's upset, so it's hard to know what she's thinking.

If I say something, maybe Nola will tell Eve that I'm questioning her ways. I can't risk it. Especially if Nola is drinking that stuff, too. Eve probably has her brainwashed like the rest of them.

"Huh? No," I say. "It's not about Zack. I, um…" I scratch the back of my neck, trying to organize my thoughts. "I'm looking for Emily."

"Emily?" Nola asks. "That young girl?"

"She's fourteen, Nola," I say, and my eyes go flat. I hate how adults talk about kids. It's like she thinks that Emily doesn't have a brain because she isn't an adult. I've been treated that way my whole life, and I won't let my friend be treated the same way.

Nola shakes her thick, poufy-haired head and it looks like she's about the try to apologize for the way she said *girl*. But then, Emily comes running up to my room and slaps two hands around my iron bars.

Both sides of her lips are touching a bar on either side. "They're coming back," she says.

"What, who?" I ask.

"The women," she says like I'm an idiot. "The ones who left Eden this morning. But I think something's wrong because Freyda's rushing over to Eve's office right now."

I blink.

"Helloooo?" she says, and she makes her jaw move from side to side while she says it. I think she's trying to be funny, but I'm not in a laughing mood.

"Let's go check it out!" she says.

I scurry past Nola and make a run for it down the corridor with Emily laughing behind me. But as I get to the main hall, I realize we're not the only ones curious about what's going on. A bunch of adults stands around in the main hall, waiting for Eve to come back with Freyda and open the front doors.

I squeeze past a few thick dresses, apologizing every time I bump into someone, and I make my way to the front of the crowd. Everyone's whispering so loud, it's as though I'm in a beehive.

I swing back around to make sure Emily followed me to the front, but as I'm turning, something hits me hard in the face and I fall flat on my butt.

My forehead's throbbing, and my vision's a bit fuzzy, but I feel okay. I rub my head and glare up toward the dark figures standing in front of me. Their shape is outlined only by the light coming from the windows on the ceiling.

Did I bump into someone?

A long arm is extended down to me, so I grab it. It's warm and soft.

"Sorry about that," he says with a crooked smile on his lips.

He doesn't let go of my arm even after he pulls me up. We stand there like we're the only two people in the room. I stare into his dark chocolate eyes, then down at the strange fuzz over his thick lips. He has curly brown hair, and his eyelashes are so dark and long that it looks like he's wearing makeup.

"I said I'm sorry," he repeats, and his smile doesn't fade one bit.

I'm a bit surprised by how white his teeth are. And they look even whiter, almost like milk, compared to his dark skin. Everyone else's teeth are either yellow or rotting.

"Oh," I say, but I can't find my words. I haven't seen a boy in over five years. I almost forgot what they look like.

"Are you okay?" he asks, and he brushes a warm thumb on my forehead.

I look at his chin, where a big red blotchy spot is swelling quickly. I must've hit my head on his chin. "I-I'm okay," I say. "What about you?"

He rubs his jaw with his long fingers, and his smile gets even bigger like he's about to laugh. "I'll live."

Then the strangest thing happens. I'm standing still with his fingers still wrapped around my forearm, and for a split second, I forget everything I've ever been taught about men. I forget that I've been taught to hate them for being the *worst possible thing to ever walk this Earth*. I forget that they're nothing but *animals* and *worthless vermin*.

For a second, Eve's opinions aren't in my head.

"I'm Zack," he says, and he slides his grip down to my hand.

"Lucinda," I say, "but you can call me Lucy."

Lucy — Flashback

"Mom, stop it!" I say, but she isn't listening. She's pulling on my wrist so hard that her knuckles are all white and my skin is burning. It feels like it's been pinched over and over again.

I try to pull away, but she's holding me too tight.

"How long will their food last?" she asks, but she isn't talking to me. She's talking to Bethany Lee, and they're walking fast down a hallway.

"A few months," Bethany says. "Enough for about a hundred boys and girls. We're giving priority to the children—"

My mom turns away from me and sticks a shaky finger in Bethany's face. "I'm doing this for my daughter and for her future. So help me God, if anything happens to her—"

Bethany Lee lifts two hands like someone does when they don't want any trouble. "I understand, Ophelia, I do. Trust me, she'll be safe here."

Safe? Here? What are they talking about? Where's my mom taking me?

"Mom?"

She starts walking fast again, and I almost trip.

"Mom, please," I say, but she's ignoring me.

I look up at her. Her face is all red and shiny, and her dark red hair is tied up into a messy bun that's wiggling around at the top of her head. I can't tell if she's sweating or if she's crying.

"Mom?"

We reach a big door at the back of the basement hallway, and my mom wraps her arms tight around me. She holds me tighter than she's ever held me before, kisses me hard on the head, then hugs me again. My forehead slides against her neck because her skin is so slimy.

"I love you, Lucy. Don't you forget that."

My throat starts to hurt and my eyes fill with tears. Why is she doing this? Why is she talking to me like she's saying goodbye?

"Mom, what's going on?" My voice cracks.

I'm so scared.

The big door opens, and a lady in a long blue dress steps out. Kids are talking, crying, and screaming behind her.

"I love you, baby," my mom says again, and the lady grabs my hand out of my mom's.

I yank my hand away and throw myself at my mom, but Bethany steps in the way.

"You'll be safe here, Lucy," she says.

"I don't want to be safe! I want my mom!" I'm crying so hard I'm barely making any sense.

"Come on, sweetheart," the lady says, and she pulls at my arm.

I try to pull away, but she won't let go this time.

"No, please!"

Bethany helps her drag me into the room, and all I can hear is my mom sobbing in the hallway. Why is she doing this? Why won't she stay with me?

"Please!"

The kids around me are all backing away because I'm kicking and screaming.

"Mom, please! I love you!"

But she doesn't come back for me, and the big

door slams shut.

CHAPTER 34 – EVE

Eve — Present Day

"Eve, you need to see this," Freyda says.

The skin on her face is pulled back, and her typical olive complexion now looks gray—zombielike, even. Something's wrong. I lunge to my feet and follow her out of my office and down toward the main hall.

The sound of my heels ticking against the hard floor is masked by what appears to be a crowd of women gathered in the hall. As I approach, several women eye me with curiosity, as if waiting to be debriefed on some important matter.

What are they all waiting for?

"Is it true?" an old woman asks, reaching for my arm.

I look down at her and at her bony, dirt-stained hands around my white sleeve. I curl my lip up. "Is what true?"

"That some women stepped outside of Eden's walls," someone else asks, slithering their way through the crowd and slipping out into the open.

The voices get louder as women try to talk over one another. It's unbelievable how fast word spreads in Eden. Someone must have overheard me speaking with Gretchin yesterday or seen them entering the main corridor this morning—the one leading to the front entrance. I gaze into the old woman's gray eyes and smile. There's no use lying to these women. They deserve to know the truth.

"Yes," I say, and the bickering starts up again.

"Eve," Freyda says impatiently, her eyes shifting from me to the main corridor.

I raise a finger at her, ordering her to keep quiet for a moment, and extend two open hands on either side of my body, symbolizing openness and transparency.

"Everyone, please." My voice carries across the room and up the high walls. "There's no need to be alarmed. I allowed four women to exit Eden's walls in search of much-needed resources. I know you're all highly intelligent women and you're well aware that we can't possibly survive inside of Eden's walls forever."

A heavy silence fills the room, and everyone's attention is centered on me.

"I believe that to survive as a society, stepping outside of Eden's walls will become crucial as we move forward. If any of you are in need of supplies that cannot be obtained inside these walls, I invite you to come see me"—I pause, gazing at everyone with tender care—"and I'll do whatever I can to accommodate your needs."

The chattering starts up again, but this time, with much enthusiasm and excitement. Anytime someone's asked me to step outside of the walls, I've denied their request. But circumstances are changing, and I know now that we can't stay here.

I'm not prepared to tell the women that yet. They've built a home for themselves here. But when the time is right, they'll come to understand.

"Eve," Freyda repeats, and I nod briefly at her.

She leads me to the main door and out toward the main gates.

"You have to see this for yourself," she says, walking me across the dry dirt and toward the watchtower.

"What's wrong?" I ask. She has me worried. Are my women hurt?

But she shakes her head and reaches a firm hand on my shoulder. I can't tell whether she's trying to prepare me or comfort me. "Go up and look for yourself."

I rush my way up the ladder, my heart pounding and my hands becoming clammy. Every step feels like a dozen. Why won't she simply tell me what's on the other side? I take my last step and pull myself up against the concrete wall, the upper half of my body bent over the hot stone.

I blink once, then twice, certain I'm hallucinating.

Standing at the front of Eden's gates are Gretchin and the three women she brought along with her, only one of them is lying unconscious in the muscular arms of a man. I slap a hand over my forehead and turn away, my mind racing in every direction imaginable.

Why are they standing next to a man, and why is he holding one of my women? Is this blackmail? Did he hurt her? Should I have allowed Freyda to train women to fight? If only I'd...

"Eve!" someone calls out from below.

I bend over the wall again, and I see Gretchin's messy orange hair. She's waving a hand at me, trying to catch my attention.

"Eve, please let us in!" she says.

Let them in? With a man? How are they even asking this of me? I pull back out of their sight, and this time, gaze down the ladder at Freyda. Her hands rest on her thick-panted waist, and she's shaking her head from side to side as if to say, "I have no idea what to think."

Jesus Christ, Gretchin. What have you done? How could you possibly betray us by bringing a man into our paradise?

"Eve!"

I move back toward the wall, my eyes fixated on the man.

"Eve, this is Gabriel," Gretchin shouts. "He saved our lives!"

"He's our angel!" the dark-skinned one says.

I pinch my eyebrow and squeeze my eyes shut.

Fuck, fuck, fuck, fuck.

I'm fighting with myself when one of the women below lets out a high-pitched shriek. I nearly throw myself over to see what's going on. The only plausible assumption is that the man's gone feral, yet I see him collapse to one knee, dropping the girl in his arms. He clutches at his ribs and lets out a grunt, before swaying from side to side and losing consciousness, his body making a *thump* against the dirt underneath him.

"Eve!" Gretchin calls out again. "He needs help!"

I want to scream—I hate being cornered into

making a life-threatening decision. If I don't let him in, these women will forever blame me for killing their so-called *hero*.

"He saved our lives, Eve!"

I wrap my fingers around the wood of the ladder, bend over to look at Freyda, and impatiently slap the air. "Open the gates!"

Eve — Flashback

I glance back at Ophelia, who looks terrified out of her mind, her mouth hanging loose and her hands brushing her greasy hair out of her face every two seconds. I've asked her to stay behind—to stay with her daughter and go back to her mom's place—but she keeps telling me this is something she *needs to do* to set an example for Lucy.

I can't believe it's happening.

I'm surrounded by women in heavy artillery gear from gas masks, to machine guns, to rocket launchers, and we're moving through the dense crowd. The sound of helicopter blades and rapid gunfire fills the air around us, and in the distance, women are screaming at the top of their lungs. I can't see what's going on near the White House because I'm still too far away, but I know that with every step I take, a life is being taken.

Women of all different ages, sizes, and ethnicity open a path for us as we move, almost the way simpletons would for royalty. They're smiling from ear to ear, but to my surprise, they aren't yelling or cheering us on. Everyone is so calm—almost eerily so. It's like they know that for our attack to succeed, they need to keep us invisible to the US military.

My legs shake, but there's no turning back now.

Vrin, an ex-sergeant of the US military, turns to me for direction. How on Earth am I qualified to lead a group of armed Rebels? I barely know how to shoot a gun. But, ever since I went above Bethany's head and divulged the information we received about the kill order, the women are treating me like their leader. It doesn't make any sense to me, but all I can do is play along.

I'm about to tell her to have her women charge at the barrier because this is where the most women are being killed, but something occurs to me.

"Vrin?" I ask.

She nods, her square jaw twitching and her sharp catlike eyes opened wide, almost as if prepared to kill herself if I were to command it.

"Is there a way inside the White House without going through the front doors?" I ask.

"Like a back door?" she asks.

"More like an underground tunnel," I say, rubbing my chin.

She smirks at me, her eyes narrowing to slits. "Actually, there is."

CHAPTER 35 – GABRIEL

Gabriel - Present Day

The air around me is cool and damp, and it smells like mildew. Where am I?

There's an excruciating pain in my ribs, and I flinch when a cold hand touches the hot skin of my torso. I'm almost entirely naked, wearing nothing but old briefs.

"Four broken ribs," a gentle voice says.

Something sparks beside me, and the smell of sulfur reaches my nostrils. The woman standing in front of me is holding a small match in between her fingers, and its flame is flicking from side to side. I can see her a bit with the flame's glow. She looks like a witch just sitting there in the darkness. Her hair is long and black and white, and she's wearing some weird, green mesh dress. Reaching beside her, she presses her match against the wick of a big wax candle. She then sticks her hand into something that looks like an old gym bag and pulls out two long leaves.

"Hold still," she says, and she rubs the dry plant along my forehead. It stings, so I'm assuming she's cleaning a wound.

"What's your name?" she asks me. Her breath is so rancid it makes me want to throw up.

"G-Gabriel," I say, and I wince when the pain in my ribs sets in.

"Gabriel," she repeats and rubs her herbs over my cut again. "I'm Perula."

Perula, I think. What a weird name. What the hell have I gotten myself into? I glance down at the beige candle. Did I wind up in some sort of devil-worshipping cult?

"The women say you saved them," she says. Her voice is so soft it almost puts me to sleep. I nod but only enough for her to see because it hurts too much to move.

"That was very noble of you," she says.

I want to say, "It's what anyone would've done in my shoes," but that would be a lie. It's not what anyone would've done. It's what anyone with half a heart and a fraction of a soul would've done. It's what Castor would've done.

I bite the inside of my cheek and try to think of anything but Castor's big, furry face. He could be so dumb sometimes, but he was such a softy. He was the kind of guy this world needs.

Perula sticks her fingers into a glass jar and pulls out a glob of cream. She rubs it on my forehead and then over my ribs.

I throw my head back.

"I know it hurts," she says, "but this will help with the inflammation."

"Who are you?" I ask through clenched teeth.

For a second, it almost looks like she's smirking. "I already told you."

"I mean..." I inhale a sharp breath through my teeth. "Where am I? And why are you helping me?"

"You're in Eden," she says, "and because that's

what I do... I heal."

"But why?" I ask. "I'm a man."

She eyes me from head to toe, looking almost impressed. "That, you are."

"What is this place?" I ask. "Are you all women?"

She brushes the back of her hand against the scruff of my beard. It looks like she's enjoying it. She then sticks her fingers in my mouth, and all I taste is a sour powder. I try to pull away, but I'm too weak.

"Get some rest, Gabriel."

And with that, she gets up, drags a fur blanket over my body, and blows out the candle. I listen to her footsteps as she walks away. I want to call out to her, but I can't. What did she do? Drug me? I close my eyes, let out a long breath, then everything disappears.

* * *

I wake up to the same familiar smell of sulfur, only this time, Perula isn't kneeling beside me. Instead, I see a pair of red leathery boots inches away from my face. I stare at the heels for a second, then slowly make my way up the white legged pants, past a white blazer, and up to the woman's face.

It's too dark in here and I can't see her features, but I can tell she has short hair. I'm about to ask her who she is, but she kneels down and rests her elbows on her knee, all while holding the match beside her face.

"Good morning, Gabriel."

If I'd been standing, I'd have fallen flat on my ass. Not because of her angelic beauty (silky blond hair, fierce blue eyes, and a smile that could melt any man's heart) but because I know this woman.

Gabriel — Flashback

The only person I can think about right now is my mom.

I should have called her, even though I wasn't allowed to. I should have visited. Checked up on her. Is she even okay? Is she a part of this rebellion?

I'm hiding in a cabinet, my eyes burning like I've had acid poured on them, and my heart's beating so hard I'm scared someone on the outside will hear it and find me. If anyone were to see me, I'd be ridiculed for the rest of my life... Me, a Black Marine, hiding like a goddamn kid in a storage cabinet.

But what alternative is there? Hundreds of women are patrolling the area, holding guns I've never even seen before. I can't tell if they're homemade or black market. And how the fuck did women manage to infiltrate the White House? I know there's more of them than us, but this just doesn't make any sense. We have men stationed everywhere. Extremely highly trained men.

I breathe in and out, feeling like I'm running out of oxygen. I don't even know how I got here. It all happened so fast. First, I received an order to get back into the White House, and then... Grenades went off, tear gas went off, and gunshots echoed all around me.

"...I repeat... Enforc... com... g in..." I hear in my earpiece, and I tear the device out of my ear. With my thumbnails, I snap the wire in two. The last thing I need is for the speaker to malfunction and give away my location.

"Call off your men!" I hear a woman shout.

"It's not that simple."

Jesus Christ, I know that voice.

"Call off your fucking army!" the woman snaps, and I hear someone cocking a gun.

Someone clears their throat, and there's a faint static sound.

"This is President Price—I repeat, President Price. Stop the attack. Hello? Stop the attack!"

He lets out a pathetic whimper, and I can only assume the gun's cold metal is pressed against his temple. Where the hell am I? The Oval Office? The president of the United States wouldn't be stupid enough to sit in his Oval Office during war... Would he? Is he that prideful? And why the hell would his protective staff have allowed it? They should have dragged his ass out of the White House a long time ago.

I slowly straighten my posture but only enough to reach my eye up to the keyhole. It's tiny, so I can't see much at all, but I can make out people moving around. Bits and pieces of military uniforms and fancy black coats litter the floor. There's no doubt in my mind that these are bodies. Probably his Protective Services Unit. Bunch of fucking idiots.

"President Price, come in," says a choppy voice through a speaker.

The president whimpers again, and instead of his voice breaking through the somber air, a woman's voice comes on.

"We have President Price," she says. She's almost too calm about it. "Stop the attack, or he dies."

I blink hard a few times, trying to go over my options. But I don't have any options because they all lead to the same thing: my death or the death of women. Realistically, though, both of these things would happen. I'd kill one or two, and then I'd get shot.

What's the point?

I thought I could make a difference. If I chose the right path, women would come to see that we're not all monsters. But where did that get me? In some cabinet, hiding from a bunch of Rebels who I know would kill me without even blinking the second I step out.

An unusual sound suddenly comes from above—it's the sound of jet engines fading and gunfire slowing down. Did they actually listen? Are they backing off for the president's life?

"President Price, come in—"

But I flinch when I hear something loud snap, almost like a twig, and the voice in the speaker cuts out. I peer through the hole, and it looks like one of the women dressed in full military gear smashed the communication device.

"Is this your big plan?" asks one of the women. She's young, has brown hair, and seems a bit out of place. It looks like she was dragged along in this whole mess. She's pacing back and forth, nervously brushing strands of hair out of her face, then lets out a loud laugh. "This is great. Just great. What're you gonna do? Kill the president of the United States?"

"That's been the plan all along," says the other woman. She's wearing a black military vest, but underneath, it looks like she has a pair of jeans and a blue shirt, unlike the rest of the women in the room, who are fully armed. Her blond hair is messily pulled back into a ponytail, and she looks nervous—like she's trying to be tough, but doesn't know what she's doing. She looks even younger than the brunette, and it's obvious she's never been trained for this.

It doesn't make sense to me. How did they get in? The only plausible explanation would be that they got in through the underground tunnel. The one that's used to pull the president out of the White House in emergency situations. But that door would have been sealed shut. Nothing would have blown past that. Not even a dozen grenades. Unless...

I slap a hand on my mouth and over the scruff of my beard. Jesus Christ. Were some of the soldiers trying to leave? Did they open the bunker tunnel up knowing this was a suicide mission? Hoping to get back to their wives, their lovers, their families?

There's no other explanation. If I don't believe in everything that President Price is doing to this country, I can't be the only one.

"Look at everything he's done," the blonde says. She's pointing a gun right at the president's temple, and he's making such an ugly face, his rolls of skin are more visible than usual.

She cocks her pistol and pushes it harder against his temple, and he raises two hands as if he's trying to convince them he's innocent.

"P-p-p-please," he begs.

I don't agree with killing him, but the man isn't innocent.

"Why should he live when so many women have died?" the blond woman says, staring at the brunette with such wildness, I'm scared she might fire the gun by accident.

"We're not *them*," the brunette says. "You don't need to do this."

One of the women dressed in full military clothing comes forward, her heavy boots stepping over a dead body. "Whatever you do, you'd better do it fast." She presses a hand over her ear and nods. "It's only a matter of time before the president's order is disobeyed. Male soldiers have already set up camps outside our perimeter." She nods again, obviously listening to a voice in her earpiece. "Navy, air force, reserves, police officers—anyone who can shoot a gun is lining up."

"What're you trying to say?" says the blonde. Her voice sounds like an unstable roller coaster. "Having the president as a hostage isn't going to do a fucking thing?"

The armed woman shakes her head. "Not for long, no."

"Hear that?" the blonde says, almost hitting the president with the barrel of her gun this time. "No one cares about you, you misogynistic piece of shit."

"Let's take him back with us," the brunette says,

but the blonde laughs out loud.

"What's that going to do? You heard Vrin! We're surrounded."

"There are millions of women out there," the brunette says. "How much military staff can there possibly be?"

The armed woman steps in, placing two hands on her hips. "Reserves included? Close to three million. But that was before they started letting go of the women, who accounted for about five hundred thousand."

"We still outnumber them!" the blonde shouts, showing everyone her teeth.

"We don't all have guns," the brunette says. "These men have missiles and bombs and equipment we've never even heard of!"

The blonde is about to go off again when something extraordinary happens. Everything turns so quiet that for a moment, I think my gun went off in the cabinet and I've gone deaf. It's almost like all sound's been removed from the Earth. I press my face harder against the keyhole and realize the lights have gone out and the room has filled with natural gray light.

"What just happened?" someone in the room says.

The blond woman laughs. "I can't fucking believe it. She pulled through."

Suddenly, a sickening rumble shakes the building, followed by screams so loud, for a second I think one of the windows is wide open.

"Oh my God," someone says.

I can't see anything outside. There are too many women blocking the windows. What the hell is going on? The sound gets louder, and it's turning into a high-pitched noise that almost sounds like something heavy falling from the sky.

"Get down!"

I slap two hands over my ears and squint my eyes shut, bracing myself for an explosion. The entire White House shakes violently, but nothing collapses. The horrific screams still fill the air around us, and everyone rushes around the president's desk to press their faces against the windows.

"Is that a—"

"F-16 fighter jet."

"The EMP worked."

EMP? Are they out of their goddamn minds? I rub my eyes and eyebrows with my clammy hands. I'm going to throw up. If they've truly pulled this off, they've now sent us back to the Dark Ages. And how the hell did they build an EMP powerful enough to take out an aircraft? How big is this thing?

I look up into the darkness of the cabinet when I hear chopper blades overhead. Within seconds, there's another shake in the building, followed by a huge explosion.

It sounds like everything's falling out of the goddamn sky. I press my face over the keyhole again.

"Let's get out of here," the brunette says.

"No, not yet," says the blonde. She walks across the Oval Office, behind the president's fancy leather sofa, and glass suddenly shatters.

Although I can't see her where she is, I'm almost certain I know what she broke—a glass box protecting the president's famous WW3 semiautomatic HK-02 rifle. I saw it hanging on the wall before I snuck inside this cabinet. It was given to him by a war veteran in 2049 and the first thing he did was to take a picture of himself holding the gun, and he blasted it all over social media. I remember that picture—the smug look on his face and the way he jokingly poked his finger against the bayonet's sharp tip with a cheesy grin.

"What're you doing?" the president asks. "Don't touch that!"

The blond woman comes back into view holding the HK-02 rifle. It's matte black with a chrome trigger and sight, and the bayonet is located right underneath the barrel. It's about three inches long, and its silver blade reflects the light coming through the windows.

"Put that down!" the president yells. He's fuming like a kid whose parents confiscated his favorite toy.

"You're not a murderer. Let this go," says the brunette.

The blonde doesn't listen. Instead, she raises the butt of the rifle and swings the entire gun across President Price's face.

Crack.

He lets out a whimper and blood drips from the corner of his lips.

"What're you going to do?" he sneers. "Beat me to death?"

"Stop it!" the brunette says. "You don't need to do this!" She reaches for the gun, but the blonde shoves her away and swings the rifle around. Its metallic frame scrapes against her rings, and she points its barrel at the president's chest.

President Price lets out a scoff. "It's not loaded, you dumb bl—"

The next thing I know, the blonde is holding the butt of the rifle with both hands over President Price's chest. I don't realize what she's done at first, but then she smirks down at the president and yanks the gun back. The silver bayonet is now dark red and the president's blue undershirt is soaked in blood over his heart.

"You don't deserve a bullet, you motherfucking—" She smashes the butt of her gun against his face again, and there's a loud crack, like the sound of cartilage being crushed, but he doesn't move.

He's already dead.

She just killed the president of the United States.

How is this happening?

"Oh, God, what did you do?" The brunette slaps two hands over her mouth.

"This is for all the women"—the blonde smashes the gun over his left ear and his head rolls to the side on the leather of his chair—"whose lives you've ruined." This time, she swings a backhanded fist at his lifeless face and it rolls the other way.

It's as if she's possessed. Her figure is hunched, her hair messy, her eyes so wild she doesn't look like the same person anymore.

The brunette reaches for her shoulder, and in one swift motion, the blonde angrily swings the gun sideways, the bayonet's tip slicing through the brunette's throat, and everything goes completely quiet.

They stare at each other, their eyes widening at the same time. The brunette slaps a hand over her throat as blood starts spurting out.

The blonde stands still, obviously in a state of shock, silent, momentarily frozen. She catches the brunette as she collapses and slowly lowers her to the ground.

"O... Jesus Christ, Ophelia. Please, no. No, no, no." She sobs, rocking who I now realize is her friend back and forth.

The sound of pain fills the room, and I stare at President Price's chalk-white face, his partially opened mouth, and his hollow eyes, which are aimed at the ceiling. I fall back into the cabinet and press a hand over my heart; it thuds against my fingertips. If I press hard, I may be able to slow it down enough to catch my breath.

Because I need to catch my breath.

I can't believe what's happened.

This woman—this beauty with silky blond hair and eyes so fierce they could melt any man's heart—has murdered the president of the United States of America.

CHAPTER 36 – LUCY

Lucy — Present Day

Mavis and Perula look a little off today. They keep bickering under their breaths so I can't hear what they're talking about. I wonder if it has to do with that Gretchin lady. I saw her talking to them outside the greenhouse, going on about how they were attacked outside of Eden's walls.

I can't tell if they're bothered by the attack, or if they're upset because they didn't get the plant they wanted. My eyes make their way back to the corner of the room, where the plant with the weird black balls looks sicker than ever.

I don't get it. I asked to be a Healer, and they're supposed to be teaching me everything they know, but they're keeping secrets from me. Why? What are they trying to protect?

Perula rests her long fingernailed hand on Mavis's arm and grins from ear to ear. "Oh, the muscles on him," she says, and Mavis looks so disgusted, you'd think she ate a spoonful of warm vomit.

What muscles? What's she talking about?

Perula catches me staring because she forces an awkward smile. "What is it, child?"

I shrug. I'm trying hard to be nice to them, but I'm getting sick of being pushed around and lied to.

"Are you all right, dear?" Perula asks.

I realize I'm glaring now, but I can't help myself. And I also can't keep my mouth shut anymore. I just can't. I hate people. I hate this place. I hate this world, and deep down, I hate Eve. She's the reason my mom's dead. If it weren't for her and her stupid beliefs, my mom would've never left me in that abandoned warehouse with Clarissa, the lady in the blue dress, and with all the other kids. I sat there for days, waiting for her to come back, but she never did. It was only Eve who came back for me. I was so grateful to have her, but I know now that I've been holding on to something for way too long: why couldn't Eve have died instead of my mom? If my mom were leading this place, things would be so much better.

"What's Devil's Breath and why are you guys making it?" I ask, my nostrils flared.

Mavis lets out a stupid laugh, then slaps a hand over her mouth. "Well, I'll be damned to eternal hell and hung by my left foot."

What's she talking about? Why does she always have to make things so complicated by saying things that make absolutely no sense?

"What?" I say, but it comes out more like a bark.

Mavis's beady eyes meet her sister's, and her colorless, wrinkled lip is curled up on one side. "The little twit's not as dumb as we thought."

I grind my teeth and bite down, my temples pulsing. "Little twit?"

"Oh, ignore Mavis." Perula flicks her wrist. She walks toward me, limping with every step. "We didn't want to implicate you," she says. Her voice is as sweet as honey, and I have to try to ignore how nice she's being because otherwise, I'll lose my anger. And I need my anger right now.

"Well I am implicated," I say. "So spit it out. Is this Eve's big idea? Is she poisoning the women?"

Perula pulls her head back and crinkles her nose. "Poisoning? Goodness, no. We use this nightshade plant"—she points her fingernails toward the dying plant in the corner—"to create scopolamine."

"I know what it is," I say. "I read up on it."

Perula looks at her sister, probably wondering where I could have possibly read something like that.

"In *Magical Herbs*," I clarify.

Perula tilts her head back, her mouth open, and black spots on her molars come into view. "Ahhh, I see."

I cross my arms and raise two impatient eyebrows.

"We use it to create Devil's Breath, as you know," Perula continues. "And then we use that to create a little tea—something we call Devil's tea." She leans her body weight against the big wooden table in the middle, trying to reduce the pain in her hips. "It makes the women of Eden... happy."

"Happy?" I say. "You mean *high*?"

"Oh shush your blabberin' mouth," Mavis goes off. "You damn kids don't know a damn thing." She slaps a hand beside her cauldron and stares me dead in the face, her pencil-thin eyebrows squishing together. "You 'ave no idea how much Eve has sacrificed to get us here! Everything she's done! Everything she's lost! Women can be stupid, especially when it comes to men."

Her face is beet red, and small blue veins stick out on her forehead.

"You think you can just come on up in 'ere and start questionin' how she gets things done?"

I swallow hard, wondering if I should've kept my mouth shut.

"Mavis..." Perula tries.

"No!" Mavis smacks another hand on the table. "The only reason we're still alive is because of Eve. So what if she wants to use a bit of herbal tea to make women happy in this miserable hellhole? To have them be more receptive and more complacent? Because God knows women like to have their way, and if it wasn't for Eve, there'd be no goddamn control in this place!" She points a crooked finger at me. "Look at you! You're a perfect example. Eve asked the children of Eden not to choose *Healer*, and what did you do? Hmmm? She gave you free will, and you *chose* to disobey!"

She's staring at me with humongous eyes and I can't help wondering if they're going to pop out and fall into her cauldron. She reaches up and scratches her matted hair. "This is exactly why," she mutters to herself. "Look at this one. Look at her. She's a friggin' teenager, and she's questioning our leader already."

She swings around. "Eve is our shepherd, and she needs us to be sheep!" Saliva spews from her mouth, and she points her stiff finger at me again. Her arm moves up and down because she's breathing so hard.

"All right, that's enough," Perula says, limping toward her sister. She reaches for her, but Mavis whips around.

"Leave me be!"

Perula looks at me with soft eyes. I can tell she feels bad about Mavis's behavior, even if I'm the one who provoked it. She pushes her chin out, and I know exactly what she's asking me to do. She's asking me to step outside so she can talk Mavis down.

I creak the big wooden door open and step down into the grass. The sun is shining bright, so I rest against the cabin, letting it warm my face, neck, and arms. I close my eyes and breathe in the smell of fresh lavender, then look up at the beautiful purple flowers.

Maybe Mavis is right. Could be I need to let it go and let Eve take charge. If it weren't for her, we wouldn't be here. I wouldn't be here. I realize that might be why she's been distant and cold with everyone... Because she's stressed out all the time. She has hundreds of women and children to take care of, including me, who disobeyed her by choosing to become a Healer.

I feel like a failure... like I'm the one who took a bite out of the apple.

"Lucy!"

I look up. It's Emily. She's running away from Ruby, who keeps barking at her and dropping on her front legs with her tail wagging in the air. Behind her, Zack is following with a big smile on his face. He keeps laughing and pointing at the dog. He's wearing cotton shorts and no top, so his light brown skin is all sweaty underneath the sun.

Maybe this is the closest thing there is to paradise in this horrible world... Friendship and laughter.

Why do I keep trying to find an answer? It's like I think that the harder I look, the closer I'll get to my mom. But she's gone, and she's never coming back.

"Come on!" Emily says.

I run to catch up, but Emily plops herself down into the grass and lies on her back. Ruby licks her all over her face, and she lets out a playful laugh.

Zack sits down beside Emily and rubs his hands over his sweaty face, then through his curly hair. "I used to have a dog," he says, and the smile on his face disappears.

"What happened?" Emily asks.

Zack shrugs. He looks heartbroken. "He ran away when all the shooting and stuff started happening."

Emily stares at the ground. "I'm so sorry," she says. He doesn't respond, so she clears her throat. "I used to have a great dad."

Zack looks at her, waiting to hear what she has to say. I'm surprised Emily's talking about her dad again. She knows the rules in Eden. Zack might not know them, but she does. And every time we talk about our pasts, we feel bad about it. I understand now why Eve says she doesn't want anyone bringing up the past. She wants us to be happy.

"You remind me of him in a weird way," she says.

He smiles big, but I can tell he's uncomfortable. "Me? What? Why?"

She giggles, sounding like she's eight years old, then points at his hair. "I think it's the hair... My dad was so hairy, and they used to call him Beaver."

"Beaver?" I ask, and I can't help but laugh because all I can picture is a man with huge front teeth. "Beavers aren't that hairy. Did he have big teeth or something?"

Even Zack is laughing now. I don't know anything about him, but he seems like a good person.

Emily shakes her head. "His name was Castor."

"I don't get it," Zack says.

Emily rolls her eyes and playfully slaps him on the arm. "It means beaver in French."

She's smiling, but it's a sad smile. I can tell that deep down, it's torturing her.

Zack's dark eyes roll toward me. "What about you? Have you lost anyone?"

I stare at him for a second, looking at the tiny mustache that's trying to grow in and at his thick eyebrows that seem perfectly combed. He looks genuine—the kind of guy who wouldn't even squish a bug. Maybe there's a reason he's here.

Then I realize something... If Eve let him into Eden, she's not all bad. It means that even though she hates men more than anything in the world, there's still a bit of humanity left in her.

That's got to count for something, right?

I lean back, resting on my palms, and smile at him. "Don't worry," I say, "there'll be plenty of time for us to get to know each other. Not like we're going anywhere, right?"

I reach for a stick in the grass and chuck it far away, watching Ruby chase it, her long tail whipping in the air.

Zack's still staring at me, looking like this is the happiest day of his life.

"I'm looking forward to it," he says.

Lucy — Flashback

"Lucy, wake up," Clarissa says.

I rub my swollen eyes and look up at her. She looks like a fuzzy ball to me right now, but I know it's her because she's wearing the same blue dress she wore the first day I met her.

"What?" I ask.

"Someone's here for you."

I sit up in my bed. Well, it's not a real bed. It's a pile of old clothes and blankets. My vision gets a bit clearer, and I rub my eyes again.

"Lucy."

My heart starts to race. Am I dreaming?

"Lucy, honey, it's me."

Clarissa pats my back and tells me it's okay. It's okay if I get up and leave. I'm not a prisoner.

"Aunty Eve?" I ask.

She's standing right in front of me, wearing torn jeans and a T-shirt full of blood. Her hair is pulled back in a messy ponytail, and she has no makeup on, but she's smiling at me like I'm the best thing she's ever seen.

"Oh, Lucy," she says and sticks her arms out on both sides.

For the first time in what's felt like weeks, the smell of pee and poop doesn't bother me. I forget that I'm dirty, that I'm hungry, and that I stink so bad sometimes I find it hard to breathe. I jump up and run straight into her arms, feeling the warm skin of her neck against mine.

I hug her tight and burst out crying. I want to

ask her where Mom is, but I'm not stupid. I know. I know she's gone. Because if she wasn't, she'd be here with me. I cry so hard that my head starts to hurt.

"Shhh, it's okay," Aunty Eve says. "I'm here, honey. I'm here. I'll protect you."

I nod against her neck, and she squeezes me tight and doesn't let go. "I'll do whatever I have to. Whatever it takes to keep you safe," she says.

I nod again, but my throat hurts too much and I can't say anything.

"Do you hear me? Whatever it takes."

CHAPTER 37 – EVE

Eve – Present Day

"Do you realize the situation you've put me in?" I say, looking down at him like the filthy vermin he is.

He looks like a beaten dog with his swollen face, bruised abdomen, and bloody forehead. I should feel sorry for him, but I don't. I should be thankful, but I'm not. The only word I can use to describe how I feel toward this man right now is *hatred*.

"I did... didn't," he tries.

"You d-d-d-didn't what?" I mock.

It takes everything in me not to jab my heel into his broken ribs.

"I don't want any trouble," he says.

I scoff. "Well, it's a bit late for that."

He doesn't respond but instead, stares into me like no one's ever done before. It's like he knows me, but I've never seen this man in my life.

"What were you doing outside of Eden's walls?" I ask.

"Eden?" he repeats.

"This place," I say. "What were you doing? Waiting to infiltrate? Or waiting for us to come out? Which one is it? You think you can stroll around this godforsaken desolate country in search of women? Like we're nothing but prizes to you?"

He shakes his head. "It's not like that," he says. "I knew about this place. I knew about Alpa"—he draws in a sharp breath—"but I was trying to help a friend find his daughter. Then my old crew... These really bad guys... I couldn't let them hurt anyone."

I throw my head back and laugh, the sound resonating throughout the cold basement. "And I'm supposed to believe you're some saint? That you're so different from all the misogynistic, testosterone-driven pieces of shit that led the world to what it is today?"

I loosen my jaw, realizing that I'm talking through teeth clenched so tight I'm barely making sense.

"Believe what you want," he says, grabbing at his ribs again. "But I'm not like them. We're not *all* like that."

I wish I could believe him, but I've seen what men are capable of. They've brought nothing but death and destruction to this world, and even if by some miracle this man were a saint, it wouldn't excuse the behavior of the other millions of men who took part in a war against women.

"I truly want to help," he says.

"How on Earth could you possibly *help*?" I say. "All you men are good for is reproduction."

He lets out a grunt and drops his head against the cold cement floor. "If I knew about Alpa," he breathes, "other men know about it, too."

My heart pulsates in my neck.

"I agree with you," he goes on. "There are a lot of bad men out there—there're a lot of bad people in this world. And some of those bad people would do anything to get their hands on a colony full of women."

He turns his black-haired head and looks at me. "I don't know if you guys—women, I mean—are even equipped. Do you have guns? Weapons? Or are you living in some made-up fantasy world where you think everything is rainbows and butterflies?"

I raise my chin and clench a fist. "I suggest you watch your tone."

He quickly raises an open hand. "I'm honestly not trying to be offensive. I'm trying to explain something to you. The world out there is still horrible... If you've been here since the war... You have no idea how messy things are right now. Men are killing each other over territory. Cutting off body parts and beating each other senseless. Women are killing, too, just trying to save their children. And it isn't only that"—he holds his stare a little longer than I like—"the surviving women will eventually make their way to you if you honestly do offer everything you've promised. This place can't possibly hold millions of women."

Millions, I think. I've been so caught up worrying about surviving—about ensuring that the few women I brought with me remain safe and happy— that I forgot about the outside world. I forgot that outside of this paradise, women are dying of disease, starvation, and dehydration every day.

I can't keep turning a blind eye to them.

I slowly stand up, my body casting a shadow over his. Even if I hate him, I realize, he could prove to be valuable for the greater good.

I swallow my pride and stretch my neck, feeling

a pleasant snap. "What do you propose?"

Eve — Flashback

"It's her."

"Are you sure?"

"That's her—that's Eve!"

"Eve!"

I squeeze Lucy's hand and pull her closer to me, refastening the blindfold over her eyes. Women begin appearing all around me, rising from piles of rubble and dead bodies. If I allow myself to take in what's going on, I'm afraid I'll drop to my knees and cry until I die.

There are so many bodies everywhere, and the smell is enough to make me want to reach into my mouth and pull out my own stomach.

And then, there's a dreadful silence in the air—a silence like no other. No airplanes fly overhead; no lights emit a soft buzzing sound; no music blares through a radio speaker; no cars drive by.

There's nothing but dead bodies and a gray overcast.

An old woman suddenly collapses in front of me, pressing her crispy lips against my bloody sneakers. "Eve, our savior!"

I pull back, violated, when someone else reaches for my hand. She's covered in dirt from head to toe, her blue eyes looking like diamonds in contrast.

"You saved us," she says. "V-V-Vrin, a lady in a uniform, told us everything."

I turn in circles, noting all the women who are coming forward, kneeling down on bruised knees as if I'm some goddess worthy of worship. They're trying to smile, but they're broken. Wet tears form silky lines on their filthy faces, and one of them lets out a sob so pained, my throat starts to ache.

It has a ripple effect, creating a unified lament powerful enough to seemingly stop time itself. I want to fall—to join these women and to cry for everything I've lost—but I can't.

I have to step into the role I've created for myself.

I have to be exactly what they need of me: a savior capable of erasing all the pain they've endured.

CHAPTER 38 – GABRIEL

Gabriel — Present Day

For the last five years, I've been playing it over and over in my head—what I'd do if I ever saw this woman again. It was my job to protect President Price, and I failed. I've been carrying a sickening guilt ever since that day... Ever since she stabbed a bayonet into President Price's chest.

It's my fault. I should've stepped out of the cabinet. I should've fought, even if it meant death. But placing blame on this woman is easier. Wanting revenge for all my anger is easier than self-loathing.

Then, I think of my mom and what she'd say to me if she knew what I was thinking: "Gabriel, *mi amor*, you are better than this."

But she isn't here.

After the war, I found her lifeless body curled up on her living room floor. She had a gray hand clutched over a cross pendant hanging from her neck. She lay there, her mouth partially open and her eyes closed. Her face looked almost white because of all the dust, and because of the sunlight overhead. Half her roof was blasted off when the jets started bombing. Her couch was sliced right down the middle, and debris, wood, and nails were everywhere. I wanted to give her a proper burial, but a few female survivors started climbing out of the rubble from the neighboring houses. I had to leave. I had to run.

I stare at the woman standing in front of me. Has the universe somehow given me a second chance? Maybe if I kill her, I'll be avenging the president and my mother.

Because right now, all I feel is anger. It's like she's triggered something for me, and all of the goodness inside me is disappearing.

"Gabriel," I know my mom would say right now. And her dark chocolate eyes would be glued to me the way they always were when she gave me a lecture. "Love is what will save this world."

"Well?" the blond woman snaps. "What's this big idea of yours? What do you propose?"

I look at her frail figure and slanted posture. She's holding one hand on her hip and resting her weight on one leg. I know I'm injured, but I'm three times her size. Maybe if I confront her about what happened. Tell her she's a piece of shit for making everything worse. Maybe...

"Mi amor," I hear my mom's voice again, something she used to repeat over and over to me, "you are the sweetest man this world has ever seen."

I don't want to be a monster.

I want to make my mother proud.

I stare into this woman's eyes, watching them narrow on me like I'm Satan himself. There's so much anger inside of her... So much hatred and resentment. How did she become like this? Who did she lose? Her nostrils expand and her chest heaves with every breath she takes. No one's born evil, and this woman's no exception. I saw her in the Oval Office. I saw how scared she was and how her hands shook when she held that gun. I can still hear her crying over her friend's body after she killed her. I've never heard anyone cry so hard before. I don't think this woman is evil. I think she's hurting and fighting a war within herself, and it's spilling out into the world.

Love is what will save this world, I tell myself.

Forgiveness.

I never once believed that men and women should be at war, and now's my chance to prove to this woman that if we work together, man and woman, or woman and man, we can accomplish a lot of good together. Gender shouldn't define us as human beings. We're all people... We all have souls and we all want the same thing—a great life full of happiness.

I take in her intense, fevered stare powerful enough to form a knot in my stomach. She hates me, but I don't care. With time and love, this woman's scars can heal.

"I know a place," I say, thinking of Area 82. "There are walls as strong as these, but the land is about twenty acres. There are vehicles, weapons, emergency supplies..."

She tilts her head to one side and looks at me like she's about to accuse me of something.

"And why would you bring us there?" she sneers. "What do you get out of this?"

I smile at her, feeling born again. "I want to be a part of the New World."

Visit **www.shadeowens.com** for more works by Shade Owens, including **Exodus**, the second book in the Garden of Evil series.

www.ingramcontent.com/pod-product-compliance
Lightning Source LLC
Chambersburg PA
CBHW031739180726
48283CB00005B/1583